The Mall of Small Frustrations

— a novel —

by graydon james

contact
graydon james
124 Queensbury Avenue
Toronto, Ontario
Canada
M1N 2X7
www.graydonjames.com

Printed in Canada

LIBRARY AND ARCHIVES CANADA CATALOGUING IN PUBLICATION

James, Graydon
The Mall of Small Frustrations / Graydon James

ISBN 978-0-9919338-0-8

I. Title.

For Simon. Anything is possible, but not everything.

"...and life [is] a son of a bitch. Sometimes you feel like a charmed twinkle, a rainbow of awesome. You are the Lord of Everything, living in a crystal palace, wearing golden underpants. Other times you feel like a frightened child, lost in the Mall of Small Frustrations."

—Principal Rory Calexico's farewell address to the students of Battleford Heights Highschool, 1983.

Chapter 1 - The Texan

Everyone knew that the Texan wasn't Texan. He didn't drawl. He didn't swagger. And Chester saw him leaving the Mega-Mart once to get into a dark green Volkswagen – a car quite possibly illegal in Texas. But he wore a cowboy hat pushed back on his round, sloping head and his belt buckle said "Texas" and in the way that all myths are generated he became the Texan.

Most Wednesdays he would roam the aisles of the Mega-Mart, a soft and smooth thumb hooked in his belt, looking at the prices on mops or deck chairs or a gross of elastic bands. The employees would surreptitiously watch him. Even Polito, in his tiny cramped security room in the back of the store, would adjust a monitor or two so he could follow the Texan's progress through the aisles.

"Look at this," he would say to Chester, if Chester happened to be lounging back there with him. Then he would point at the unmistakable profile of the cowboy hat in the flickering grey monochrome of monitor 9. "Why doesn't he buy something?"

"Why should he?" Chester asked.

"Don't it seem weird? Walking around, looking. Never buying."

"I don't buy anything here. I just walk around and look."

"But you work here."

"I work for the mall," Chester explained carefully.

"Aw, shut up."

"Do you buy anything here?"

"Sometimes," Polito said defensively.

Chester slid further down in his chair. He tried to get some sleep.

"Now he's in housewares," said Polito.

There was something subversive about the Texan. He never spent too much time in one area. He didn't have a pattern to follow. Sometimes he just walked straight through the Mega-Mart and out into the rest of the mall, without even glancing to one side or the other.

He wore a leathery looking jacket that used to be white but was starting to jaundice, and would swing his arms a bit too high. Sometimes it seemed like he didn't even notice that he was in a store with other people, and then suddenly he would help an old woman find where the Mason jar lids were kept. He might muse over a stuffed animal for 10 or 15 minutes, delicate fingers stroking his clean-shaven chin, before turning and decisively walking right out of the store. He had a wedding ring, but it was not ostentatious, nor did he ever adjust it. It seemed like it must always be fitting him just right. Chester admired that about him.

The myth of the Texan had been old before Chester arrived at the Mega-Mart, and word had it that the only person who'd been there when the Texan first arrived was Guy Tuffray, the manager of Mega-Mart. Guy Tuffray was an insufferable and opulently idiotic micro-dictator. He never spoke about the Texan, except when you were first hired, at which time he would tell you never to talk to the Texan. Otherwise, he would deny that any such person ever came into the store.

"I heard he tried to talk to him once," said Kipling, on one of the many occasions Chester saw him in the food court.

"Tuffray tried to talk to the Texan?"

"Apparently."

"What did he say?"

"Who?"

"I don't know, what did they say to each other?" Chester asked, testily.

"Oh. I don't know," Kipling said laconically, rewrapping his chicken soft taco with the expert adroitness of an avid pot smoker.

Chester rubbed the bridge of his nose.

"But apparently," Kipling continued, "that's why he never goes on the floor when the Texan is there."

"How do you know?"

"Polito told me."

"When do you talk to Polito?"

"Every Sunday afternoon. He does his once-around and finishes by the Emporium." Kipling was the sole employee of the Amphibian Emporium, a specialty pet store in the mall.

He was an iconoclastic figure with a wild rumple of dark hair already streaked with grey at the tender age of twenty-one, and he had an exceptionally mild demeanor. Although each would deny it, he and Chester were best friends.

"Why didn't he tell me?"

"Who?" asked Kipling, biting into his taco.

"Who have we just been talking about? Polito."

"Oh. Not surprising. He doesn't like you."

"He doesn't like me?"

"No."

"What's not to like?"

"He says you ask too many questions."

Chester knocked three quick times on the door to the back security room at the Mega-Mart. He waited a second for Polito to say "Come in" and then opened the door and stood in the doorway.

"Hey, I heard you said you don't like me," he said accusingly.

"Shh," said Polito, frowning. "I can almost see into one of the change rooms." He indicated on the monitor where he had aimed a camera at one of the mirrors on the back wall of change room 17, and could see the head and shoulders of a middle-aged woman as she tried on track pants. Chester sighed, shook his head, and then took his usual seat. Polito stared at the monitor. Polito was a terrible security guard because he was easily distracted, but the thing he hated most about his job was not the dulling effect of ad nauseum watchfulness; it was the uniform.

To Polito the uniform was a polyester monstrosity, despite the crisp lines of the creases that seemed permanent or, at least, unflappable in the face of the mere power of the modern washing machine. Despite, too, the fact that with his broad shoulders and narrow waist, he looked damn good in the uniform. Virtually no one suspected that Polito was actually quite a clothes-horse. He had an eye for colour and texture and balance, and he ordered his shirts from Italy, to be sent to him by his cousins. His pants came specially tailored from Germany, his underwear was Egyptian cotton, and his suits were cut by the local haberdasher from cloth purchased in Japan or Brazil. One of the reasons Polito was obsessed with the Texan was due to a sort of sartorial jealousy. He needed to know where the Texan bought his pants. Chester was afflicted with a form of jealousy for the Texan as well – he needed to know how the Texan had such a profound effect on those around him.

Later that week when the Texan came in, black jeans making crisp sounds as he walked slowly around the store, Chester noticed that Guy Tuffray was nowhere to be found. That was another thing for which he admired the Texan.

The Texan wasn't a stunningly dangerous-looking man. In fact, he seemed mild, his large soft eyes and his large soft hands. He had laugh lines around his mouth and his eyes, and they were worn easily like comfortable shoes. Sometimes for no reason he would step into his laugh lines while staring at Tupperware or bath towels, and they would crinkle into an amused topography. He seemed affable. He could put his hands in his pockets and just stand and slowly scan a row of toasters without looking like he was killing time.

He seemed to be a man with no schedule, no concern, no agenda, and yet someone who could fit in no matter the social situation. Fit in wasn't even an apt characterization, he would slip in to any group or gathering and casually take the reins with a natural candour. It seemed that any loosely assembled smattering of dog-eared riffraff would cohere into a disciplined democracy under his gentle, distant guidance given a short montage sequence.

Chester could imagine he had a warm chuckle, and if you heard it you would be reminded of a crackling fire. The sound of wood snapping discreetly and collapsing delicately into ash. He wanted to talk to the Texan. Perhaps walk over slowly, stand beside him, admire the fishing lures for a moment, and then say: "So, what do you think?" But Guy Tuffray had made a special point of mentioning personally to each staff member that they were not to talk to the Texan.

Normally that wouldn't have mattered. No one had any particular amount of respect for Guy Tuffray. But everyone had at least a grudging respect for the Texan. Even Easter, the youngest cashier at 16, and by far the most rebellious, would hold her tongue if he walked past while she was stocking a shelf. But she would stare brazenly at him, watch him as he perused prices. Chester thought her unbroken spirit was a joy to see. It was a moment of purity in a place fouled up by pretension.

Guy Tuffray, for example, with his thin strawberry blond hair and his tasteless mustache, was forever bloated on his own importance. He often clashed with Chester over the tender topic of Chester's employment and chain-of-command, levelling a pathetically annoyed sneer at him and calling him over with a short: "Ches!"

"What now?"

"You didn't stock these shelves correctly," he said, adjusting a package of diapers. "The smiling baby looks out, see?"

"So what?"

"Listen, I don't need your attitude, Chester. You are on thin ice with me as it is, what with this re-shelving error."

"They're diapers. They're not an impulse item. People will buy them if they need them."

"I don't need your lip, Chester. I don't need your attitude and I don't need your lip."

"What's the difference?"

"And I don't need your smart mouth, either!" Guy Tuffray's face was turning the same shade as his thin hair and his wiry mustache.

"Do you need my hands or feet at all? 'Cause I'd like to go home."

"Oh, I can send you home, mister. I can send you packing."

"No you can't Guy."

"It's pronounced Guy," he said sharply. "Rhymes with key."

"Okay, Guy."

"That's it. I don't want you in my store one more second. You are fired!"

Chester sighed. "You can't fire me."

"Well I am! Now march out of here, mister."

"Only Ipswitch can fire me. I'm a floater."

"Well then you're suspended!" Tuffray spat. "One week. No pay!"

"Great, then I can head home."

"No! Not until you re-shelve these diapers, every last one of them."

"So, I'm not suspended?"

"You're on my last nerve, Chester. Get shelving."

"And what if I don't't?"

"Then I will suspend you, oh, don't think I won't!"

Chester shrugged. "I could use the break."

"I want to see smiling babies. I demand to see smiling babies!"

"Well, then you should probably hop to it and get these diapers re-shelved."

Guy Tuffray glared at him with his watery eyes, trying to look either angry or tough. His fists trembled.

"I am going to report you to Ipswitch and recommend that you be kicked out of here on your smart little ass!" he declared, storming away. His entire face and neck was suffused in red. Chester shrugged and watched him leave and then went back to the security room to watch the monitors with Polito.

Ipswitch was the staff manager for the entire mall. He had a personality like a cannon: explosive and intractable, prepared to withstand the siege and batter the walls of his employees' excuses with an inexhaustible supply of pure, iron-hard questions launched in volleys at high speed. His great failing was that he did not understand the simple rule that the recoil could do more damage than the missile. It went without saying that he was unpopular.

His head was square and his hair was smooth and dark. He parted it in a ruler-straight line on the left, and it swept over his scalp in a wave despite the pomade he used to tamp it down. He was clean-shaven to a fault, with olive skin that complemented his green eyes, and his suits and shirts were pressed, severe, and dark-coloured but not black. His ties were plain or striped, nothing fancy. All of his clothes were bought for him by his wife, who had a conservative taste. In college Ipswitch had worn jeans and button-down shirts, sometimes with a sweater, sometimes with a blazer. He had actually been borderline stylish.

Ipswitch hired the floaters. They were the people not assigned to any particular store, but who helped balance the load, especially around the holidays. Chester had been hired as a floater three years ago and had manoeuvred by blind luck into a fireproof position. Guy Tuffray hated Chester but didn't have the authority to fire him, and Ipswitch hated Tuffray with a furious passion that was almost inspiring to Chester.

Whenever Tuffray went to Ipswitch to complain

about Chester, the conversation was always more or less the same. Tuffray would be made to wait and Ipswitch's secretary, an efficiently sour woman named Consuela, would watch him until he stood up to go to the bathroom. She was told to wait for this, and instructed to bark at him that Ipswitch was ready to see him right now.

Mumbling, self-conscious, Tuffray would enter Ipswitch's office with his bladder on the edge of uncomfortable fullness. In the time that he had been waiting, Ipswitch would have the guest chairs removed from his office so Tuffray would have to stand, shifting back and forth foot to foot as Ipswitch talked on the phone, looked over some papers, typed on his computer. After fifteen minutes of this he would finally turn to Tuffray, whose legs were, by this time, turning to gelatin.

"Yes?"

"It's about that floater, sir. Chester."

"Yes?" Ipswitch was obviously annoyed.

"He has no respect for authority, sir. I simply cannot work with him. He can't do the easiest jobs. He isn't a team player. He forgets to face items when he's re-shelving them, he gets the price wrong when he is re-pricing them, he is useless in the stock room and useless on the floor. He can't be trusted as a cashier, and when he cleans something it is dirtier than before he touched it. He—"

"Slow down, slow down. Honestly." Ipswitch glared at him and waited for a slow count of ten. "Now tell me what your problem is with this Chester, and slowly."

Knees shaking, Tuffray repeated what he had said.

"So what?"

"So what? Sir, he needs to be fired."

"Tuffray," he said with a note of warning in his voice. "I did the hiring and I will do the firing. I don't need you to tell me who to fire."

"Sorry, sir. Whom, sir."

"What?"

"Whom to fire. You said who to fire."

"I just told you, you don't tell me who to fire!"

"I know, sir." Tuffray paused, his face nearly grey. "It's whom, sir."

"Whom what?"

"Whom to f-fire," he said quietly.

"Listen, Tuffray," Ipswitch began in a rage, "I decide who gets fired and who doesn't when it comes to the floaters. You hear me? If you can't handle your own workers then maybe I should be firing you. Now stand there and look me in the eye like a man and tell me you have things under control. And then get out of this office and don't come back unless you have something important to talk about!"

Gasping quietly, Tuffray would turn and flee before his bladder exploded.

After he had sent him on his way, Ipswitch would lean back in his chair and chuckle in his rich baritone. And when the next floater schedule came out Chester would invariably be spending at least four days out of six at Mega-Mart.

The only way Chester could leave was if he quit, but he didn't have it in him to go to Ipswitch and serve notice. Ipswitch was mean, irascible; he was also possessed of the stately tenacity of an asteroid plunging through the atmosphere. Regardless of heat, friction, or plain common sense, once Ipswitch was on a path he followed it to the inevitable moment of impact. If it so happened that a few species wound up extinct, so be it. To Ipswitch there was no difference between death and uselessness.

Chester knew which was the worse fate. At least when you died you got a funeral, a parade, a notice in the newspaper, something. Some shining outward display for your personal suffering. Chester sometimes daydreamed that his ultimate end would cause a public outcry matched only by the paroxysm of national grief that occurred when Elvis got drafted and all those beautiful women wept on TV. But he wasn't one to be picky about it. He'd be happy if he got a single tear from January Chajkowksi, who worked as a sales clerk at Candida's Fashion in the mall.

Death and utility were far removed from Chester's future, though, because Ipswitch needed Chester. He needed him to be the thorn in Tuffray's side, the vinegar in his milk. Ipswitch needed Chester for revenge, and Chester was just the blunt instrument for the job. Ipswitch's idea of revenge was so frigidly soulless and protracted that it made the ice ages look like a balmy long weekend.

As it turned, out the Texan gave Chester his chance to be free. That was another thing that Chester admired about him.

Chapter 2 - Gina

Kipling loved the food court because it was the most anonymous place in the mall. It was the axis, the point about which all visits to the mall revolved, and this was by design, because most suburban developers understood the intricacies of the Pavlovian response when entangled with the structure of Maslow's hierarchy. That it takes the stoicism of a Windsor Palace guard to pass the Cinnabon without succumbing to the power of concentrated cinnamon bun vapour, wafting through the air like a cartoon scent off a window-silled pie.

Whenever he had the chance, which was often, he would stroll past the colourful façades of the different eateries and inhale the stratified ephemera of their unhealthy fare. He marveled at the way that, as you passed Arby's and began to cross the border into McDonald's, the smell would slowly shift from day-old, sliced roast beef to overcooked ground beef and special sauce. By the time you were squarely in front of McDonald's there was no trace of Arby's, right next door.

Chester, by contrast, hated the food court, and spent as little time there as possible. It was, however, the only place close by to eat.

"It's convenient," he said to Kipling, and then narrowed his eyes. "Too convenient."

Kipling knew almost all of the noontime staff and would nod to each as he passed. Homelina at New York Fries, then Zari at Subway, followed by Julio at KFC, and Singer at Great American Steakery. Pratesh worked at Jimmy The Greek, then Piper at the Pizza Plaza, and then Ameesha at the Canton Kitchen. They were followed by Carmen at Booster Juice, Tony Delillo at Manchu Wok, Vanderwaal at A&W, Igliuk at Arby's, Maya Mankiewicz at McDonald's, and Shayna at Second Cup. And then there was Gina at the Taco Bell.

In its way the food court of the mall was the epitome of the melting pot mentality of North American culture. Although it wasn't driven by the love and celebration of individual differences and unique backgrounds, but rather by the absolute indifference to those things.

Kipling wondered why the worker was never matched to the store. Julio should be at Taco Bell. Piper at the Canton Kitchen or Manchu Wok, or even Sushi Express, depending on if she was Japanese. Zari at New York Fries. Homelina at Great American Steakery. Singer and Tony Delillo at the Pizza Plaza. Ameesha at KFC. He kept these thoughts private even though he didn't fully understand them to be of the sort of background racism that children absorb from their parents unwittingly and without artifice. He would be embarrassed if anyone had pointed it out to him. Kipling was nothing if not open-minded. It worked to his detriment in cases when logic was replaced by inculcated ideas, entrenched in ignorance and married to an unfortunate amount of social acceptability.

He did consider it a lucky blink of coincidence and fate that Gina worked at the Taco Bell, because he liked Gina best and he always bought tacos for lunch.

Gina was a short, nimble 18-year old with the kind of small elfin features you would find on an anime character. Her eyes even had a penchant for quivering moistly like she was close to tears, or overexcited. Her skin was pale and perfectly smooth, a fact of which she was proud and was due to her strict regimen of exfoliating every morning before school and every night before bed. While she was not beautiful, she was certainly not unattractive, and had the peppy mannerisms shared by certain cute, middle-class, teenage girls who are slightly overeager to please. Adolescence being a hellish war zone whose main assault weapon was shame, any survival strategy was viable, and so she had learned that being inoffensive and cheerful allowed her to slip through high school largely unnoticed. This was good, and it was bad.

Now that she had finally graduated, Gina was determined that someone should notice her. The thought made her uncomfortable, but she liked the idea so much that it consumed her daydreams, which made her uncomfortable, which was a sign that she was pushing her own boundaries, which she had always thought was a sexy thing to do, which, in turn, made her uncomfortable.

Kipling was not attracted to Gina sexually. Kipling was not attracted to anyone sexually, even though he was bisexual and had a body literally chock-a-block with hormones. It confused Chester. It was one of the many things they argued about when they met frequently in the food court, or were just hanging out.

"But you think she's cute, right?"

"Yeah."

"But you're not attracted to her?"

"No."

"But you talk to her all the time!"

"Yeah."

"But you don't want to do her?"

"No."

"Is there something wrong with you?"

Kipling shrugged. "Maybe."

"Do you want to do anyone?" Chester asked exasperatedly.

"I've thought about doing you," he said musingly.

"Oh?"

"Yeah."

Chester hesitated. "What's stopping you?"

"I don't really like you."

"You don't?"

"No."

"Then why do you hang out with me?"

"You seem so interested in stuff." Kipling abstractly punched buttons on his calculator watch. He was figuring out how many weeks it would take him to save up 2,431 dollars and 23 cents. He subtracted his known expenses.

"What do you mean?"

"Well," Kipling paused, stopped working on his calculations. They were leaning against the fountain near the middle of the mall, surrounded by the bustle of the food court. Above them the skylight was glowing a kind of golden from the slanted rays of the setting sun. "You ask so many questions."

Chester nodded. "I'm a curious guy."

Gina visited Kipling at the Amphibian Emporium in the early afternoons, usually, after the lunch rush. She considered him a friend because they talked once or twice a week and he seemed gentle. When she arrived late one day Kipling was feeding the salamanders, dropping crickets into the large glass enclosures and watching the results with an interest he normally had to fake for other tasks. Kipling was so laid back he formed his own micro-universe that rarely intersected with the real interests of other people. But he liked answering questions.

"How's it going?" Gina asked.

Kipling nodded. "Yeah, things are happening. What's up with you?"

Gina was smiling too much. Her ears were slightly pink from a mild blush. "Oh, just coming by to say hello. You know...I'm finished work. Just waiting for my dad to pick me up."

Kipling was leaning back against the salamander case, the box of crickets resting on his hip. He straightened his arm, which pulled his sleeve back enough that he could look at his watch. "Five already," he said distractedly. There were moments when he wondered how time could pass so quickly.

"What are these?" Gina pointed at the salamanders.

"Salamanders."

"What's that one?"

"An Eastern Red-backed Salamander."

"He's eating that cricket."

Kipling nodded. His conversations with Gina were never about anything, which seemed to suit both of them. There were pauses, but they were never awkward.

"Do they just give you one uniform?" he asked.

Gina looked down at her Taco Bell uniform, which was a dishwater-grey shirt with tan pants. The shirt was the smallest size they had, but it was still too big. The short sleeves came down to her elbows. Self-consciously she touched her hair, which was up in a loose ponytail with wild, reddish-brown strands loosely frizzed in a late-afternoon, long-day kind of way.

"Well, they just give us the shirt, but I have two." She thought for a moment. "When do you think we'll have uniforms for everyone?"

"Hm?"

"Like, in the future. Like in movies in the future everyone wears the same uniform."

"Those are B movies," Kipling replied.

"Okay. But I still wonder."

"Well, they'd have to get rid of the fashion industry first, so I'm going to guess never." They were taking turns watching the salamanders dart at their prey, and watching each other.

"Never?"

"Well," Kipling began airily, "Old Navy posted a strong third quarter, so...I can't see it happening."

"Nothing lasts forever, Kipling."

"I was speaking functionally," he replied. "If we're speaking categorically, well, you're probably right. I suppose. For now."

Gina's brow creased as she looked at Kipling. "Why do you have to be so weird?" She said it amiably.

Kipling shrugged. “You say weird, I say precise.”

“Yeah. You say precise, I say weird-o.” Gina gave the last word a kind of sing-song quality.

“Well, only a weird-o would think that we could get rid of the fashion industry and all wear sparkly jumpsuits.”

“I think I’d almost like that,” Gina laughed.

Kipling nodded. “Probably be fewer eating disorders.”

“Yeah, and fewer models.”

“They would all have to find other jobs,” he said, and his eyes glassed over as he imagined it.

“So, is your friend Chester single or something?”

“Yeah.”

“He doesn’t have a girlfriend?”

“No. He finds it hard to keep girlfriends.”

“Oh, yeah? Why is that?”

“I think he can be demanding, maybe.”

“Hm.”

“Watch the one with the yellow stripe on his back. That’s a California Slender Salamander.”

“He’s cute though.”

“Even when he’s chewing on a cricket?”

“I mean Chester,” Gina laughed, punching Kipling’s shoulder.

“Oh. Yeah, he is.”

“Would he ask me out, do you think?”

“Maybe, if he knew that you would say yes.”

Gina put her hands on the glass case, leaning forward, studying the movements of the animals. They seemed to like their habitat. One ran, in their off-kilter way, up a mossy section of log angled in the corner.

“Do they ever eat each other?”

“Sometimes,” Kipling said.

Gina was not necessarily nervous around boys, but she found Chester’s brusque manner intimidating. He ate almost daily in the food court, and she would watch him argue with himself over which place to order from.

Sometimes he got very impassioned, almost yelling at himself as he tried to make a decision. Whenever he would look in the direction of the Taco Bell she would blush.

Her blushes were like a sunset, they seemed to start at the top of her face and work their way down, touching her forehead first then the tops of her ears, which stuck out slightly. By the time the blush had reached her cheeks it would have darkened from a delicate pink to a luscious scarlet. Her moist eyes would creep even closer to tears. She would pat her hair, smoothing it.

It took Gina a long time to make friends. She liked Modesta Mae, the other security guard besides Polito. Mo, as she preferred to be called, was a barrel-chested black woman who wore too much lipstick and smiled whenever she wasn't chewing someone out. She often had to chew out the scrappy, rebellious teens that liked to hang around the mall and who would try to bring their skateboards inside. Polito hated chewing anyone out. He just wasn't good at it. Mo had a knack, but her tongue-lashings were always fairly good-natured and protective in a motherly sort of way. The kids liked her, and respected her after their fashion. Her and Gina were friends in part because they lived just down the street from each other, and because Gina always felt like Mo was looking out for her and Mo liked being protective of Gina. The two often came to work together in Mo's dark green Citroen, or when Gina borrowed her mother's faded red Ford Taurus.

"How you doing today, baby?" Mo often said as Gina climbed in the passenger side of the Citroen, the door making sounds like an animatronic dinosaur as the hinges protested their use.

"I'm good, thanks," Gina replied with a smile like she might give an older sister if she had an older sister. She liked being referred to as "baby".

Gina had a fear that some day both Mo and Chester would be at the Taco Bell at the same time. She was afraid that Mo would chew out Chester for being moderately impolite when ordering, and then it would make it even more embarrassing to try to ask him out. Or, more to the point, to try to trick him into asking her out.

At last year's staff Christmas party, the same one where Ipswitch broke his finger, Gina had decided to go even though she didn't have a date, and was embarrassed to arrive and find that everyone else had brought someone. She spent the night trying to avoid conversations, especially with Ipswitch or her manager, Clyde Saphoria, both of whom scared her no end. She noticed that there was mistletoe hanging from the ceiling. The party was held in one of the meeting rooms in the office section of the mall. The mistletoe was hung in the centre of the ceiling, and so she stayed in a corner and avoided making eye contact with anyone remotely close to the festive sprig. She had been told before that she was a bad kisser, by both of her ex-boyfriends, but that was only part of the reason she avoided the sprig of holiday foliage. The other part was her natural inclination to fade into the background, like a professional wallflower.

At midnight when her father had arrived to pick her up she felt a flood of relief and left without taking her coat, which she never saw again. It seemed a small price to pay.

Halfway through the party Dusty, the clerk at the games and hobby store, which kept changing names, tried to engage her in a conversation. It was the only tolerable part of the evening.

"Eggnog?" he offered, holding up a second glass he had brought across the room for her.

"Oh, no thanks. Wait...is there any alcohol in it?"

"No."

"Oh, then no thanks."

"So," he began, holding both glasses of eggnog and feeling kind of foolish, "finished your shopping yet?"

She liked his lopsided grin, and gave him as cheery a smile as she could manage. "Oh, no. I haven't started." They both nodded.

"Yeah, working at a mall, you know, the last thing I want to do is shop." She gave him a small laugh, which was close to being the best Christmas gift he got that year. Then they stood and looked around awkwardly: at the other employees, at the inoffensive art prints on the wall, at the floor, which was nicely carpeted in a tightly-knapped royal blue. Dusty drained one glass of eggnog, then, after a pause, the other.

"I'm going to go get some more eggnog," he said.

"Okay, sure."

She watched him try to bring a glass of eggnog to Dove Anquanita, who worked at the HMV and was almost taller than Dusty, who was 5'10". Dove had a curvaceous body wrapped sexily in a shimmering black dress, but she had a thin, long, hooked nose that made people double-take when they saw her. Because of this, when she was standing she affected a posture of complete uncaring, with her knees twisted inward and her hips angled, and usually with one hand resting on her thin waist, right where it slanted out to become her well-rounded hip. Gina watched Dusty offer the eggnog, and saw Dove shake her head.

Behind the counter of the Taco Bell Gina tried to stand the way that Dove had. Immediately her knee ached. Kipling was delicately holding his chin, musing as he stared at the Taco Bell menu. She was never sure why it took him so long to choose – he always ordered the same thing.

"What do you think of Dove?" she asked.

"Anquanita?"

"Yeah."

"I will have...three chicken soft tacos please." Gina had already made four chicken soft tacos. She blinked at Kipling, then placed three of them on his tray. He noticed, but seemed lazily unconcerned. "I don't know her that well. Ask Puck, they used to go out."

"Puck never eats here, he thinks tacos are chick food," Gina said with a sour expression.

"You don't like Puck?"

"We used to go out," she said. Kipling nodded. He

had his tray in his hands, it looked like he was about to leave, but he wasn't going anywhere. He seemed just a bit confused, which Gina thought was endearing. Kipling sensed that there was more that she wanted to say.

Finally she leaned closer and said, "He told me I was a bad kisser."

"Are you?"

"I don't know."

Kipling thought about it. "It might behoove you to find out."

"What does behoove mean?"

"I don't know. Use it in a sentence."

Gina chuckled. "You just used it in a sentence."

"Did I?" And then he walked away slowly, trying to find an empty table.

Kipling knew that there was no good method for finding an empty table in a food court at a mall. You had to wander, and wait, and believe in luck or fate or both. He found it easy to believe in anything and everything, and so he got a table almost immediately. From where he sat he could see down the corridor on one of the axes of the mall, past the information booth behind which sat the Sumerian.

The mall was shaped like a giant X. At the nexus of the two corridors, both nearly a half-mile long, was the information booth. The only person who ever worked at the info booth was the Sumerian, who was as Sumerian as the Texan was Texan. No one knew the Sumerian's real name because virtually no one ever talked to the Sumerian. It was a faux pas of the highest order to be seen talking to the Sumerian, because no matter what you were actually talking about it always looked like you were asking for directions.

It was paramount among the employees to appear knowledgeable of the geography of the mall at all times. It was, however, perfectly acceptable to air any and all opinions on which stores were going to be the next to close up, shutter their doors, be sequestered behind plywood facade, renovated, and revealed with some lame grand opening foofarah. There was one store that had been sealed away for almost a year: the old popcorn place, Colonel Kernel's Popcorn Express. Rumour had it that the mall was finally getting one of those trendy, high-end coffee joints called Starbucks.

Only two people could ever talk to the Sumerian without reprisal. One was Ipswitch, who, as staff manager of the mall, sometimes needed to talk to the Sumerian. Besides which, under his thunderhead of anger he could talk to whomever he damn well wanted whenever he damn well felt like it. The other was Chester, who, as the only floater still employed by the mall, was both part of every facet and above every boundary. It was a status he was completely unaware of, and this lack of awareness made it acceptable for him to have it.

As Kipling re-rolled his chicken soft tacos one by one, he watched Chester leaning back against the counter of the info booth like a '50s greaser, talking to the Sumerian. The Sumerian's wide, impassive face remained motionless as Chester talked, giving no sign of what the conversation was about. He didn't move an eyebrow, possibly because they looked like they had once been part of Stonehenge, they were so slab-like and mossy with hair. The Sumerian had yellowed skin that was creased like a piece of paper that just came out of the laundry. He didn't seem old so much as he seemed timeless.

"I'll tell you man, you have it pretty sweet here. No manager, no stocking, no inventory," Chester said. He was looking down the long corridor that ended at the Mega-Mart.

The Sumerian said nothing.

"But I suppose it's all memory work. You must have a great memory."

The Sumerian remained completely still, save for his steady breathing. He was imperturbable.

"That's one thing I would like to have, you know? I feel like my head's all stuffed up with useless junk. Yesterday I almost forgot my own phone number, you know?" They both took a healthy pause. "Yeah, it's a pretty sweet deal here. My job, I got Guy Tuffray telling me what to do and then telling me that I did everything wrong and I have to redo it. Sometimes it makes me so angry."

The Sumerian shook his head a few millimetres back and forth, in a sympathetic way.

For Gina it was the Sumerian who changed her life, although she never got to thank him. But she got Chester to ask her out all by herself.

Chapter 3 - Chester the Molester

Everyone had a nickname for everything at the mall. Well, almost.

The mall wasn't even called the mall, it was called TM, which became Trademark, which became Mark, which became Mark's House, which became Le Maison, which became Frenchie's, which became The Mustard, which became The Colonel, which became The Conservatory, then, briefly, the Royal Donkey Conservatory (because it housed all the asses), then the RDC, then the Riddick, then Ol' Vin's Place, then Cueball, then Q-mall, then Cue The Mall, and finally the mall again. And that was just one slow Sunday afternoon.

The process was expedited by the superfluence of cell phones with text messaging among the employees of the mall – it was the trendy new gadget. Mya, the spike-haired half-Asian manager at the Aldo, would text Areola, the curly-maned hairstylist at VictorStyle. She would text Puck, with his slicked forward black coif and three-colour athletic wristbands. Puck would text a half-dozen people, including January, who worked at Candida's Fashion and endeavored, futilely, to be the nerve centre of all intra-mall communication. She failed for two reasons, first because she didn't like sending text messages. She had immaculate nails, with carefully applied designs of stars or hearts or flowers or whatever struck her fancy that particular morning. Text messaging and delicate nails did not go together, in January's notion of the universe. Secondly, she was a social pariah. The only reason Puck texted her was because he was trying to sleep with her.

January was beautiful, and she knew she was beautiful, so she truly did not fathom the depths of her unpopularity. Her best friends were her parents. She was an only child. Her mother was extremely over-protective and her father was indifferent and so, by the time she was six years old she had never been on a sleep-over, never gone to another kid's birthday party, never had a friend over to visit. She barely understood how to interact with people. She thought it consisted of telling them what to do and how to do it, although she was beginning to see an inkling of a hint that what she was doing was alienating the people around her.

Because of that January was only superficially aware of the nicknames, hearing them in passing in conversations of which she was not involved. The nicknaming process was highly personal and, like deciding on a style of fashion to adopt and wear, it was important that everyone else recognize the nicknames that you selected for things. So while Homelina might refer to Chester as the Russkie and Dove might refer to him as Chaz, both were expected to acknowledge the other's choice and respect it.

If Homelina said, "I saw the Russkie downtown yesterday," it would be a deeply wounding slight for Dove to say, "Who?"

Chester himself was aware of less than half of his nicknames, of which he had over 50 among the staff. He was the Jazzman, Katmandu, Chest, the Chessman, Mork, Ip's-bitch, or Momo. Sometimes he was Hester, Blue, Tallboy, Q&A, Chezzy, Chas, Chuckles, Cheeseball, or C-Note. More obliquely he was Thunder, Eagle-Eye, Detective Dan Dermack, Dizzy (or Gillespie), Flambé, or Pencils McGee. For one memorable day he was The Jizzmaster 9000.

Even though he was ignorant of half his taxonomy,

he had yet to offend anyone when they referred to him by some nickname. Chester was always ready to believe that someone was waving to him, regardless of the name they called out.

There were certain of the employees who did not like to use nicknames for anything. Gina, for example, was very concerned about using the exact proper names for everyone. When she was introduced to people she would double- and triple-check that she had got their name right.

Puck, on the other hand, rarely used anyone's real name. Having his own handle for everything was beyond important to him: it was his defining characteristic. He would sometimes come up with one-off nicknames based on frivolously embarrassing moments. Like when he was lunching with Rose McDougall, the large-breasted but mousy older cashier at the Grand & Toy, and she dropped a fry twice before managing to eat it. The next time he was talking to someone about her he used the nickname Droppy McFries, but only that one time.

Droppy McFries was never heard again.

Puck was afforded this companionable quality because he loved people and was genetically predisposed to being your pal. He was charming and confident, shorter than average, with a spastic, little-brother kind of energy. He was an inveterate dater, and had gone out with just about every available girl who had worked at the mall. He was 22 and he thought his life would never change, which only fed his confidence.

Puck's ability to nickname was unique, though. Most of the managers, for example, had an entirely different code of nicknaming. Ipswitch would use one of three nicknames for everyone, depending on how he felt about them at the moment. If he hated you, he would call you Numbskull. If he wanted something from you, you became Buddy. In the event that neither of those situations described how he felt about you, then you were You. As in, "How are things, You?" or "What's the meaning of this, You?"

Of the managers, only one successfully crossed the invisible staff border between management and employees without being perceived as an enemy by both sides, and that was Mya. She did it in two ways. First, she had started as an employee and had shared foxholes with her fellows for many years – weathering layoffs, staffing shortages, and the dreaded Wheel of Fun. Second, after she had crossed over to the other side, normally her foxholes would have been covered over, and a short memorial service among the remaining low-level employees would have ensured her disappearance from their camaraderie; however, she joined the band started by a few musically-minded employees and became the lead singer and bass player. Besides which, due to her nose ring and long jet-black hair that she wore in Astroboy-style spikes, the Aldo outlet that she managed had a lax, hip dress code.

Guy Tuffray tried to follow her example, but simply couldn't pull it off. He saw how she acted like one of the employees, so he attempted the same. He tried to emulate the regular employees' way of nicknaming, but his selected pseudonyms were snickeringly derided as lame. He referred to Shorsky – the oldest of the cashiers at the Mega-Mart, at the arm-wattle-inducing age of 71 – as Babyface. It took Guy some time to realize that he was absolutely the worst at nicknaming people, and it was because of a conversation he had with Chester.

"Hey, Breadstick," Guy said, strolling down the sports and leisure aisle of the Mega-Mart, with all the bicycles lining one side.

Chester turned. "Are you referring to me?" He was assembling a pink bicycle with a wireframe basket that had a flower on it. He sort of wanted it for himself, but he was going to have to put it up on display with the rest of the bikes.

"Yeah, you're Breadstick!"

"Why am I 'Breadstick'?"

Guy shrugged, feeling the creeping tendrils of nervousness. "Because. You— Look at you, with your um... Don't you eat Italian food?"

"What does that have to do with it?"

"Listen, Breadstick, I don't need to explain myself to you."

Chester sighed and went back to assembling the bike. "Whatever, Guy."

"It's pronounced Guy," Tuffray said angrily. "Can't you remember that?"

"Sure, Guy."

Tuffray made a sound in the back of his throat, kind of like a growl but more phlegmatic. "Jesus, Breadstick, if you can't pronounce my name why don't you give me a nickname?"

Chester turned. There was very nearly a light bulb over his head. "Why don't you give yourself a nickname, Guy?"

"Howsabout Managerio the Magnificent?" Tuffray smiled wolfishly.

"No, Guy. Nicknames are not about your job, they should speak to who you are as a person. Your inner qualities. Come on, you can think of something, can't you?"

"Well," Tuffray paused. "I like...TV. You know, watch the old boob tube."

"Great. 'Boob Tube' it is. Now if you don't mind," Chester rang the bell on the bike as he stood up with it and threw one leg over, straddling the curved pink seat, "I'm going to take this baby for a spin."

Eventually Guy came to a tacit agreement with the employees. They didn't refer to him as Boob Tube, and, because of his desperate lack of nicknaming ability, he never referred to anyone by any kind of name other than the one they had chosen for their name tag. He had even gone so far as to call Chester "Watson" for the entire day that Chester had to borrow Watson's uniform.

Watson, who did not even look remotely like Chester. It was all the more surprising that Watson's uniform fit, but such is the nature of men's fashion. Watson was tall, he was raven-haired, and he had thin eyebrows that arched chaotically as he talked to you. He was very animated when talking and very restless when listening. It made people enjoy talking to him initially but quickly lose heart. It took too much energy to have a conversation with him. Watson's eyes were a heavy-lidded brown, usually rimmed in red from lack of sleep. Watson played online games and, every once in a while, played poker at online casinos. Puck called him Diamond Jack Watson, even though Watson was his first name: Watson Huffernanny.

Watson was also older than most of the other employees at the Mega-Mart, and in the mall in general. He was in his mid-20's and had yet to discover his purpose in life. It made his relationship with Easter, who was the youngest cashier at the Mega-Mart, all the more scandalous. She was 16 and knew exactly what she wanted to do with her life. The only mystery with Easter was why she was dating Watson Huffernanny. He was lanky, a cinephile, and had his strongest opinions about pop culture.

Chester, on the other hand, was medium build, slight, with curly blond hair that was halfway between Art Garfunkel's tight kinky afro and Owen Wilson's disheveled waves. He had blue eyes. They were not rimmed with the redness that comes from late-night online game playing, or substance abuse, both of which led to Watson Huffernanny's nervy stare. They might, however, be described as being rimmed with that brand of cynicism that leads to long talks about The Way Things Should Be. He was not animated when he spoke, but rather, impassioned. He might leave his hands in his pockets, but those blue, cynical eyes would flash.

Chester had opinions about everything and everyone, and was not afraid to share them. It was to his credit that he also asked people what their opinions were – all the better to begin a debate. Conversation with Chester was free-flowing, filled with questions, and came forth in a chaotic stream that made sense only in aftermath.

He was of the moment. He didn't deliberately avoid planning things, but the idea of forethought was foreign to him. Everything could be figured out as you went, and if not, it could be avoided. The most effort he ever put into any endeavor was his long project to ask January out on a date.

Chester had first seen January in the food court not long after he had begun working at the mall. He had just finished eating lunch by himself, sitting at one of the two-seat tables along one side of the food court, and when he stood up he saw January alone at the last two-seat table. Without looking away from her, because she was quite a vision in a white turtleneck sweater with her caramel hair spilling straight down her shoulders, he turned to the person sitting at the table behind him.

"Who is that?" he asked.

"Hm? Oh, that's January."

"She's beautiful."

"That's relative."

Chester looked down into the grey-green, bored eyes of a young man with disheveled dark hair who was wearing hand-me-down bell bottoms and a smock over top of a t-shirt. The smock said "Amphibian Emporium" in a lizardly scrawl.

"Relative? No, no. I mean I could agree with you in theory but this is fact. She's absolutely beautiful."

"Meh."

"Meh? You know even if you happen to be gay, which I don't know if you are or not, but surely it's possible, but even if you are, it doesn't hurt you to admit that she is a beautiful woman."

"How does it help me?"

"I don't know. How does it hurt you?"

"Ah," the young man held up one finger, "but how does it help me?"

"Hmph." Chester stood and stared at January for a moment. "Fuck that eye of the beholder crap, can't beauty be absolute?"

"Nope."

"You sure?"

"Absolutely."

Chester mulled that. "What's your name?"

"Kipling."

"I'm Chester."

"I didn't ask."

"I noticed. What's with those marks on your arm?"

Kipling looked at the inside of his wrist. "I work with amphibians," he said.

"Yeah, so do I. One of them's named Guy Tuffray."

"You know it's pronounced Guy? Like the French way."

"Not to me it's not."

Kipling nodded. "I like that," he said.

That was Kipling's tenth anniversary of working at the mall. And Kipling's last day, the day that Chester wore Watson's uniform, was the same day that the Sumerian gave the two fast friends their freedom. Chester knew something auspicious would happen that day as soon as he put on Watson's uniform. He found twenty empty condom packages in the pockets.

Chapter 4 - Jasper

Chester found every opportunity he could to walk past Candida's Fashion, which was almost at the opposite end of the mall from the Mega-Mart. If anyone needed anything from anywhere Chester would volunteer quickly, and then chart a circuitous path that would take him past the intensely potpourried women's clothing store. He felt like a big game hunter. He felt like a spy. He felt like he had something of his own.

Candida, the owner and manager of the store, was the only one who worked there who didn't notice what was going on. She rarely came into the store, and when she did she was stunningly oblivious to everything except the sound of her own voice. She was middle-aged, eastern European, and very rich. She treated the store like her personal closet, which it sort of was. She was exceedingly lucky that the store manager, Susanna, was as on the ball as a highly trained seal.

Susanna did not care for Chester, and would silently fume at his appearance, slinking past the store front, because he was a distraction for her employees. Peoria and Michaela, the only other employees besides January, would spot Chester slowing down as he passed and they would subtly indicate his presence with a tilt of the head, a cock of the eyebrow, to January.

"Hey," one of them would whisper.

She would try to ignore them.

"It's Boy Genius, over there, in front of the Shopper's. He's checking you out."

"I don't care," she would sing-song. In reality she cared a great deal, but she knew Peoria and Michaela were making fun of her.

Chester was one of the only employees at the mall who hadn't grown up in the town, so he was an unknown quantity. January had gone through school with everyone else and they all treated her the same. She was the social equivalent of a recently deceased skunk. Chester held some promise, some sliver of hope, and January was absolutely unwilling to talk to him for that very reason.

If January wasn't in sight when Chester walked past he would slip into the Shopper's Drug Mart across the way and pretend to be looking at cough medicines or lipstick. If his timing had been right, that would have been how he saw Ipswitch's accident that put him in a neck brace for eight weeks, and he might have caught the moment when Mya accidentally kissed January. But his timing was all wrong, and instead he met Jasper.

"May I help you sir?"

"Yeah, kid, you can leave me alone," Chester replied, not even turning his head from his careful scrutiny of the interior of Candida's. January was in the back, trying to find a different size of jacket for a middle-aged woman trying on lavender power suits.

"That one is for children," said Jasper, gamely. He had pluck.

Chester turned to look at him, then looked at what he had in his hand. He was holding a bottle of cough medicine, and indeed, it was a children's strength bottle.

"May I suggest this one, sir?" Jasper pulled a nondescript box down from the shelf. "I find it eases coughing, aching, stuffy nose, fever, congestion, phlegmatic build up, mucous, uh, build up, and pretty much all of the other symptoms you might experience with a cough, cold, or chest infection."

Chester gave him an appraising look. Jasper was slim, and wore high-top sneakers loosely laced. He had glasses with thin, silver metallic frames and a close-cropped head of brown hair the colour of mahogany. His nose was very evenly proportioned, but he had a slight scar on his bottom lip, which he had received once in a race with his brother to see who could get from the upstairs bedrooms to the basement the fastest. Jasper would have won that race, despite being four years younger, but his brother tripped him and now he had a thin scar marring his lip line.

He had an air of willing acceptance about him. It was an almost child-like acknowledgement that you were the leader and he was the follower. Partially this came from being the youngest of three, but Jasper was also just inherently a listener with a deep sense of empathy. His open and simple honesty, plain-spoken attitude, and ready smile made him the sort of amiable chap that everyone knew but no one really remembered. Because of this, Jasper longed for the deep acceptance that comes with intense friendship. He wanted to be able to argue with someone and still remain good friends.

His job at the Shopper's Drug Mart was getting him no place in that regard – everyone else who worked there was twice his age and had no place in their lives for new friendship, beyond comments about the weather. When he had seen Chester enter the store, for the tenth time in as many days, he decided to approach. Now Chester stood, looking him up and down, and Jasper was suddenly very aware of the bright pink colour of his button-up shirt, and the oversized qualities of his hand-me-down jeans. He wore a white smock with the name tag, "Diane".

"I see you replaced Diane," Chester noted.

"Oh, yes." Jasper smiled and self-consciously covered the name tag.

"You know she abused her behind-the-counter privileges."

"I wasn't told about–"

"Well she did," Chester warned. "She was pretty sly. She would undercount one, maybe two pills, and then pocket them. Over the course of years she must have amassed quite a collection, one or two at a time. You know, pill here, pill there. Hoping that some customer would come in and order a gross of Celexa, or Jantoven, or Lipitor, or Pancof EXP, or Balsalazide Disodium, also known as Colazal, so she could top up the bottle she had going."

"Wow," said Jasper, impressed, "you sure know your prescription drugs."

"And you ask a lot of questions," Chester said defensively. He looked back across to Candida's. Still no sign of January.

Jasper thought about it, "That wasn't a question, sir."

"Call me Chester."

"I'm Jasper." He shook hands emphatically, his head nodding. "So, what are you looking at?"

"Ah, there's this girl that likes me," Chester said, leaning out, trying to see further into the back of Candida's.

"Oh, that's lucky," said Jasper, "I wish a girl liked me."

Chester shook his head, turning to look at him. "Ah, kid. I was like you once." He raised one finger, sternly. "Once."

"Yeah?" Jasper said, eyebrows raised.

"Listen, let me teach you some things."

"Oh, geez. That'd be cool, thanks."

"Okay. Let me ask you – you're into girls, right? – what kind of music do you like?"

"Oh, right now I'm kinda into like older stuff. Jackson Five and Smokey Robinson and the Miracles and—"

"Okay, okay." Chester held up a hand. "I didn't ask for your life story."

"Sorry."

"Listen: you can't like that music."

"No?"

"No," he shook his head, closed his eyes like he was tired. "Girls don't like that kind of music. You've got to like, uh, you know the Spice Girls and 50 Cent. Junk like that. Celine Dion."

"Oh, really?"

Chester nodded sagely.

"My parents told me that I should be myself."

"Hey," Chester spun around angrily, his finger in the air, locking eyes with Jasper, "forget that. That's loser advice."

"But—"

"You've been yourself, right? I mean, you haven't been anything but yourself. And how has that been working out for you? Hm?"

"Well—"

"I don't see girls hanging off your arms. Hear what I'm saying?"

"Yeah."

"Being yourself is clearly not working. It's bad advice, no offense to your parents. The you that you are is just not attractive to women."

"Right."

"So you gotta change. You try something new. They say be yourself, well I say don't be yourself. Be anything but yourself."

"Uh-huh."

"Be the opposite of yourself. Try that for a while, and see how it works out."

"Okay."

"Okay?"

"Okay."

Chester nodded. He looked across to Candida's and still couldn't see January.

"Quick question," Jasper interrupted.

"What?"

"How do I be the opposite of myself? I mean, I am myself, no matter what. Right? It seems to me that it might be impossible."

"Well of course it is, if you have that kind of

attitude."

Jasper blinked confusedly.

"Listen, if you aren't gonna be can-do about this thing – about this whole process – then you're already a lost cause," Chester said.

"Oh. I don't want to be a lost cause."

"You're damned right you don't." Chester was only half paying attention. His gaze was focused on Candida's because he thought he saw a glimpse of January's signature white turtleneck. His heart was halfway up his throat, stopped only by his suddenly thick, sweaty tongue. He felt immediately awkward and not at all himself.

"So...how is this," Jasper motioned with his hands to indicate Chester's stalking of January, "part of the whole system? Are you being yourself or the opposite of–"

"Christ, you ask a lot of questions, don't you?" Chester snapped defensively.

"No, just the one. Well, two."

"This is field research," he explained, obviously irritated.

"Sorry."

"You aren't ready for this level, yet."

"Okay."

Chester looked back and watched January, who was now folding blouses. "Field research," he repeated. "Here, hold this," he said this to Jasper, pulling a small notebook from his back pocket. It was bent in the way that all things shoved into a back pocket eventually bend. "You have a pen?" Chester asked.

"I may have to get back to work soon," Jasper mumbled.

"Shhhh. Write this down: singing along with muzak, looks like maybe Billy Joel. Or Shania Twain."

Jasper diligently made the note. Chester watched him with a flavour of fatherly pride.

"You know, kid," he said, smiling, "you're gonna learn a lot. I'm gonna take you under my wing."

"Thanks!" said Jasper.

"Have you ever had a mentor?"

Jasper thought. "Well, I like Captain Planet."

Chester nodded. "Enough chit-chat, let's get back to bacon." Jasper hunkered down to make more notes.

Jasper's other sibling was a sister who was two years older, and who was not nearly as mean-spirited as their mutual older brother. Still, Jasper had grown up being the wingman, being told what to do at tea parties, being bossed about, never having much say in what shows were watched or what seat he got in the car. Without Chester's help he would have grown into a fine young man that sensible girls would enjoy hanging out with. A funny, happy, practical family man with a strong internal sense of interdependence on his loved ones and a good ear for listening to people.

Under Chester's tutelage he began to see the use in standing up for oneself, even if it meant bowling over other people. He also saw the collateral damage that such an attitude eventually causes much more clearly than Chester ever did. At times Chester's influence would cause Jasper to assert too much, to try too hard, to become overbearing. He had to learn for himself where the balance lay, but he was happy to have a friend who seemed to be looking out for him, and trying to improve his lot in life.

That Chester's mentorship was destined to end in tragedy was no one's fault.

It brought Jasper out of his shell a little and gave him enough confidence to start conversations with some of the other employees at the mall. He talked to Kel Urquhart in the food court until he caught Chester's eye and saw him shaking his head, trying to warn him off. Kel was a shabbily rotund manager's assistant at the Barnes & Noble, the kind of person who would never allow a backpack in the store and who took a vast, unstoppable pride in always pricing everything absolutely correctly. He had a circular mop of brown hair set on top of his smooth-cheeked face.

He was cute in the same way that anyone who grows to be 21 and still keeps his baby fat is cute. Women generally liked him well enough until they got to know him, and he would grouse at them for wearing the wrong kind of footwear in the Barnes & Noble. Guys never really liked him. Chester had a special kind of hate for him.

"He's my nemesis," he said to Kipling as they leaned against the wall in the arcade, waiting for the *Crazy Taxi* game to become available.

"You said that about Guy Tuffray, last week," Kipling replied, lazily typing numbers into his calculator watch.

"Well Guy Tuffray is my nemesis," Chester argued.

"I think you can only have one nemesis," Kipling drawled.

"Maybe regular people can only have one nemesis, but look at me." Chester held his arms wide, Kipling obliged by looking at him. "You know? They're trying to bring me down. They need two nemesisses."

"Nemeses."

"Yeah. Two of them."

"Hm," said Kipling, nodding, going back to his calculator watch.

"How many nemeses do you have?" Chester asked conversationally.

"None, I think."

"Lucky."

Kipling continued punching in numbers, then abruptly said, "What about Dr. Pointree?"

"Hell, yeah, how could I forget about her? She's my nemesis too!"

Dr. Pointree was an orthodontic surgeon who ran an office on the second floor of the mall. She inexplicably hated Chester. Had, in fact, walked up to him out of the blue at the end of the day when he was mopping an aisle in the Mega-Mart and told him so. She would tell him a second time a couple of months later, and add a hard slap right across Chester's nonchalant cheek, when he was standing just outside the Mega-Mart with Jasper. She was East Indian, with richly coloured skin, large doe-like eyes, lips like plush couches, a narrow chin, a surprisingly powerful right arm, an omnipresent clipboard, and apparently a great and unqualified loathing for Chester.

"Should I have a nemesis?" asked Jasper, who had been standing just beside the two, trying to absorb their mannerisms.

"Why's this kid here?" asked Kipling.

"He's a friend of mine," explained Chester, then leaned out and addressed Jasper. "You don't want a nemesis, kid."

Kipling turned to Jasper. "Unless you feel like you don't have enough to complain about. Hey, I'm Kipling."

"Jasper. Pleased to meet you."

They shook hands.

"Are you accusing me of complaining?" Chester said.

"That's like accusing you of breathing."

"Fair enough."

"Where do you work, kid?"

"Me? The Shopper's."

"But you know I'm right," Chester interjected.

"Oh, you're Diane's replacement," Kipling said to Jasper, then he turned to Chester. "And what I know is that the traditional nemesis relationship is one-to-one."

"When have I ever done things traditionally?"

Jasper shyly covered his name tag.

"There's a point, but it's a point in favour of tradition," Kipling said. After a pause he turned to Jasper and asked, "Do you know where I can get a thousand postcards?"

Jasper began hanging out with the two at the food court during lunch, whenever he could find the time to join them. Because of his happy-go-lucky nature and his winning personality he soon became indispensable, and was the first person to find out about Homelina's cervical cancer. He managed to assuage some of her fears with a few tender words. Everything he said was heartfelt because he could no more fake an emotion then he could manage to get a girlfriend these days. Inexplicably, after his first foray into dating he had hit an unmanageable dry spell. But then, he had hurt his first girlfriend's feelings, and perhaps the subsequent years were penance.

But Homelina appreciated the short talk they had, and said, "Someday you gonna make some woman a fine husband." She would have added, "Or maybe some man a fine husband," because Jasper was slightly androgynous that way, but she decided against it. She would have called it a tactful decision.

Jasper became a regular fixture next to Chester, and managed to become fast friends with Kipling as well. It was Jasper who managed to find a thousand postcards for Kipling after he had given up all hope. It was Jasper who unwittingly gave Gina the information she needed to persuade Chester to ask her out. It was Jasper who laid down in front of Chester and noticed how it had become suddenly cold. And it was Jasper who proved how the raccoons got into the Bulk Barn. Indispensable Jasper.

At the Shopper's Drug Mart Jasper proved himself equally indispensable and managed to gain behind-the-counter privileges, with a name tag all his own. From the slight height that was added to his modest frame by being behind the pharmaceuticals counter, he could see straight across into Candida's Fashion, and his notes for Chester became that much more robust.

Naturally the customer came first, though, so he missed the moment when January accidentally kissed Mya.

Chapter 5 - Kipling

Kipling had a list of words in his pocket. Kipling was the only one who knew the names of all the pets in the Amphibian Emporium. Kipling thought it was important to be well-rounded and well informed, and so he had several magazine subscriptions to general interest magazines that were actually special interest magazines written in a populist style, like Scientific American, Art History Digest, The Economist, The New Yorker, and National Geographic.

He was the one to make epic proclamations in a quiet, laconic drawl. Paradigms were shifted by his off-hand comments. He understood much, and knew very little. On days off he would crawl through used bookstores on his hands and knees in the back corners finding thin, dusty manuscripts published in the '70s with titles like “Diethylene Parachloride and You” or “The Exciting World of Mathematical Topography: from Dietrich spheres to double-helix functions: an introductory primer”.

He was an inveterate consumer of hand-me-downs. The vast majority of his clothes had once belonged to his older brother, and he wore them out of necessity. If he had a choice he would have burned the bell-bottomed jeans, the tight t-shirts, the button-down shirts with the too-short sleeves. Kipling lived with his parents, who owned the Amphibian Emporium and were thus fairly poor: it did not turn much of a profit. His brother had yet to move out of the house, his father had chronic pain from glaucoma, and his mother was an undiagnosed depressive with an irrational fear of hospitals. They were living hand-to-mouth in the worst way, and Kipling was the only one willing and responsible enough to keep their family store up and running. Considering the pressures he was under, the fact that he stole some of his father's medicinal marijuana to stay relaxed was remarkably level-headed of him.

When he was fourteen Kipling had invested in a very strong set of locks and installed them on his bedroom door himself. He was a loner by nature, but even loners needed social contact now and then, and he was grateful in his way for Chester's blunt friendship. He didn't want much to do with his family, for a variety of reasons.

"He seems cool, but I don't know. He never gets excited about anything, you know?" said Areola to Dove Anquanita, shaking her hair and making her curly semi-afro bounce. She was standing behind Dove, cutting her hair. Areola was a senior stylist at VictorStyle. Distant, generic house music drifted through the air of the massive, open-concept salon and mingled with the nauseating chemical potpourri of sprays, perfumes, fixers, spritzes, looseners, straighteners, curlers, and permanents. Dove hated Areola's hair because she was jealous of it. Dove had thin, bodiless, straight, hazelnut brown hair that suited her perfectly and which she thus despised.

At least, Dove thought to herself, I'm taller than her. But she replied, "Yeah. He was, like, totally asking for weeks about this CD that he ordered. He kept coming in and he would go on and on about it, like, it was like he was in love with this CD or something. And then when it came in he was like, 'Oh, okay.' Like he didn't even really give a damn." Dove tilted her head as Areola pushed it gently and set about sculpting Dove's hair with scissors and fine-toothed comb, angling herself this way and that to see it from all sides. She made an exploratory snip.

"Did I tell you Polito bought me a membership to the Indie Club?" Areola asked.

"Oh, fuck," Dove replied, her shoulders slumping.

"What?"

"Please just, like, don't ask me to explain how it works, okay?" Dove worked at the HMV and they had just launched a new initiative known as the Indie Club, which had the most Machiavellian system of discounts and rewards of any incentive program in the known universe. It was specifically designed to discourage its members from using it. The employees at the HMV were quickly learning to discern the perplexed look, the slightly furrowed brow, that meant a customer was about to say the five words they most despised: "So, how does this work?"

"Well, how does it work?" Areola flicked the comb professionally through Dove's hair.

"Listen, I want to help you, but, like, this is only a 45-minute cut-and-style," Dove said. "We don't have enough time. We'll need, like, a whole evening or something. And even then..." She trailed off.

Areola stopped cutting and put her hand on her hip. "What, do you think I'm stupid? Jesus, Dove!"

"No, of course I don't," Dove began, although that's exactly what she did think, "it's just, like, a totally ridiculous program. You know, like, we all had to take this, like, week-long course just to learn how it worked!"

"Whatever. You just like having this to hold over my head."

"It's not like that."

Areola went back to styling Dove's hair in silence.

Dove sighed. "I, like, hate my job," she muttered.

"You don't have to work at the HMV," Areola said.

"It was totally fine before this."

"Totally fine? Totally fine?!"

"What?"

"How many times have I heard you bitch and moan

about that job!"

"Well. Yeah, like, it sucked but it didn't suck like this sucks."

Areola smiled despite herself. "You have a way with words, girl." Then she added slyly, "You could always work at the Barnes & Noble."

Dove shot her a look in the mirror through the wet strands of her hair. "Like, I totally hope you are joking!"

"Why?"

"Kel Fucking Urquhart is why!" Areola cracked a smile, and Dove was laughing to herself. Their friendship had begun as a mutual hatred of Kel Fucking Urquhart, as they invariably called him.

After a little while Dove said, "You know who you could ask?"

"Hm?"

"Kipling. He's the only person I know who I think actually, like, understands the Indie Club."

Areola tilted her head and thought about it. "I don't know, I've barely talked to him, you know? To just walk up and be, like, 'Hey, tell me how this works', won't it be weird?"

"Well, yeah," said Dove, "but you're a weird chiquita, you can pull it off."

"He's weird, too."

"Yeah."

"He's a smart guy, though," she said.

"Yeah," agreed Dove, "totally a smart guy."

Chester disagreed.

"You're an idiot," he said to Kipling as they ate their lunch in the food court. Kipling had just told Chester that Polito didn't like him.

Kipling shrugged. "I'm just telling you what he told me."

"What if I don't believe you?"

"You can believe what you want to believe," Kipling replied. He said it like he was mulling over the thought, working it into his personal philosophy.

"Come on. Everybody likes me. What's not to like?"

"I have to pick one?"

"You like me."

"Actually, I already told you that I don't." Kipling finished his chicken soft taco and picked up the second of the quartet.

"Oh," said Chester, nonplussed. "What about Rose McDougall, at the stationery store?"

"No, she thinks you don't like listening to her stories."

"Well her stories are boring, they don't go anywhere," Chester said exasperatedly.

Kipling shrugged.

"What about Nordquist?" Nordquist was head of the janitorial staff, a tall, lanky man with short, battleship-grey hair and tattoos on his arms and chest. He was a 50-something family man now, but he had spent many years in the merchant marines before settling down and being hired at the mall. He was a contemplative and contented fellow, and his swabbing the deck skills were exemplary. Plus he seemed to enjoy the work. He whistled a lot.

"No."

"Why not?"

"Do you recall what you said about his book club?"

"Which time?"

"When he told you who else was in it."

"Oh. And I said if you put a grenade in the middle of that circle it would be a mad dash to see who could pull the pin first?"

"That's it."

"How could he hate me for that?"

Kipling shrugged. "I don't know. Accuracy, perhaps. I'm just telling you what he told me."

"Does Chelsea like me?"

"Nope."

"Starla?"

"Nope."

"Mazy?" Chester was reaching for straws now.

"No, she doesn't like how you ask her out every time you see her."

Chester thought about it. "What about Stanswick?"

"Stanswick who works at the Moore's or Stanswick who works at the popcorn place?"

"Stanswick who works at the Moore's, retard. The other Stanswick got fired, like, a year ago. And Colonel Kernel's closed down."

"I know that, I was just double-checking. And don't say 'retard', it's uncouth."

"Sorry."

"Anyway, he hates you."

"Well what about the other Stanswick?"

"He hates you, too. You got him fired."

"I didn't get him fired. He got himself fired."

"You provoked him."

"That's not true."

"I'm just telling you what he told me."

Chester paused. "When did you see Stanswick?"

"Which one?"

"Arrrgh," said Chester, grabbing the table and shaking it enough to rattle the bolts holding it to the floor.

"He comes by the Emporium every once in a while. You know he's an entrepreneur now."

"Entrepreneur?"

"It's French. I think it means 'between jobs'."

"So he just drops by?"

"Well, he bought Dr. Osterhosen." Kipling finished his second chicken soft taco and began on the third.

"You know I think it's weird, the names you give those lizards."

"Amphibians," Kipling calmly corrected. "And they're not really names, it's just what I call them."

Chester put his head down on the table, moaned loudly. After a good moment he pulled his head back up and took a sip of his drink. Kipling finished off his last chicken soft taco.

"What about Mr. deHavilland?" Mr. deHavilland was an elderly man who arrived at the mall early every morning with a chessboard under his arm. Polito or Modesta Mae would let him in as they were opening the doors and he would shuffle to the food court and set up the chess board at the same table every day and slowly play chess until the mall closed. Kipling had noticed that it seemed like he was playing the same game over and over, altering one or two moves each day.

"No one's ever talked to Mr. deHavilland," Kipling said, brushing his hands together like a cowboy who just finished a dusty job. "But if I had to guess, I would say that he didn't like you."

Chester was not as universally reviled as Kipling made it seem. Kipling felt it necessary and potentially useful to test Chester's mettle. Chester, ever confrontational, would usually find a time to challenge his erstwhile hater, who, it would usually turn out, didn't actually hate Chester, but just didn't like certain things about him. Slowly, like a glacier receding and leaving a remarkably changed landscape, Chester became a better, or at least more likeable, person.

Kipling, too, was not universally loved.

"He just gets under my skin. He's so laid-back with his stupid voice and his stupid way of talking," Kel Urquhart said to Guy Tuffray after an early morning manager's meeting during which Ipswitch had welcomed Tuffray to his new promotion as manager at the Mega-Mart.

"Listen, Kel," Tuffray began, "you're just a manager's assistant. Okay? I'm a manager." Tuffray invested the word manager with the importance some people might put on the words President of the United States. "Okay? If you have a managerial issue to ask for my help with, that's excellent. Otherwise, shut your mouth."

Kel's face immediately flushed a bright red, and he turned and left with a tight-lipped grimace. Tuffray felt good. He turned back to Clyde Saphoria, the manager of the Taco Bell, who was a short and remarkably thin man with tiny feet clad in small patent black leather shoes. He was balding, but wore a hairpiece that had obviously been constructed for a much larger man's head. The edges of the wig overlapped his ears. Saphoria looked up at Tuffray.

"Where was I?" said Tuffray.

"You were telling me about this turddropper, Chester, and his friend Kipling," Saphoria bellowed.

He made up for his small stature by speaking in a gigantic yell. Whenever Gina heard his voice, which could be heard halfway across the mall on a slow midmorning, she would cringe in anticipation of a physical blow. He never hit her, it just somehow felt like he was on the brink of doing so.

"Yeah, they get up to no end of trouble: slacking off, lazing about. They're ne'er-do-wells I tell you, and we've got to get rid of them."

"Can't you discipline them?"

"I've tried, with Chester, but he knows that I can't fire him. I haven't brought it up to Mr. Ipswitch yet. I'd like to try to handle the issue myself."

"Just give 'em a good talking-to. Always works for me." Saphoria balled his hands into tiny fists and planted them on his hips.

"Yes!" Tuffray said, exultant, "maybe you could talk to them for me. Specifically to Chester, actually. Kipling isn't the bad one. I don't think he would do anything without Chester. That one," Tuffray shook his head. "He's a bad seed. He's such a pain in my ass I'm going to have to start taking Tylenol suppositories." Tuffray chuckled at his own joke.

"Naw, naw. I'm too busy to solve your problems, too." Saphoria crossed his arms.

"No, no, I don't want you to solve my problems, I—"

"Listen you gotta learn to handle it yourself," Saphoria yelled with a nod.

"Can you please keep it down?" Tuffray asked, looking around at the milling managers talking in hushed tones, casting annoyed glances in his direction. Fortunately Ipswitch had left already. Tuffray couldn't face an angry tirade during his first week as a manager.

"I'm not doing clean-up for your incompetence," Saphoria added.

"I'm not asking—"

"Learn to control your own staffing issues, son. A good talking-to, that's all they need." He gave another nod and a knowing wink and then stalked out of the meeting room.

Tuffray, embarrassed, looking around apologetically at the other managers, moved back into the corner of the meeting room near the large plastic potted tree. He stopped there for a second, sighed, and looked down to see Gina's peppery grey-black winter coat. He picked it up and said, "Huh."

Kipling was the kind of person who would have known whose coat it was. He had an eye for detail and he had a knack for listening. He might have made a good detective except that he tended to believe almost everything that people told him. As such, he had agglomerated a wide selection of varying beliefs and managed to shoehorn them into his own personal philosophy.

He believed that plastic particles could get into your lungs if you drank with a straw. He believed that many young kids carried handguns, but he wanted to give them the benefit of the doubt and assumed they used them for personal protection only. He believed that humans were amphibians before being born.

"How can you believe that?" Chester asked.

"Well, the amniotic sac is filled with fluid when we are developing in the womb. That's essentially the same as the tadpole stage – we even have these gill-looking kind of things to breathe before the umbilical cord develops," Kipling explained.

"Okay, now you're freaking me out," Chester said as he stood and dumped his lunch tray into the garbage bin.

Kipling believed that if you wish hard enough you can make something happen through the sheer application of force of will. He believed there were GPS tracking devices in the heels of his shoes. He believed that banks ruled the world.

"Consider: they consistently turn a profit, and they get away with murder. Look at bank fees," said Polito at the end of his once-around, standing by the entrance to the Amphibian Emporium. Kipling nodded.

He believed that pot should be legalized. He believed that there were either mutants, crocodiles, or mutant crocodiles in the sewers of large cities. He believed that teachers assigned marks using some archaic formula that was based on the letters in your name, or at least your initials. He believed it was not necessary to wear matching socks. Some days he believed that he could read minds.

He would be the first to admit that some of his beliefs did not make sense. But he would hasten to add, "You can believe what you want to believe."

"All I believe is that girl's don't like me," replied Dusty.

Kipling stopped punching buttons on his calculator watch. The tinny beeping sounds were not conducive to in-depth discussions. "Why do you say that?"

"I don't know. They don't seem interested," Dusty said. They were sitting on the cold concrete floor of the security corridor that ran behind all of the stores. The games and hobby store, which kept changing its name, was right next to the Amphibian Emporium, and the two employees would take breaks at the same time. Fifteen-minute snippets of friendly conversation.

"You just need more confidence."

"How do I get more confidence?"

"Well," Kipling shrugged. "You go out with girls."

"But I can't go out with girls," Dusty said, exasperated.

"Why not?"

"Because they're not interested in me."

"But you've got a lot going for you. You're a nice guy, easy to talk to, good sense of humour, a decent job, going to school, saving some money for college."

"Yeah, I guess."

"You just need more confidence," Kipling said, tracing with his finger on the rough concrete.

"Yeah," Dusty sighed. "I guess. I'm back to square one."

"Where did you start?"

Dusty looked up at him. "Well, square one."

"Ah, I see."

"How else can I get confidence?"

"Have you tried dating?"

Dusty sighed.

There was a momentary pause, then Kipling asked, "Is there anyone you're interested in?"

Dusty hemmed and hawed. "There's one girl."

"Who?"

"It's Dove Anquanita. You know, she's at the HMV."

"Yeah, I know her."

"Yeah, she's so hot. And she's got really cool taste in music and stuff."

Kipling hesitated, and then said, "What about her nose?"

"What about it?"

"Well..."

"Is there something wrong with her nose?" Dusty asked, genuinely concerned.

"It's just a little...over-sized," Kipling said as tactfully as possible.

"Is it?" Dusty was flabbergasted, picturing Dove in his mind, trying to remember. "I didn't notice," he said.

"Forget I said anything," Kipling said, dismissing his comment with a casual wave of his hand. "So are you going to ask her out?"

"I can't, man."

"Dusty," Kipling said with a note of potential irritation. He didn't want to hear that kind of talk.

"No, I just can't. It's too nerve-wracking. It destroys me just trying to meet her eyes when I walk past her."

"Have you ever talked to her?"

"Once, at a staff Christmas party thing."

"So what happened?"

"I offered her some eggnog. She said no thanks." Dusty ran a hand through his bedraggled, straw-coloured hair. It maintained its shape, like a stiff meringue.

"Well, see, at least you have some history together."

Dusty thought about it. "Do you think she might want some eggnog now?"

"No, probably not. It's September." Kipling put a hand on Dusty's shoulder, patted it a few times.

"Damn," said Dusty, "I thought I had my in, man."

Kipling was never good at giving advice. Customers would ask him for his opinion on which amphibian to purchase as a potential pet. Which were the most cuddly? Which were the hardest to care for? Which ones could you housebreak? Those questions he could answer. Which one is meant for me? That question was much harder. It would haunt him for the rest of the day.

As the mall closed down and Kipling mopped the floor of the Amphibian Emporium he would try to work out a good answer. Somewhere in the depths of the mall Mo pulled the switch to turn off half the lights, marking the official closing time, and with a heavy clunk Kipling was plunged into a fluorescent twilight. Looking up he spotted Kel Urquhart at the far end of the food court, sipping menacingly from an Orange Julius. He waved, and watched as Kel turned on his heel and stormed away. Then he went back to mopping and pondering.

Jasper stopped by as Kipling was locking the metal security grid that slid across the entrance to the Emporium.

"What are you doing here?" Kipling asked suspiciously.

"I'm walking home with you," Jasper replied. They'd been walking home together for the past four months, and went through the same conversation almost every night.

"Oh. What's the notebook for?"

"Chester gave it to me. He wants me to make notes

on January. You know: field research."

Kipling dropped the keys in his pocket, began walking, and Jasper fell in beside him. "Where are you going?" Kipling asked.

"Home," Jasper explained. "I'm walking home with you. We live down the street from each other."

"Ah."

"Did you know that Mo and Gina live down the street from each other, too? And Tuffray lives with his parents, across the street from Ipswitch."

"Yeah, I heard that."

"Isn't that a weird coincidence?" Jasper pushed the door open and held it for Kipling as they exited the mall.

"You can't pick your neighbours," said Kipling as he breathed in the sharp autumn evening air. It smelled like fallen leaves and shuttered houses.

"I thought it was you can't pick your family?"

"That too," Kipling said, with an odd quality to his voice.

"So who can you pick?"

"Your friends," Kipling said, putting his hands in his pockets. "Supposedly." There was a quiet reflection between the two. As they came upon a pile of leaves Kipling swept them up into the air with the side of his shoe. Jasper kicked his feet creating a dust devil of leaves that swirled down the street.

"I love fall," said Jasper.

"Are you following me?" Kipling asked.

"No, I'm walking home with you. We live down the street from each other."

"Oh. Do you know where I can get a thousand postcards?"

"Actually I did find a place," Jasper replied. "Why do you need a thousand postcards, anyway?"

Kipling thought of Chester, and replied, "Why wouldn't I?"

Chapter 6 - Ipswitch

What happened to Guy Tuffray after he found Gina's coat, left by accident in her mad rush to leave the Christmas party, was bad luck or kismet, depending on how much you liked Guy Tuffray. For Polito and Chester, sitting in the cramped back room watching the security monitors, there was no discussion. It was kismet, karma, the blind hand of justice. It was retribution. And they didn't even know the full story, nor would they ever. It took a little more than a year for it all to play out. From their perspective, Ipswitch just hated Tuffray. That was natural.

"C'mon fellas, don't you think you should give the poor guy a break?" asked Jasper, one hand in his pocket, the other clutching his notebook, looking from Polito back to Chester.

It was a sticky summer day and the mall's ancient air conditioning system was labouring like Hercules to break the steamy damp quality of the air. It didn't help that Ipswitch ran the old beast at the lowest possible setting to try to save money. Chester was lounging on a folding metal chair, wishing he had a sombrero to pull over his eyes so he could ignore everyone and catch some zees.

Polito slowly looked over his shoulder at Jasper. "What the fuck is wrong with you, man?"

"Polito," Chester said in mild rebuke, eyes closed,

leaning back, legs crossed.

Polito turned a little further to give Chester the crook eye, but Chester was settling in to saw some logs and didn't notice. Polito turned back to the monitors shaking his head.

"What did I say?" asked Jasper, feeling ashamed.

"It's okay Jasper, you just don't know what you're saying. You don't know Guy Tuffray."

"Damn skippy you don't know him," said Polito, maneuvering a camera to try to see into change room 17.

"What's so bad about Guy?"

"Guy Tuffray. You have to say his whole name. And try to say it like it's dripping with hatred. Like in a comic book," Chester explained, arms folded comfortably, looking serene as he relaxed his face.

"Guy Tuffray."

"That's weak," said Polito.

"Polito."

"Guy Tuffray," said Jasper.

"That's a bit better. That's more sarcasm than hatred but we'll work on it," said Chester.

"So what's so bad about him?"

Polito made a sound between a snort and a pfft.

"I think what our friend Polito is trying to say is what isn't wrong with him? But it's a story for another time, kid. Right now you should think about getting some sleep." Chester settled in more comfortably, his spine forming a sort of bowed triangle with the chair seat and back.

Ipswitch chose that moment to burst into the already crowded room, his eyes nearly smoking with impotent rage. "Polito!" he snarled, slamming the door with the authority of a prison guard. Polito shot into the air, up on his feet in a second.

"Yes, sir!"

"Raccoons broke into the Bulk Barn last night. They got into the nuts, the candy, the dried fruits. The place is a mess, an absolute cock-up! Now where the hell were you?" He stabbed a thick, meaty finger into

Polito's chest. It was his left index, which had been broken six months before. Now that it was fully healed and no longer pained him, Ipswitch had taken to jabbing it into people's chests when he was angry.

"I was at home, sir," he said hesitantly. He wasn't sure if that was the right answer. It wasn't.

"Home? What the hell were you doing piddly-dancing at home when there were raccoons breaking into the Bulk Barn?"

"I didn't know there were raccoons breaking into the Bulk Barn."

"You didn't know? It's your job to know."

"Mr. Ipswitch, you were the one who fired the night security staff and told Mo and I to lock the doors and go home when the mall closed."

"I don't need a recap of my life, numbskull, I know what I did. That doesn't excuse the fact that you are head of mall security."

"Yes."

"And it is your job to know what is going on in this mall, in a security sense. Right?"

"Yes," Polito answered reluctantly.

"And having a break-in by a bunch of animals is a goddamned security issue, isn't it, numbskull?"

"Yes," Polito said with resignation.

He had learned long ago that there was no escaping the inevitability of a guilty verdict from the kangaroo court where Ipswitch was judge, jury, and court stenographer. It was, in a very real way, just part of his job. Mo had been offered the head of mall security position first. She had turned it down. Polito now knew her to be the wiser of the two.

"Get over there right now and help them clean up the mess," Ipswitch barked, turning to leave.

"Yes, sir."

He whirled around, "And find out how those raccoons are getting in and stop them!" He turned to stomp away under a black cloud.

"Yes, sir," Polito said under his breath.

Ipswitch pirouetted neatly back, with surprising

agility. He barked, "And Chester!"

"Mm?" said Chester sleepily, not opening his eyes or getting up out of the chair.

"Keep up the good work." Ipswitch whipped around on his heel a final time and marched away glowering and muttering. He walked the way you might imagine an annoying upstairs neighbour would walk, lifting his knees and stomping his feet down flat on the ground.

"God damn it," said Polito. He glanced back at the monitors wistfully, "I almost had the angle just right. See? Change room 17." He sighed noisily, grabbed his jacket from the back of the door and took a walkie-talkie from the recharging unit on the desk.

"Can I come with you?" Jasper asked, excited. He'd never been involved in an investigation before. He clutched his notebook in both hands excitedly.

"Whatever," Polito said.

"Do I get a walkie-talkie?" Jasper asked innocently.

"No!"

"Please?"

Polito didn't respond, he just tugged his uniform into place, wiped his sweaty brow, and the two strode purposefully, if wearily on Polito's part, away and left Chester to snore lightly as January got undressed in change room 17. Another missed opportunity.

Ipswitch's hatred for Tuffray had bloomed from a short series of coincidences. When Tuffray put Gina's coat in the back of his car, he tossed it in haphazardly and didn't notice that it landed fairly flat on the backseat. Because Tuffray always arrived before Ipswitch his car was parked closer to the mall. That fact changed when Ipswitch had the parking lot repainted so he could have a private space right next to the entrance. He put Tuffray's spot in the far back corner. The repainting was a cost-cutting endeavor which, as everyone agreed, made it nearly impossible to navigate the parking lot without ramming into at least two cars and a couple of pedestrians.

As Ipswitch walked past Tuffray's car he saw the coat draped across the backseat, and mistook it for his own wife's coat. It was easy to mistake, Gina and Ipswitch's wife did own the same coat, they both shopped at the mall. Due to the suggestive placement Ipswitch imagined that it had been taken off of his wife by Tuffray while she was lying supine in the back seat of Tuffray's car. Her long milky legs wrapped around Tuffray's beanpole hips. Her dark, wavy hair cascading across his plaid upholstered backseat. Her hands holding his pale, columnar face, topped with its ratty dust trap of thin, carrot-coloured hair and adorned with his desperate mustache. The image almost made Ipswitch's nervous system melt. His whole body shook, and blood zoomed around inside him, up into his face, and into his muscles as he clenched them spasmodically. A tiny mushroom cloud very nearly appeared over his head. His first impulse was to kill Guy Tuffray by ripping his appendages off and force-feeding them to him until his gut exploded. But he stopped himself.

No, Ipswitch thought with a sadistic gleam in his eye, that would be too good for him.

He noted, too, that he didn't have enough proof, necessarily, to condemn Tuffray just yet. But all he needed was one iota more. He got into his car and peeled off a layer of rubber from his tires in leaving the parking lot.

Tuffray was blissfully unaware of his fate. He left work whistling to himself, feeling satisfied about a good day of managing. The Mega-Mart staff, he felt, were beginning to respect his authority and his leadership. He had managed to fire all the rabble-rouser types except Chester, and if he could just get on Ipswitch's good side he felt he had a decent chance of keeping the floater out of his store. If he could, then he could probably operate the Mega-Mart cleanly and efficiently, and going to work every day would be a small joy he could savour like a warm cup of hot chocolate after a nice long cross-country ski.

When he got to his car he got the coat out and went to the information booth to propose an exciting new idea to the Sumerian. He had never been able to talk to the Sumerian before, but now he was a manager.

“Hi,” he said brightly, leaning against the counter of the info booth, the coat draped over his arm. “I’m Guy Tuffray, the new manager at the Mega-Mart.” He held out his hand to shake. The Sumerian gave him a long appraising stare.

Unfazed, Tuffray continued, “Listen, I found this coat in one of the, uh, meeting rooms. And, yes, I um thought it might be a good idea to start a lost and found.” He swallowed heavily under the Sumerian’s unflinching gaze. “What do y-you think?”

The Sumerian very slowly shook his head.

“Not interested, huh?” he laughed nervously. He had no idea the trouble that he was in. Suddenly Rose McDougall plucked at his sleeve and fortuitously saved him from further embarrassment. She had overheard him proposing the idea to the Sumerian.

“I’d be interested in starting a lost and found, I think that’s a good idea,” she said. She was about a decade older than most of the employees of the mall, and had been working there ever since giving up her dreams in her second year of college. She was a mature, responsible, boring woman who told mature, responsible, boring stories.

“Oh, great,” said Guy Tuffray, realizing she had saved him from the creeping red prickling sensation that meant he was blushing all over his face and halfway down his upper torso. He walked with her towards the Grand & Toy and spared a moment to look over his shoulder and say, “Thanks anyway!” to the Sumerian.

Underneath the counter of the information booth, the Sumerian lowered his Glock 9mm.

Meanwhile Ipswitch, his breath hot in his throat, his powerful meaty hands turning the doorknob, entered his house through the garage. His wife was in the kitchen, and she breezed out in a cloud of luscious perfume with a beatific smile and gave him a kiss on the cheek.

"Hi, honey. Dinner is on the table, I've got to go out but I'll be back in a couple of hours, okay?" She rattled the words out as if they were well-rehearsed: precisely and without inflection.

"Huh? What do you have to go out for?" Ipswitch's deep-set green eyes were like craters in his moon-shaped face, and he narrowed those craters at his wife.

"Oh, I'm just...going to the neighbour's," she said. She put on a scarf.

"For what?"

"For a visit, you old silly! Now go eat your dinner and be good. And take care of that finger," she said, indicating the splint on his left index. It was wrapped with tensor bandage up past his wrist.

She was sweetly mothering in a completely unselfconscious way. She kissed him again, this time her pouted, freshly lipsticked lips against his thrust-out, resolute bottom lip. She patted his shoulder, and then left the same way he had come in.

He turned to go to the kitchen, and then thought better of it and came back as he heard her car start and the garage door opener trundle to life. He opened the door and stepped out to see her backing out, not wearing her coat.

"Wait!" he yelled, starting after her, but she was looking over her shoulder as she backed out and the garage door was already coming down. He was too respectable to shoulder roll underneath the door, so he cursed, stymied, as the door came down in front of his face.

Back inside he went to the living room window and fingered the blinds apart with his unsullied right index and middle fingers. He squinted through, his lips pulling back over his square teeth in a slight snarl. Across the street he could see that Guy Tuffray's car wasn't in the driveway. Going to see the neighbours indeed, he thought murderously.

Four hours later he was sitting on the flower-print

couch in the living room in complete darkness, his eyes fixed on the door to the garage, where his wife would enter. The rage inside his body had reached the point of fusion, and was combining with fury, patience, cleverness, and cruelty to form new compound emotions of dizzying power. It was the fuel that would drive his engine of revenge.

The door opened. His wife entered, thinking herself alone, humming. She was wearing her coat. Then she closed the door and the square of light from the garage disappeared.

She was in light spirits, he saw. He was willing to bide his time. All his thermonuclear bombs of impassioned hatred had gone off, and he was now irradiated with the kind of slow-cooling malevolence that had a half-life of millions of years. She turned on a light, and he noticed that her skin was slightly flushed. She began to cross to the kitchen.

"So," he said conversationally.

She shrieked. "Oh, god, you scared me!" she said, her hand holding her chest to keep it from visibly pounding.

"Did I?"

"What are you doing sitting here in the dark?" she asked.

"Heightening my senses," he answered with a cruel smile.

"Well did you have any dinner?" she asked, walking towards him and leaning down to give him a kiss on the forehead.

"So who did you visit?" he asked, ignoring her question.

"I went to see Mary."

"Mary lives two doors down from us. Why did you have to drive?"

"Oh, um, we went out for coffee." She busied herself, pulling off gloves, scarf, boots.

"Oh, where did you go?"

"The Have-a-Java. I mean, the Second Cup."

"Well, which one was it?"

"The...the Second Cup."

"You seem hesitant. Maybe I should call Mary and ask," he said, his eyes narrowing to slits. His jaw was so tense he could have crushed diamond. He shifted down the couch, towards the phone.

"I'll just give her a quick call," he said.

"What?" his wife said, confused. "Why would you call Mary right now? It's almost midnight."

"Very well," he conceded, dropping the phone back onto its cradle.

"You're acting weird," his wife declared. "I'm going upstairs."

"I'll join you in a minute," Ipswitch replied, his mouth twisted sourly.

She began climbing the carpeted steps, making the dull thumping sounds of stockings on carpet, and said, "Don't forget we have that dinner with your parents tomorrow for your birthday."

"Hmph," he replied, scornfully. He went to the window again, pushed a thick finger between the slats and looked out. Tuffray's car was just gliding down the street, devil-may-care, and turned into the driveway opposite. Ipswitch's cheek twitched as he watched Tuffray get out of his car, whistling.

Ipswitch looked back over his shoulder, up the stairs, his eyes trying to burn through the floor directly into his wife's cold, stony heart.

The next night, when his wife pretended to be lost and drove them into the parking lot of the local Knights of Columbus guild hall and led him begrudgingly to the door to "ask directions", and he was greeted by a hundred of his closest acquaintances yelling "Surprise!", he still didn't put two and two together. He had seen things the way that he wanted to see them.

And when he saw Guy Tuffray there, with his parents, he began to give Tuffray a taste of what his life would be like for the next thousand or so years. They shook hands and Tuffray said, "Happy birthday, Mr. Ipswitch!"

Ipswitch replied, "Tuffray, I'm thinking that the

floater, Chester is it? He should probably be helping you out at the Mega-Mart more often. Don't you agree?”

Chapter 7 - January

Jasper only let Chester down once, and it happened after he went with Polito to the Bulk Barn to see how the raccoons got in. They arrived and Polito immediately set to asking the tough questions while Jasper helped the other employees clean up the spilled nuts, candies, and dried fruits.

"So...what happened?" Polito asked, hands on his belt, looking down at the group of pissed off Bulk Barn employees who were on their knees sweeping up bulk produce. Sullenly they cleaned up the mess, ignoring his question, until one girl piped up and said, "Some raccoons broke in." She had long black hair and pale skin. She was obviously a goth when she wasn't forced to wear the unnaturally purple Bulk Barn shirt.

"No shit, Sherlock," Polito snapped. He lifted his head, surveying, and spoke with his most authoritarian voice, "Does anyone know how the raccoons got in here?" He was greeted with stony silence. He wished Mo didn't have the day off. She had a way of asking questions so that people answered. It was like everyone could tell that Polito was too lazy to hassle them that much. That he would tire of it before they would. Which is exactly what everyone knew.

Polito left to investigate, which meant eating handfuls of bulk candy and dried apricots without paying for them and hemming and hawing as he looked around at the floor, leaning this way and that to try to gather clues. It seemed so much easier on CSI. You just showed up on the crime scene and bingo, there was the small piece of thread that would eventually tie up the whole case for you.

Jasper finished helping the other employees clean up and felt a mild sense of dissatisfaction. For some reason he had expected cloak and dagger work, tense interrogations under hot lights, maybe a chase through the back lanes and loading docks of the stores along this side of the mall. He realized his expectations might have been unrealistic, and with a self-conscious shrug he went to the food court for a quick lunch before he had to start work at the Shopper's Drug Mart. He had his notebook under his arm and opened it to thumb through his recent notes on January as he waited in line at the Taco Bell.

When he got to the front Gina said, "What's that?"

"Oh," said Jasper distractedly, rereading an entry from the other day, "it's just a notebook."

"I know that," she said rolling her eyes. "What's it for?"

"Oh, Chester wants me to keep notes on January," he replied. Then his head snapped up and he clapped the notebook closed. "Um," he said. He felt horrible: he'd just broken a promise he'd made to Chester to "never breathe a word of this to anyone," in Chester's words.

Gina frowned. "Why does Chester want you to keep notes on January? Does he have a crush on her or—"

"No, no, forget I said anything," Jasper backpedalled quickly, waving his hands in her face, looking around to make sure no one had heard.

"That son of a bitch has a crush on her, doesn't he?" Gina said, tearing her flimsy plastic food prep gloves off and slamming her hat down on the counter.

"No, no, Gina...Gina calm down," Jasper said. He wasn't sure he understood why Gina was upset, but he knew he had to contain the situation.

Gina paced back and forth behind the counter like

she was practicing for the drum corps, stomping back and forth with her lower lip set in anger. "Oh, god, how could I be so stupid?" she asked herself.

"Gina, no, you don't understand," said Jasper.

"Of course he has a crush on her, why wouldn't he have a crush on that stupid, bitchy, arrogant, stuck-up, egotistical, snooty—"

"No, Gina, he doesn't have a crush on January, she has a crush on him," Jasper explained. That stopped Gina short.

"She has a crush on him?" She wasn't sure if that was better or worse.

"Yes," sighed Jasper. "He just has me doing some fieldwork for him to...help him out."

"Does he like her?"

"Um, well. Don't tell anyone," Jasper said, leaning closer, "but I think he's going to ask her out."

Gina felt a cold little explosion in her heart, like it had been frozen and then hit with a hammer, bursting into pieces. "Oh," she said, giving Jasper a sad smile. Jasper smiled back, thinking: crisis averted. Gina quietly put her hat back on and got new plastic gloves from the small dispenser on the counter.

"Anyway. Could I get the number four, please? With extra sour cream?"

Gina wandered away slowly, feeling a bit numb and dazed. It seemed like her chances were gone. It seemed like she should pack it in, let bygones be bygones, call it a night, cash in her chips, etc. January was arguably one of the most beautiful employees at the mall, at least physically. She was also a cold, ruthless, self-inflated asshole, too stuck up to even say "hi" back to Gina when she had gone out of her way to be nice and try to strike up a conversation with her when she saw her in the food court. But she was hot. Even Gina, who understood awkwardness, didn't understand that January didn't get into conversation with people because she had no idea what to say or how to say it. January maintained what she would call an aloof mystique and all the other employees at the mall called bald-faced bitchiness.

It didn't help that January was attractive. The combination of beauty and stalwart social avoidance had become a barrier of mythology that January thought she was too good for everyone else. That she was somehow too beautiful to speak to the lowly peons. With that mentality firmly in Gina's mind, how was she supposed to compete? Better to save face, be mature, use it as a growing experience. But there was something, some niggling doubt that touched the back of her mind and made her think there was a way to turn everything around. And then suddenly it hit her.

When she came back to Jasper with his order she was smiling. "You know," she began, "I don't think Chester will have much chance just asking January straight out like that."

"Why not?" Jasper asked, putting his notebook on the tray and taking the tray in both hands.

"Well, she gets asked out a lot, you know."

"I've never seen her get asked out," Jasper said.

"That's what I mean. Everyone knows she's got a screening process."

"Screening process?"

"Yeah." She said it like he'd just asked if Taco Bell served tacos.

"What's the screening process?"

"She always gets a friend of hers to go out with the guy first – on, like, a trial date – and then her friend tells her whether the guy is worth going out with or not. If he does a good job on the date and is, like, super-sweet and nice and everything then he gets the best rating."

"The best rating?" Jasper asked naively.

"Oh, it's all about the rating," Gina gushed. "Like if you want to get to have a date with January you've got to get at least a triple A plus rating."

"Wow, that sounds pretty high." Jasper looked slightly crestfallen.

"Yeah. You have to make sure you act right on the date with January's friend."

"Who is this friend of hers that goes on all these dates?"

Gina smiled angelically. "Me."

Besides some certain conversations that Chester had with Kipling, Jasper's and Gina's chat had been the longest anyone had talked about January at the mall. She was completely unpopular for the same reason that some people are exceedingly popular, which is no good reason at all.

Being a bitch was certainly no barrier to popularity, since Dove Anquanita was quite popular and also, most agreed, a full-on bitch salad. Even social awkwardness was not particularly a barrier. Chester, for example, was popular even though he could turn a good conversation sour with his penchant for asking blunt questions. And Watson Huffernanny was at virtually every party – by invitation, no less! – even though he would often spend the entire time corralling people into a corner so he could expound on his thoughts about the casting of the last *Star Wars* movie.

No one talked about January, not even disparagingly. Had she known, she would have preferred that people say something, even hateful things. She was blissfully unaware of her complete lack of importance in everyone's lives. She thought they must be talking about her, either enviously or hopefully. She didn't think she was put out of mind, she thought they were all jealous or intimidated. That may have been the case years ago, but by this point everyone was too sick and tired of her supposed attitude, and so she had been cast out. It was like a genteel version of being excluded from Amish society; a kind of Shunning Lite.

Too, it wasn't just that she was rarely asked out, she had never been asked out. Even Puck, who had once jokingly asked out Shorsky, even though she was 71 and had an odd lump growing just under her jawline, had never asked January out. He had spent a fruitless week trying to sleep with her by dropping subtle hints, but she never picked up on it. She had, in fact, been quite afraid to bump into Puck during that week because he kept trying to talk to her and it made her nervous.

No one asked her to go get some coffee, no one asked her if she was busy, no one invited her to their parties. Peoria, who had a party almost every week, refused to invite January. After all, January was more attractive than her, and she was boring, snobbish, prudish, egotistical, loud, desperate, and a real bitch sometimes. January was on the receiving end of a lot of adjectives that didn't necessarily apply to her in real life. But since no one ever really talked to her, no one ever learned that she wasn't, for example, a shrewish, frigid, cruel, hectoring, shallow racist. She had been accused, in absentia, of all of those qualities.

January missed a lot by not being invited to Peoria's parties. Colin Hanks, the son of Tom Hanks, had been at one of Peoria's sprawling, weekend-long boozefests. He had regaled the crowd with hilarious tales of hanging out with Freddie Prinze, Jr. How the two of them tried to find haemorrhoid cream for Prinze's best friend's mom at three in the morning in LA. The time they accidentally wound up naked on the seventh hole of the golf course inside the Luxor Hotel in Las Vegas. Their road trip up to the giant redwood forests north of San Francisco when they got lost on the wrong side of the Santa Lucia mountain range and had to drive through an airforce base to get back to Highway 1 and had their backpacks confiscated by a suspicious lieutenant.

He also told stories about meeting Keaton and Cali Scolari, and shooting a pilot for a sitcom with them that involved a creepy-looking robot that they built with the help of two wacky scientists played by their actual fathers.

No one knew who Keaton and Cali Scolari were, but they weren't about to ask questions and look like idiots.

For months afterward people talked about that party. January had no idea there had even been a party.

She was a 21-year old pariah. It seemed that no one wanted much of anything to do with her. And yet she was lyrically beautiful, stunningly tall with long, lithe legs and suggestive hips like sexual parentheses. She had soft, caramel hair and eyes that looked like the earth as seen from space: misty and blue.

She was brutally conceited as a method of survival. If she hadn't bolstered her own ego – and it was easy to do with long, indulgent looks in the mirror – it would have disappeared, starved by a diet of ignored conversations and opinions greeted with complete indifference. Everyone had learned the hard way that it wasn't worth it to talk to January Chajkowski.

She was the Woman That Popularity Forgot. And she felt utterly alone in the world.

Her most meaningful conversations were with her parents, who were becoming increasingly concerned every night their daughter stayed home to help clean up after dinner and made up stories about interesting things that had happened at work. When she sensed that her continual proximity was weirding them out she would excuse herself and retreat to her room, where she was surrounded by enough stuffed animals that most people would have thought they'd stepped onto the set of some '80s horror movie.

The combined effect of a thousand pairs of blankly staring eyes had ceased being anything but homey for January. She would choose one or two favourite stuffed friends and enact scenes with them.

More and more often they were dates or even full-blown on-again off-again relationships between two unlikely animals. A mouse and a panda, for instance. Or a cheetah and a walrus.

Like some people who have reached a certain time in their life without passing that significant milestone, she dreamt about being kissed, touched, loved. What would it be like? She began to feel a real sense of desperation that was unseemly and was starting to make her do brash things.

Of course she had suffered the indignity of a few

small forays into the world of kissing. She remembered the turtle-like, hard kisses of Davis Moone; the overpowering, wet, lip-swallowing kisses of Shae Stevenson; and the prim, sour-tasting kisses of Horace Dengelly.

But the last time she had been kissed, slobberingly, by Shae, she had been fourteen. Besides, she thought of those as trials. She had yet to successfully invent kissing in her life. So when Mya accidentally kissed her she was surprised as much that she was being kissed as by the fact that it was a half-Asian woman who played bass and was a manager at the Aldo. That is: someone who was cool.

Chester was equally surprised when Jasper told him about January's supposed screening process.

"Gina?" he said.

"Yeah. I thought I should let you know," said Jasper. He was holding his lunch tray, gasping for air because he'd jogged from the food court.

"Well thanks, kid. You did a good job. I think I can handle it from here." Chester put a hand on his belt buckle, took a breath in, paused heroically. Jasper fled without littering his wake with superlatives the way Chester was hoping, but then the kid was late for work.

"So, let's go out," Chester said to Gina. He had come to the food court directly after hearing the news from Jasper. He still had a hand on his belt buckle. The look he was aiming for was irresistibly licentious, but he looked like he had a stomach ache.

Gina cantilevered her hip and her eyebrow at the same time, indicating extreme scepticism. With her hand on her hip she said, "Is that how you would ask January out?"

"Well, no."

"You've gotta treat me like you would treat her. Otherwise, I simply can't make a fair assessment, and I'll have to give you a very shoddy rating."

"How shoddy?"

"Very," she paused for effect, "shoddy."

This was serious. Chester turned away, then turned back, and looked her in the eye. This was very serious. He muttered, "Consarn it!" under his breath and punched the air in frustration.

He went to the Mega-Mart flower section and selected a robust bouquet of mostly purple, orange, and yellow flowers that he couldn't name if you held a gun to his privates. He went to the candy section and found a box of caramel nougat walnut confections called Snugglehuggs. He passed Guy Tuffray, who was wordlessly apoplectic.

Tuffray found his voice when Chester was about ten feet past him. "What are you doing?" he yelled, frightening an old woman and her granddaughter as they walked past.

Chester stopped, looked around slightly dumbfounded. "What does it look like? I'm going to go practice asking a girl out."

Tuffray looked at his watch exaggeratedly. "It's the middle of the afternoon!"

"Oh, is it? Then I guess you'd better find someone to clean the bathrooms for me. Or better yet, do it yourself. Mr. Hands-on." Chester turned and walked away, half-hoping he would feel Guy Tuffray's dishwater hand on his shoulder so he could spin around and clock him one.

Tuffray pointed after Chester, yelling, "I'm going to dock your pay! Don't you think I won't dock your pay! You can't get away with this smart-aleck behaviour!"

Chester crossed the food court, reached the Taco Bell, and held out the flowers and candy. "Now can we go out?" he asked.

Gina folded her arms, tilted her head in a critical way. "You'd ask January out wearing your Mega-Mart uniform?" she asked. Chester looked down at the blue smock, the name tag, his jeans with the worn-out knee. He shook his head slowly and blew out a breath of air.

"What do you suggest I wear?"

"A tux would be nice," said Gina.

"A tux."

"Mm-hmm." Gina nodded.

Chester sighed. "A tux," he muttered, turning away. He headed to the Moore's, stalking determinedly. He'd get a triple A plus rating or kill several innocent bystanders trying. There was a tuxedo and suit section in the Mega-Mart, but only homeless people would get their clothes there. The Moore's wasn't that much better, but it was the best that the mall had to offer.

When Chester arrived at the Moore's he saw Stanswick's blond head bobbing and swaying around the upper stratosphere of the store. Stanswick was a foot taller than was strictly necessary, and moved like a stilt walker with vertigo. Even from this distance Chester could tell he was in a bad mood. Stanswick was always in a completely foul mood.

Puck, on the other hand, was in a whimsical mood. He was sitting next to Mya, both of them looking down at his foot, which was clad in a brown Oxford.

"It's not really you," said Mya.

"Yeah, I'm more a hightop kinda guy," said Puck, smiling at her. He was in the midst of trying to impress her because, of all the girls in the mall, she was the only one who had said no when he asked her out. Today, he felt, was going to be different. Today he could conquer Mount Everest.

Mya was bored, and didn't much want to talk to Puck. Puck with his professionally mussed hair saturated with "product". Puck with his wrists adorned with red, white, and green athletic wristbands. Puck with his baggy pants and a smile that made babies gurgle. He was adorable, but Mya didn't care about that. She knew he was going to ask her out, and all she could think about was January.

Mya had a crush on January. A completely unexpected thing that had bloomed when she saw January eating at the food court by herself one noontime. She had looked so perfect and perfectly alone. The way Mya sometimes felt because she had only come out to one other person, Piper, who worked at the Pizza Pizza, and being homosexual in a small city in the mid-west was not a wild and delirious party. It was hard and lonely and confusing.

Mya sighed, "Maybe you want to see the other ones again?"

"No, no, that's all right," said Puck, taking off the Oxford and replacing it with a Converse. "Hey, what's up, you sound tired."

"I don't know. Maybe I'm tired," she said with a mix of disdain and sarcasm. Puck missed her tone.

"You wanna talk about it? You can talk to me," he said, smiling his sweet smile. "I'm a good listener. I know a tonne of stuff about the people here at the mall."

"Oh, yeah, like what?" She was partially trying to forestall him asking her out, but she was also curious to know if anyone thought she was a lesbian.

"Well," he said conspiratorially and looked around as he leaned in a bit, "I heard Mr. D used to own this mall." Mr. D was his nickname for Mr. deHavilland, the old man who played chess in the food court with himself and would greet a polite hello with a wrinkled stare of quiet annoyance.

"Oh yeah, I heard that."

Puck pressed on, trying to find the tidbit that would impress her. "Did you hear that Mickey got a sex change operation when she was, like, four?" He was referring to Michaela, the tall, lantern-jawed saleswoman who worked at Candida's and who wore false lashes that made her seem more transsexual than she actually was. She had, in fact, had sex reassignment surgery at age four because she had a terrible accident that irrevocably marred her former genitalia. Only Michaela knew that her accident had not actually been an accident.

"Yeah, I knew that."

"Well," he paused, "did you hear that Che's got a crush on the Ice Queen?" In Puck's parlance that meant Chester had a crush on January.

Mya startled Puck by jerking her head up and

staring at him intently. “What?” she said.

“Yeah, that’s what I heard, anyway. Apparently she likes him too.”

Mya’s mouth was open, her face slightly ashen. Puck thought he had found the impressive tidbit he needed.

“I think he’s supposed to be asking her out, like, today or something,” he continued, and then shook his head. “Poor guy, he's only lived in town for a few years so I guess he doesn't really know her like we do.”

Mya stood up. She looked out into the moving sea of people just outside the Aldo. “Hey,” said Puck, “what’s up?”

She didn’t answer, just anxiously toyed with her fingers, which were rough from playing bass for hours on end in Watson’s garage.

Puck looked down to his Converse for a second and Mya left, heading for Candida’s. Puck didn’t see her leave and said, “So, I was wondering, maybe you’d like to go out sometime?” He looked up to where Mya used to be and was dumbfounded. She was gone. He looked around.

“Mya?” he said, because he was so out-of-sorts he forgot to use her nickname: Angelou. It was hard to conquer Mount Everest when it left the room as soon as you started nearing the top.

Mya made a quick stop in the washroom and straightened herself and fixed her hair and adjusted her tanktops, which were worn one over the other. She was cute. She had gigantic eyes that were so darkly brown they seemed to absorb sound as well as light. Her neck was a delicate, smooth movement in the lithe, tan symphony that was her body. Many men and a few women had longed to gently massage that neck. If Rodin had seen it he would have immediately smashed all his previous sculptures and spent the rest of his days trying to capture the curving moments of that neck. It was pretty nice, and Mya’s dangling silver and lapis lazuli earrings offset it beautifully.

She found January easily enough at Candida’s, folding sweaters, alone, and said, “Hey sunshine, what's up?" She tried to keep her voice light, but she was nervous.

January was pleasantly surprised that someone had decided to grab enough initiative to start a conversation with her, and especially that it was Mya, who was popular and cool. Her feeling of desperation had become more acute, and the idea of spending another night making up relationships for her stuffed animals was almost enough to make her scream. Lately January had been trying to start conversations, she had been pushed to that level of brashness, but it was like jogging through a minefield. If she said, "How was your weekend?" she might be asked the same question in return and have to make up the details of some pretend hot date or social event. Any misstep would cause the conversation to explode, raining gory bits of social awkwardness over all involved. It was trying. She felt like she was walking a knife-edge, trying to fool everyone into thinking she was a social butterfly. She needn't have worried: she was fooling no one.

Candida, who was as blunt as a club-footed kickboxer, had said to her once, "You. You are not too popular," in her Slovakian accent. January had tried responding with a light-hearted laugh, but it fell flat. Fortunately only the two of them had been in the store at the time.

"Hi Mya, not much, you know. Work." She immediately felt disappointed in her answer. "What's up with you?"

"Nothing, no, I'm fine. I'm normal." Mya cursed herself. "Has Chester come by today?"

"No, are you looking for him?" January nodded to herself. If she could keep asking questions she could keep the focus strictly off her and on Mya. She wondered airily if Chester walked past Candida's so often because maybe he was meeting Mya on the sly.

Mya breathed in relief. "Oh, no," she said, then realized she didn't know what else to say. "What are you up to tonight?" she said after a moment.

"Nothing. Or, I mean," January laughed like she was

silly for forgetting, “I’ve got some thing, but, you know, I can cancel it.”

“You don’t have a date tonight?”

“No, not tonight,” January said judiciously. “Do you?” She wanted Mya to ask her to go somewhere, to ask her to be friends. She envisioned her and Mya hanging out, chatting, laughing, being joined by other cool people who worked at the mall, carousing, dancing, enjoying everything.

“Do you...have a boyfriend?” Mya asked. She suddenly felt very shy. She was used to being on the receiving end of a proposition. Now that she was making one it seemed hard to get to the punch line.

“Well, you know, a lot of guys are trying, but, um, no. Not at the moment.” January was worried that maybe having a boyfriend was a prerequisite for hanging out. Maybe she could find someone to pretend.

“Really? Do you have a crush on anyone?” she fished.

“Oh,” January blushed slightly, “yeah...”

This was maybe good news, maybe bad news. “Who?”

“I don’t want to say,” said January. She started playing with the cardigan on the mannequin next to her, straightening it. “It’s embarrassing.” She was starting to feel flustered, out of her depth. She struggled to think of a question to ask and failed.

“Is it me?” Mya asked, smiling.

January just laughed appreciatively. Mya didn’t know how to read that, yet.

“You’ve never had a crush on a girl?”

“Oh, I don’t know...I’ve thought about it,” said January vaguely, looking down. She had, in an extremely abstract way. She was lonely enough and desperate enough to imagine many different situations, but she was also as straight as a prairie highway.

Mya had worked her way around the sweaters, tracing the designs on the front idly with one finger, until she was standing next to January. Mya noticed that with her platform shoes on there wasn’t that much difference in their height. “Would you ever kiss a girl?” she asked softly.

January couldn't bring herself to raise her head. She looked down shyly, and said, “Oh. I don’t know—”

Mya kissed her.

It was a quick movement, an impulse. Mya ducked her head slightly, came at January's lips from underneath, and because January was not looking up and not expecting anything she stood stock still with her mouth parted in shock. Jasper, across the way in the Shopper’s, was answering an old man’s questions about ear medicine. He missed the whole thing.

January felt the kiss, felt her lips against Mya’s soft, full pout. For a second she didn’t move, was immensely surprised, noticed that it felt good, and then realized that it was Mya she was kissing. She pulled back.

“What the hell was that?” January said breathlessly.

Mya was confused. “I kissed you.”

“Why?”

“You...dared me to...”

“I said I don’t know!”

“Oh. I thought you said I dare you,” Mya said defensively.

“No, I... I said I don’t know.” January felt her face getting hot, turning red. She wanted to react differently, she wanted to be cool with it, but she was far too flustered.

“Well, fine,” said Mya, hurt. Then she tried, “Do you know now?”

“No!” said January, confused. “I mean yes. I mean,” she tried to gather her thoughts. “What are you asking me?”

“Well, would you kiss a girl?”

January wrung her hands. “I don't... I mean we only just—I, I, I can't... I'm not, you know—I haven't—” She had no idea what to say. All she knew was she felt completely taken aback in seven different ways.

“Well neither would I!” said Mya, defensively angry in the face of what she thought was January vacillating.

“But you just kissed me!”

"I thought you said I dare you," Mya enunciated to indicate there was no other way she would have kissed January.

"Well I didn't," January enunciated in the same way, angry now herself because it felt like the easiest emotion to get a hold on.

"Fine."

"Fine!"

"Goodbye!" Mya yelled, turning, storming out, feeling embarrassed and exposed and hurt and angry. She went to find Piper at the Pizza Plaza and they went into the security hallway that ran behind the stores and made out for a while. Piper was Asian, sensible, short, chubby, with eyes that were slightly crossed and slightly exophthalmic, so it looked like she was always being surprised by something hovering an inch in front of her cute-as-a-button nose. She was the only other lesbian Mya had found at the mall. They were like sisters, except that they made out sometimes.

January felt extremely bad about getting so upset with Mya. She realized that she had pushed her away and could only become friends with her if she made a huge effort and reached out, but she already felt exposed, vulnerable. She didn't have the courage in her to make reparations with Mya.

Chester, meanwhile, was receiving the full blunt force of Stanswick's ire.

Chapter 8 - Rose McDougall

"Why can't you help me out for five seconds," Chester said, almost nose to nose with Stanswick, who was bent over with his hands on his hips, red in the face. Chester shifted the flowers he was holding and put the box of chocolates under his arm.

"I can't let you just take a tux, Chester," he explained again.

"I'm just borrowing it, geez! I'll bring it back in two seconds."

"I'm sorry, you've got to pay for a full rental. Otherwise I can't let you take the tux."

"Why do you gotta be so pig-headed about this?"

Stanswick bent over even further, got his face a little bit closer to Chester's. "Because I don't like you Chester," he said quietly, his eyes burning a hole in the bridge of Chester's nose.

"But what's not to like?" Chester asked simply.

Stanswick nearly lost it. His body thrashed around as his face went a dark and dangerous red and his fists pumped the air. "Ask Augusta, you complete nincompoop!"

"Augusta?"

"Augusta Pointree. Dr. Pointree. The dentist!" Stanswick yelled, punctuating his reply by jabbing his finger against Chester's chest.

"Ow," Chester replied, rubbing his chest. Stanswick

was breathing hard. “Why doesn’t Augusta like me?” Chester asked.

“Dr. Pointree,” Stanswick corrected him angrily.

“How come you get to call her Augusta?”

Stanswick closed his eyes, buried his face in his hands. He lifted one long, thin arm and pointed to the door of the Moore’s. “Please, just go Chester.”

“But I need to get a tux,” he said pleadingly.

“You’ve got to rent one. I can’t just give you one, you son of a bitch.” Stanswick said it without rancor. He seemed spent, tired.

Chester thought about it. “Can I just try it on first? See how it looks?”

“Fine!” Stanswick measured him irritably, muttering to himself, and then disappeared for a few minutes. When he came back he was holding a hanger off which hung a garment bag. He could almost hold it at his hip level and it wouldn’t brush the ground. “Here,” he said, thrusting the bag into Chester, who gripped it solemnly.

“Thanks, Stanswick.”

Stanswick just grunted in reply and stalked away, shaking his head.

Chester went to the change room, set down the flowers and took the box of chocolates out from under his arm. He changed quickly, grabbed the presents, and slid under the door of the change room, leaving it locked closed behind him with his clothes in it. Instead of exiting to the store’s main floor Chester went through the staff door into a small office. He passed through the office and opened the back door into the stockroom. From there he went out into the security hall that ran behind all the stores. He went next door, to the Grand & Toy, went through the security door into their stockroom, and out onto their main floor. He swept past Rose McDougall, whistling, and gave her a quick wink. He cut a pretty mean figure: tux, flowers, and chocolates. He guessed he had maybe two minutes before Stanswick would discover he’d stolen the tux, but he only needed a few seconds, really.

Rose McDougall was flabbergasted by the odd sight of Chester swooshing past, flowers in hand, chocolates in the other, dressed to the nines. She blinked a few times. The cashier working next to her, a nameless young teenaged boy with a cowlick of blond hair who she would have to fire within a week due to extreme incompetence, asked, "Who was that?"

"Remember," said Rose mechanically, trying to watch where Chester was going, "relevant questions only. Relevant questions, my dear." She lost sight of Chester before she had a chance to ask him what was happening, so she straightened up and shook her head as if that was enough rebuke. She almost tsked. She turned to the incompetent young boy. "Did I tell you about the time I bought my father an accordion?" she asked.

He groaned inwardly and thought, oh god, not another story.

"What was your name again?" she asked.

He told her and she promptly forgot it.

Rose had a rotating cycle of stories that she told, all of them meandering tales of small triumphs or losses in her life. So far she had only found one person who actually liked her stories, but she hated dead air and strove to fill it in any way she could. After any significant pause she would begin, "Did I tell you about the time..." and watch the listener's eyes glaze over. But she persevered. She had faith in stories. She had loved to read as a child, but nowadays couldn't find the time to settle down with a book like she once had. It was questionable what the hell filled up all of her time. She certainly didn't know. It seemed like time was being deliberately cruel, stretching out on the long afternoons when she had to work with some immature and incompetent teenaged boy, and then disappearing once she was by herself.

Chester could almost distill a type of rocket fuel from the hatred he had for Rose's stories. Every once in a long while he would be assigned to the Grand & Toy while they tried to hire someone who could do more than gape like a yawning hippopotamus at a simple request for a package of printing paper. He would drag himself into the store like a dead man walking. Rose would be chipper. She had slightly reworked versions of the same old stories to try on him.

"Did I tell you about the time I went to buy yarn?" she would ask, and Chester's heart would stop.

"Yes, Rose. Yes, I have heard that story!"

"Well, you heard the old version. I completely forgot the part about my bus transfer. Listen."

Even Chester did not have the kind of blind tenacity that Rose did. The only way he got through the stories was by tuning out Rose's voice and nodding appreciatively at her ample bosom.

There were certain stories that she kept to herself. She never said, "Did I tell you about the time I gave Guy Tuffray a blowjob?" Nor did she say, "Did I tell you about the time I banged up my car in the parking lot, after Ipswitch repainted the parking spaces?" She didn't even tell those stories to Dusty, who was the only one who liked hearing her epic yet pointless tales.

"I like that one," he would say, after she finished telling him about the time she finished a whole crossword by herself at the laundromat.

"It just felt good, you know?" she said, gazing fondly at his acne-speckled face, his windblown blond hair beginning to grow down into his eyes so he had to swipe it out of the way every ten seconds.

Dusty nodded, brushed the hair out of his eyes, said, "Anything new in the Lost and Found?"

"No, but that's probably a good thing."

"Hm?"

"Do you know, not one person has ever come in to claim something?"

"Really?"

"It's almost like no one else knows it exists," she said, which was exactly the case.

"What do you do if no one comes in to claim anything?" Dusty asked. When Rose looked away for a second he stole a glance at her breasts, but he really didn't mean anything by it.

"I don't know, give the stuff to Goodwill?"

"What kind of stuff have you got?"

"Well, there's this," said Rose, pulling out Gina's peppery grey and black winter coat. Dusty nearly gasped. "I've had this ever since the Lost and Found started. It was my first item. I've had it for...like, well over a year now. Maybe almost two years."

Dusty said, "Can I see it?" and his hands almost trembled as he took it. He remembered the staff Christmas party where he'd seen Gina wearing this coat. The same party where Ipswitch broke his finger. The same party where his year-long crush on Gina had slowly started being replaced by a year-long crush on Dove Anquanita. "Can I keep this?" he asked.

"Is it yours?"

"Well, no," Dusty admitted. "But I know whose it is."

"Sure," said Rose, "I don't see why not." And then she had the story about the time she got rid of her first item from the Lost and Found.

Dusty took the coat with every intention of giving it to Gina. He stored it in his locker at the games and hobby store that kept changing its name, and then realized that it might be hard to explain why he had her coat so long after she'd lost it. He supposed that he had Rose to back him up, but then he'd have to give the coat away. And it kinda seemed to fit him all right. Anyway, Gina had a boyfriend now. Many things had changed after the incident at the Mega-Mart. Dusty felt like moving on, but didn't mind holding on to a relatively innocent piece of the past. Simpler times, and such.

Modesta Mae noticed the new coat, and said, "Not too shabby, Dusty."

"Thanks, Mo," he said, locking up the sliding metal accordion door of the games and hobby store that kept changing its name.

Mo's hand rested on her belt where her gun would be, except that her gun had been replaced by a taser wand. It was due to be re-replaced by a gun again, but it was on back order. At least she had her new uniform. She still wasn't used to it, but she liked it better than the previous uniforms that had cut across her midsection unflatteringly. The old uniforms were from the bygone era when Ipswitch had continuously slashed the security budget like a price-conscious samurai.

In those days Mo would have already begun the closing-up process by throwing the giant switch that shut off half the fluorescent lights in the mall. Then she would have escorted Dusty and any remaining employees to the outside doors in the fluorescent half-light. She would have set the alarm system, and then she would leave herself, and the rest of the mall lights would shut off automatically, and the whole place would be dark and deserted except for the raccoons that would break into the Bulk Barn.

Now mall security was swimming in money, and Modesta Mae was the head of the night shift. They had gone from having two security guards for the whole mall to a team of twenty working in shifts. After the Mega-Mart incident everyone had talked about being pro-active. They were actually being completely reactive.

"You know that looks a bit like Gina's old coat," Mo added.

"Does it?" Dusty laughed. He dropped his keys, and grabbed them up quickly. "Clumsy me," he muttered.

"Aw, what I don't know about fashion," Mo chuckled. It was true. She felt out of place wearing anything but the dark navy pants and light blue shirt of the security officer uniform.

Rose, too, was not exactly a fashion plate. She liked handmade sweaters in the winter, and wore ill-fitting jeans that made her thighs look large and her butt look flat. She got nervous in the spring, as the weather warmed up and she had to reveal more and more skin to stay comfortable. By the summer she would be wearing t-shirts and crossing her arms more often.

Then fall rolled around and she would relax a bit, wearing rugby shirts, button-up blouses, and a pair of beat-up corduroys that felt comfortable and accentuated her nice curves.

Dove Anquanita, on the other hand, saw fashion as yet another place to compete with other women. She kept a close watch on Areola's wardrobe, and haughtily enjoyed the fact that her clothes were funkier, newer, and smaller than Areola's. For her part, Areola wore what was comfortable and moderately sexy. If it was one and not the other she would take a pair of scissors to it and make it both. Her stitching was only passable but she could cut up a dowdy outfit to make it look artful and sassy.

When January was feeling particularly brash, she took a special pride in putting down anyone who wasn't wearing exactly the same as what she was wearing. And if they were wearing the exact same thing she would never speak to them again, because that was inexcusable. She tried to take a chunk out of everybody with equal precision and thereby raise herself up by that amount, but everyone saw through her game and refused to listen to her.

"I don't understand," she would say, crying, to Mr. Toad or Professor Bunny Bun, two of her favourite stuffed friends. "I keep telling everyone what they're doing wrong but they still don't want to be friends with me."

Chester was not known for his fashion sense. He tended to wear cardigans that made people chuckle and earned him another dozen nicknames like Grandpa Ches and the Old Geezer. So it was certainly surprising for Rose to see him swoosh past in a tuxedo, looking quite dapper. So surprising that she didn't even make a story out of it.

Chester waltzed into the food court and caught Kipling's eye. He gave a nod and a raffish smile, and Kipling just shook his head. He saw Kel Urquhart just seating himself with a tray from Great American Steakery and another from Canton Kitchen. Kel stared at him for a second, mouth slightly open, looking like a child at Christmas who has just received a half-dozen subscriptions to magazines. It was kind of like a dazed, what-the-hell-is-this look. Chester wasted no time on him, and headed straight for the Taco Bell.

He had to wait in line. Gina saw him and had to suppress her laughter as she served the next customer. Eventually he got to the front.

"Make it good," Gina said before he began. She was smiling self-indulgently.

Chester went down on one knee. "Gina, you are the light that fills my heart. You are the moon, pulling me towards you like the mighty oceans swelling. Your hair is really nice today. Would you please do me the favour of consenting to dine with me this Friday eve? My heart shall burst with joy if you say yes, and it shall shatter into a million pieces if you decline, for my love for you is as great as the sun and twice as powerful." He proffered the flowers and candy.

Gina took them both, smelled the flowers with eyes closed. "Sure, all right," she said.

"M'lady," said Chester, standing and bowing. People all around were staring at them. "Shall I squire you about town beginning at, say, eight in the PM?"

"Can't we eat at, like, six-thirty or something reasonable?"

"Your merest wish is like a declaration from above, and I shall inscribe it upon a stone tablet. Six it is."

"I said six-thirty," Gina chuckled.

"That is of course what I meant to state. Six and then thirty!" Chester swooped around and walked off regally, leaving whispering commotion in his impressive wake.

"What was that all about?" asked Kipling as Chester passed.

"That was all about grandiosity. That was resplendent. Positively baronial."

"Baronial?"

"Baronial, my friend." Chester hurried on his way, hoping Stanswick hadn't discovered that he was missing yet. Kipling took the piece of paper out of his pocket, and a pen. He wrote down "baronial" and then went back to his lunch. He wondered absently where Jasper was – they were supposed to eat together.

Jasper was at the Grand & Toy, at the counter, listening to one of Rose's stories and nodding intently. He was trying to pay attention, he really was, but he kept drifting out of it. Her voice droned like cicadas on a hot July day. He had gone there to inquire about the price of 1000 postcards, a task Kipling had saddled him with and who was expecting him to report his results at lunch.

"And then— Did I tell you about the time the old man hit on me?" Rose asked, interrupting her own story.

"Huh? No, I don't, um... When?"

"Well, okay. I was thinking about going out but I was like, where do I go? You know? I just wasn't sure what I wanted to do. This was on a Friday night. And so I thought maybe, I don't know, why not go to maybe see a movie, right? But I didn't have anyone to go with. So I am driving to the movies, going all by myself, right, and then I turn left on Delmore and then I keep driving and heading towards the movie theatre. Anyway, I get there after a while and then I'm like— Oh, wait, I forgot a part. No, wait, okay, sorry, I was wearing this brown coat that my mom bought but it didn't fit her anymore because my other coat was dirty because my mom wore it. Anyway, but that's not really important to the story..."

Then Chester tore through wearing a tux, and Jasper was shaken out of his stupor.

"Chester, what—?"

"Can't talk, I stole this tux. Don't listen to her stories. Gotta run!" Chester yelled as he flew past.

Rose was flummoxed.

Jasper seized his opportunity and said, "I'm terribly sorry, I'm extremely late for a lunch appointment.

Would it be okay if you told me the rest of the story another time?"

"Oh," Rose was impressed by his politeness, "sure. I'll remember where I was, don't you worry!" She smiled after him as he took off at the same speed as Chester but in the opposite direction. "What a nice boy," she said off-handedly. Then she turned to the mouth-breathing simpleton beside her and smacked him one across the shoulder. "Why can't you be more like that?" she asked.

He shrugged like a teenager.

He reminded her of Puck, who shrugged in the same way. Complete indifference, like possibly he didn't even comprehend the question he was being asked, he just knew that that heartless shrug would dissuade whomever it was from talking to him anymore.

The two had dated for a month and a half, and when Puck had broken it off she had been more upset than she thought she should be. For Puck it had been a case of older woman, younger man. He was excited by the prospect of dating someone in her thirties. Besides which, Rose was essentially the next on his list. For Rose it had been too long coming back to an empty apartment with no messages on her answering machine and no one to spend time with on long, interminable weekend nights. She kept making pasta for two and throwing out a lot of leftovers.

Puck had a system whereby he always had three girls in various stages of courtship. He felt like a world-class chef preparing a difficult tri-partite meal. One girl was his current flame, kept on the front burner at a steady simmer of bubbling sexual experimentation. The second was being brought to boil on a back burner and would be shifted to the front burner as soon as it became overcooked. The third was just being put on the other back burner, and being warmed up. It required an extensively developed sense of timing and lack of pathos to manage all three girls.

When Rose and Puck broke up he was going out

with Ameesha the next day, and that compounded the destructive impact of the break-up for Rose. Afterward she felt miserable sitting alone in her apartment, or at the laundromat, or grocery shopping for one. Further adding to the devastation was the fact that she had dropped out of her second year of college, forever abandoning her dreams. She did this for an eclectic combination of reasons. One was Puck. Another was Kel Urquhart, and his connection to an expired student card.

Chapter 9 - Kel Urquhart

"He's a complete bastard," said Chester vehemently.
"How do I know?" Kipling asked laconically.
"Because I'm telling you."
"If my existence was limited to what you told me, it would be a pretty piss-poor life."
"Ask Jasper then. Go on, Jasper, tell him."
"Um, he, uh," Jasper stopped, looking from Chester to Kipling and back. "He doesn't seem very nice, I suppose."
"Bah!" Chester exclaimed. "He's a bastard. A complete one."
"What did he ever do to you?" asked Kipling. He crossed his arms as he leaned back against the wall of the arcade, where they were waiting for the game *1945* to become available. The arcade was predominantly lit by black-light and neon fluorescents, so their skin was a gruesome shade of blue. The robotic chirping of arcade games surrounded them.
"What's he ever done *for* me?" Chester countered.
"Didn't he give you part of his lunch one time, when you didn't have enough money to buy one?" Jasper recalled dimly.
"No, that was Singer, from Great American Steakery," Kipling noted. "But I thought he gave you a lift home last week when it was pouring like a banshee."

"No, that was Polito," said Jasper. "But wasn't there that time when your shoe came apart and he fixed it with his gum, or something?"

"No," said Kipling, wagging a finger, "that was me."

"Guys. Shut up," said Chester. He had his head tilted back, eyes closed, rubbing his temples. "Kel Urquhart," he said darkly, "is a complete bastard. I'm telling you."

"If my existence was limited to what—" Kipling began.

"Okay, guys, I'm done. I'm out of quarters," said Areola, bouncing her curly hair as she stepped away from the video game.

"Great. Finally," said Chester.

"Say hi to Polito for us," said Jasper as Areola twirled in her bright white sneakers and waved goodbye. The sneakers made a high-pitched, plastic squawk and she nearly fell over. Jasper raised his hand to return the wave but she was already spinning back to face front. She was used to ignoring her clumsy moments.

"Hey, I will. And he says thanks!" Areola yelled back.

Kipling and Chester stepped up to the machine and plugged it with quarters. The rule was whomever died had to step aside and let the third person take over their next life. That meant that Chester and Jasper rotated position often.

"Why did you say that?" asked Kipling as he concentrated on the screen.

"Hm?" asked Jasper, watching the two set about the grim business of dogfighting over the verdant jungle.

"You said say hi to Polito for us. Why'd you say that?"

"Oh, Areola and Polito are dating. They've been seeing each other for almost a year."

"What?" said Chester, turning to look at Jasper. His airplane exploded and he swatted at the controls. Jasper stepped in. "How come we don't know this stuff?" Chester continued.

"Well, I don't know," said Jasper.

"Maybe you're too busy hating Guy Tuffray and Kel Urquhart and pretty much everyone else to really get to know anyone," Kipling answered, smoothly avoiding enemy fire.

He was as laid back about arcade games as he was about everything else, but the thing that annoyed Chester about it was that he was good without real effort. If you were good at something it should be because you yelled and raged and cursed it roundly with every atom of your body screaming with pure adrenaline. Otherwise what was the point?

"What do you know. Your dime-store psychology that you picked up second-hand from a used bookstore," Chester retorted.

Kipling shrugged because Chester was exactly right about where he got his knowledge. Jasper's plane exploded and he stepped aside with an unconscious shrug.

"Finally!" said Chester.

"Hey, wait a second. Why did Areola say that Polito says thanks?" Kipling asked. There was a lull in the game as the first end-level boss exploded repeatedly and Kipling took a moment to lean against the game and look at Jasper, who was standing just behind Chester.

"Oh," said Jasper, growing pinker and looking down shyly. "I kinda helped him find out how the raccoons were getting into the Bulk Barn."

Kipling nodded.

"Actually," Jasper continued, "you fellows might be interested to hear how they were getting in because it's why I think Kel Urquhart's not a very nice guy."

Chester looked over his shoulder at Jasper. "We're listening," he said.

Kel Urquhart felt cheated. He felt vengeful. He felt like he was owed, and it was all because of an off-hand comment Kipling had made to Ipswitch on Kel's very first day working at the Barnes & Noble. Kipling was working two jobs at the time, his regular shift at the Amphibian Emporium plus a late-night restocking and reshelving shift at the Barnes & Noble. Kel had been hired for the same shift and Ipswitch was there to enact his own personal brand of pointless cruelty, this time in the form of a competition between the two to see who would be the assistant manager in charge of the overnight crew, which was the two of them.

After Ipswitch had explained the process and the outcome of the competition, Kipling had drawled, "Are you crazy? Only a complete idiot would want that job."

Kel had immediately said, "I want that job, Mr. Ipswitch!" Then he realized how that had sounded. Ipswitch laughed.

Kipling remained impassive but he had pointed at Kel and added, "That's not management material."

"Well, the idiot gets the job," Ipswitch said. "Kipling, you're fired. Get back to the lizards."

"Amphibians."

"I don't care."

Kel had not risen above assistant manager since that time, and it was all Kipling's fault. He still boiled at the memory. He was not a vindictive person, but he had an elaborate sense of what was fair and what was not, and any imbalance would make him lock his fists and fire his blood until his jowly cheeks shook with frustration.

For example, whenever he saw Puck with a different girlfriend – and Puck averaged 23 girlfriends per year – he would get twitchy. Whenever he saw grapes on sale at the grocery store shortly after he had bought grapes at regular price at the other grocery store, he would get fired up. Whenever he saw one of the employees of the Barnes & Noble with their shirt untucked, their smock untied, their name tag left in the change room, or wearing sneakers instead of the regulation black dress shoes, he would get incensed. And when he saw Kipling he became rigidly apoplectic.

In the four years since Kipling had ruined Kel's

ambitions with his languid response to Ipswitch, Kel had managed to work his way up to assistant manager of the day shift. He should have been junior assistant staff manager of the entire Barnes & Noble chain, working out of an office in Manhattan or Chicago or Seattle by now. The schedule of life goals Kel had pinned up on his bulletin board kept getting angrily revised with murderous scratches of red pen as Kel suffered setback after setback to his future career thanks to Kipling.

It didn't help that the bulletin board his schedule was pinned to was located in his bedroom in the basement of his parent's house. It was a house of despair, lethargy, and silent suffering. No one could succeed in their ambitions living in such a house. It was a place Kel was desperate to move away from at all costs, except he couldn't ever save up enough to afford to move out, because he couldn't get a raise, because Kipling had soured Ipswitch's first impression of him.

His parents were constantly at war, and they used him as a sort of reverse bargaining chip.

"If you don't get the hell out of my space right now," his mother might roar at his father, "I swear to god I will leave you here, alone, with that boy."

"You leave me with that boy and I will make goddamned sure I hunt you down and deposit him right on your doorstep!" his father would yell back.

That boy would disappear down into his room in the basement and carefully re-plot exactly how he was going to afford to leave home. He had tried to get out of the house as much as possible to avoid hearing the hours-long arguments between his parents, but he found himself sometimes inexplicably angry with people he tried to hang out with. And the people he tried to hang out with didn't much care for that sort of behaviour and ditched him as often as possible.

So Kel would walk slowly around the town by himself, his chubby cheeks nipped to a healthy pink by the chill air, his floppy brown mop of hair tossed this way and that playfully by the wind. And because he liked books he would stop at the library and read for several hours sitting quietly at a table by himself, or hunkered down in the aisles, leaning his back against a rack of literature. He enjoyed the well-ordered atmosphere of the library, but was eventually asked to curtail his visitations because he kept telling the other patrons to be quiet, not re-shelve the books themselves, not spend more than twenty minutes on the self-serve computers, not take the newspaper until it had been returned to the circulation desk, and not to use their uncle's library card because they didn't have their own.

Removed from the library, he stuffed his hands in the pockets of his puffy down jacket and wandered slowly to the bridge that ran over the train tracks. He thought about jumping. He thought about being crushed under the shiny steel wheels of the long, rattling trains. He thought about the crowd that would form, or wouldn't form. He thought about his parents. He couldn't jump, not when he had a chance to possibly escape everything and find happiness as a junior executive in some big city somewhere.

Except that his chance was denied him. By that arrogant fool, Kipling and by that other arrogant fool, Ipswitch. So he started stealing inventory from the Barnes & Noble.

He started small, taking knick-knacks that he then sold to second-hand stores for a pittance. It wasn't much, but it gave him a thrill like he was finally putting a finger on the scales and tipping them in his favour. The knick-knacks were easily hidden under his shirt or in his jacket. Then he tried slipping a few CDs and DVDs out, after carefully removing the magnetization on the cases while he was supposedly counting inventory. He made a bit more from selling those to second-hand music stores. But he realized quickly that the big money was in turning over books, which required a more sophisticated system. Some of the books were bulky, especially the high-priced textbooks and gigantically padded self-help books, both of which were easy to sell to a used book dealer or specialty second-hand store.

Being assistant manager and being such a damnable stickler for the tiniest details certainly made him no friends among the employees, but it afforded him excellent opportunities to steal inventory. He would gather the grumbling, sleepy, irresponsible teens and college students early on a Saturday morning and tell them to be prepared to stay late that night so they could categorize and inventory the entire store. By Saturday evening, as the mall was just beginning to close down, he would be as alone as if he were on a desert island. He was often rather impressed – it didn't seem like the employees were on the brink of dashing out the door, but if he turned his back for one second he would look again and they would have disappeared as inexplicably, quickly, and soundlessly as Batman's shadow.

Then he would smile as he imagined himself slipping the blindfold on Justice herself, and he would carefully miscount the inventory and make a few dozen books disappear from the storeroom. He had a system. It only required privacy and time.

Jasper, meanwhile, had finished his Saturday shift at the Shopper's Drug Mart slightly early, and, emboldened by something Modesta Mae had told him, he headed directly for the Bulk Barn to once and for all solve the mystery of the raccoons. The Bulk Barn was just beginning to close up, the cashiers were balancing their floats, and a young man with a curly mullet so bushy that it seemed to be trying to push his Bulk Barn baseball cap off his head was sweeping the aisles, his mouth parted and his lips wet from overproduction of saliva. His name was Ben Outhwaite, he was mentally challenged and his brother was the manager of the Bulk Barn.

Jasper nodded to the employees, and said, "Hi, Ben. Where's Horne?"

Ben turned, pointed soundlessly towards the back, and Jasper gave him a friendly smile as he strode towards the stock room. He swung the door open and almost ran into the manager, Horne Outhwaite, and said, "Oh, hi Horne."

"What are you doing, Jasper?" Horne asked sullenly. He had thick-rimmed brown glasses and a freckled face with a short shock of brown hair that looked like a badly mowed lawn. His image was not helped by the sort of thin, pointed shoulders that made every shirt look ill at ease while he was wearing it.

At sixteen he was by far the youngest manager in the whole mall, but he was something of a prodigy and liked to beat Ipswitch at chess. They played three times a week. The fact that Horne always won was not particularly surprising. The fact that Ipswitch found some perverse pleasure in losing at chess to a teenaged boy was unexpected, to say the least. Ipswitch allowed Horne certain leniencies that no other manager enjoyed – like hiring Horne's older brother to work at the Bulk Barn.

Horne was on the school chess team, and he was the kind of chess player who wore his chess team t-shirt every time he played a game. He did not go in for subtlety in fashion. He did not understand that there could be a subtlety to fashion. He was smart in the specific ways that make you a bona fide nerd, which made him extremely suspicious of nice people. In his experience nice people were only nice until they got the required help they needed on their math homework, and then pantsed him.

"I'm going to try to find out how the raccoons are getting in."

"It's no use, Einstein," Horne said. "If I can't figure it out I don't see how you can."

"Fair enough, Horne," Jasper admitted. "But it doesn't hurt to let me look around does it?"

"Yes, it does."

"Oh." Jasper paused. "How?"

"It wastes man-hours, Jasper," Horne said like he was talking to a child. "Besides, someone has to stay late to lock up and watch out and make sure you don't mess things up."

"I won't be five minutes—"

"That's right, you'll be zero minutes." Horne was pushing him gently towards the door. Actually, he was pushing as hard as he could, but it felt gentle to Jasper, who was himself considered slight. Horne's shoulders bunched up near his ears.

"Isn't there any way you'll let me just take a look around?" Jasper asked.

Horne stopped pushing, looked Jasper in the eye, then glanced from side to side and lowered his voice as he motioned him to lean in.

"No."

"I'll do anything you'd like," Jasper pleaded.

Horne thought about it. "Okay, Jasper. You can look around. But," he said, and held up one finger and his features took on a calculating air, "you owe me a favour."

"Sure, sure," said Jasper, and they shook hands decisively. It was to Horne's despair that his carefully calculated favour would never be returned.

"Take a look around," Horne said lightly. "Let me know if you find anything."

Horne struggled his way through the door and Jasper looked across the storage area and walked around slowly, peering in the dusky half-light at the dim corners and stacked slats of bulk food. He opened the door to the security corridor that ran behind the stores and felt a draft whistling along briskly. Curious, he headed for the source of the cold air mass, the wind mussing his hair like a careless brother at a funeral.

He'd only walked a short distance when he came across the raccoons, chattering and squeaking, their eyes shining in the dim overhead light. They looked up at him, three of them, fumbling their hands over their noses and trying to discern if he was a threat or not. He moved towards them and they scattered back the way they had come, making harsh chuckling sounds like they were scolding him. Jasper took off after them, racing to keep up with their shambling, arch-backed retreat.

He found the source of the draft at the same time as he lost the raccoons, because one of the doors to the parking lot at the back of the mall was propped open with a cinder block. The raccoons piled over the cinder block and out the door, and by the time Jasper hit the door and it burst wide open they were halfway across the parking lot, heading from one pool of lamp light to another, making for the forest behind the mall.

Jasper, breathing hard, his breath crystallizing in the air, turned slightly to see Kel Urquhart loading books into the trunk of his car, the snow swirling about him as he stood stock still. Some books slid out of his arms and into the box at his feet. The box rested on a dolly. In the trunk of the car Jasper could see a mound of book covers, shining dully in the yellow parking lot lights.

"What's up, Kel?"

Kel came toward him, menacingly, but Jasper didn't react. He still held the door wide, the snow hitting his eyelashes, making him blink. Kel pointed at him with one mittened hand.

"I'm just taking some of these to give to a charity," he said.

"I'm not an idiot, Kel," Jasper replied calmly, putting his hands up.

"Yeah, well you'd better just keep your mouth shut. I can make your life a complete hell, and don't think I won't. This has got nothing to do with you, so just keep out of it."

"You know you let those raccoons in."

"What the fuck—? What are you talking about?"

"Those raccoons, they've been stealing food from the Bulk Barn," Jasper explained.

"Listen," Kel shoved Jasper, pushing him inside, "I don't give a giant bearded rat's ass what the fuck raccoons do. I'm just telling you, if you breathe a word of this to anyone I will take you down. I will take you downtown. You understand me?"

"I'm no snitch, Kel. But you could be a little nicer about this."

"Nicer?"

"Yeah. You could ask me politely not to tell anyone."

"I'm telling you, you four-flushing codswollop, you'd better not speak a goddamned word."

"That's fine, but you've gotta stop letting those raccoons in."

"What?"

"Don't prop the door open with a cinder block. You're letting raccoons into the mall. Someone else is going to find out if you don't stop it."

"Is that a threat, little man?" Kel pulled his mittens off, unzipped his jacket. He'd been getting closer and closer to Jasper, edging him into the corridor, and the door closed behind them, bumping against the cinder block.

"It's not a threat, Kel," Jasper said simply.

Kel glared at him for a moment. "Oh," he said.

"Just find another way to keep the door ajar. Or something."

"Fine," he said petulantly. He turned to go back outside and finish loading his car, but then whipped back around and pointed an accusatory finger at Jasper. "I better not hear you told anybody about this, or so help me..."

"Have a good night, Kel." Jasper walked back to the Bulk Barn, shaking his head, his hands in his pockets trying to warm up.

"Did you find anything?" asked Horne smugly.

"Well, I think you won't be bothered by raccoons anymore," said Jasper, smiling cherubically.

He smiled the same smile at Chester and Kipling in the arcade as he finished the story, with the strobing lights and raucous sound effects adding a frenetic element to his narrative. Both Chester and Kipling were, however, locked in a grim dogfight for freedom several hundred feet above the verdant terrain of Asia in 1945. They had heard the story, but they missed the smile.

"A complete bastard," muttered Chester, shaking his head. Then his plane exploded. "Aw, c'mon!" he yelled at the game. Jasper moved in smoothly to take over.

Just passing the arcade, moving smoothly herself, was Ameesha. She was practicing her walk, which was a sort of liquid motion that involved keeping the head level and swiveling the hips like a belly dancer. Ameesha worked at the Canton Kitchen during the day, but at night she worked a second job in order to save up enough money to go to college full time. She wanted to be a dentist, and she had a wide, full mouth of smooth, shining, perfect white teeth. Her gums were healthy and well maintained, and her lips and tongue were delicate and clean. She was a model of oral hygiene, and gargled regularly with salt water. Ameesha had dark, dusky skin and a dark, dusky voice to match. She didn't look like a whiskey drinker, but she sounded like one. She was in her early twenties, with long eyelashes, and her body had no sharp edges, just curves, curves, and curves. Although she was relatively chaste in her personal life, she was almost perfectly built for seduction.

Oddly enough she was the reason that Kel Urquhart and Tamara, who worked at the Mega-Mart, met. Tamara was 39, and wading through a messy divorce that was being dragged out like a clumsy cowboy behind a galloping horse. She was normally chipper, with her short brown hair sticking up for itself in even the gamest wind. Her body was thin and small and seemed to be attached to a power outlet via a worn, old, braided cable. She moved slightly spastically and jerked her limbs very minutely. But she was obviously depressed late one Friday night as she walked with Ameesha out to her car in the parking lot.

"Hey babes, what are you up to right now?" Ameesha asked. She knew Tamara's personal situation because of Tamara's great love of faux Cantonese cuisine. Almost every day Tamara, buzzing with so much energy that it looked like her hair was shivering, would belly up to the Canton Kitchen counter with her tray and order from the selection of delectable dishes ruined by copious amounts of MSG.

"I guess I'm going home," Tamara replied. She said it like a cynic might say "I guess I'm going to go vote."

"Hey, why don't we go someplace? You follow me, girl, we're gonna go out, okay?" She gave Tamara her best smile, which, considering her beautiful teeth, was something of a doozy.

Tamara gave a shy smile back, and said, "Oh, all right. Be good to have some fun for a change."

So they went to The Paradise Club, which is where Ameesha worked as an exotic dancer. Tamara chuckled to herself as they went inside, because she hadn't been completely aware of Ameesha's personal situation, but she was an easygoing person who felt that as long as people were happy then everything was all right.

Inside, much to his dismay, they found Kel Urquhart sitting alone in a booth stirring a Long Island iced tea. Ameesha didn't have to work for almost an hour, so the three sat together with Kel's smooth babyish cheeks getting pink as he stared at the circular current he was creating in his drink.

"I don't, ahem, I don't come here, uh, often," Kel began.

"I know," said Ameesha. "It's the first time I ever seen you here."

"You come here a lot?" He was surprised, his thin and sensitive eyebrows rose ever so slightly.

"I work here," Ameesha said, smiling. "But you don't tell anyone and I won't tell anyone how you would know that." They shared a laugh at that.

"It's my first time here, too," Tamara added.

Ameesha looked from Tamara to Kel, and saw the flicker of a look that sparked between them. She wisely made a quick excuse and left them alone. They talked for a few minutes and then Tamara said, "Do you wanna get out of here, hon?"

No one had ever called Kel by any endearment before, and he felt an odd sense of pride and a strong attraction to Tamara. He said, "Sure," and they were gone without even thinking about saying goodbye to Ameesha. They pulled out of the parking lot in Tamara's car about ten minutes before Puck swung in and parked his Jeep.

Tamara's ex-husband was tall, thin, mean-spirited when he was drunk, and prone to jealousy – a small-minded man with no ambitions and a singular idea of what made a good time. Kel never once remotely reminded Tamara of her ex-husband, and so she developed an echo of the attraction he had for her. They had sex, and Kel made the mistake of becoming clingy afterward, and Tamara made the mistake of rebounding every once in a while into his needy arms.

Lying awake in each other's arms after, Kel told Tamara about the three novels that he was working on while Tamara gently fell into peaceful sleep. This was, in a way, the exact opposite of how Gina and Chester's date ended.

Chapter 10 - Nordquist

There's no two bones about it, thought Nordquist, this mall is a goddamned sty.

He stood, leaning on his mop, his beautiful 188-strand Kenora-Sevelton mop with the fiberglass handle, by one of the entrances to the mall. He was watching teenagers tramp in with mud and slush and dirt and filth and muck and haphazard waste on their shoes. One teen, with long blond hair hanging like a curtain over his face, had a skateboard in his hand and tossed it forward as soon as he came through the doors. He hopped nimbly onto it and coasted about a foot before Modesta Mae caught his eye.

"You get off that skateboard, son," she said decisively.

"Who's gonna make me?" he chided, good-naturedly. They both knew he would obey, eventually, it was just a matter of when. Some of the more rebellious types wondered exactly how far it was safe to push.

"You better believe I'm gonna haul you by your hair right off that thing and then use it to light a fire under your ass. I am a mother, I know how to make a young man's life a living hell." She stood with her arms folded. She had large arms – she was a large woman – and although they were fleshy it was also clear that they were powerful. And when she crossed her arms they were like a force field that repelled disrespect. He got off the skateboard, ducked his head.

"Sorry, ma'am," he said. He sensed that maybe he had gone too far.

Mo gave him a smile of forbearance. "It's okay, hon, you just take care now, all right? Ride that thing to your death outside my mall, okay?" She gave him a playful swat on the shoulder and pushed him off in the direction of the arcade.

Nordquist noted that the kid's shoe had a wet leaf stuck to it, and it was leaving a trail of muddy water behind him as he slouched toward the arcade, using his skateboard like a cane. He plunged the mop in the wheeled bucket of warm soapy water and went to swab the deck.

Nordquist was a tall drink of water with short, iron-grey hair that bristled out of his eczemic and slightly oversized head. He maintained yesterday's five o'clock shadow because, after being honourably discharged from the merchant marines, he was no longer required to submit to the tyranny of daily shaving. When he had been on the ship he was a model of strict observance of the rules and rituals of a seaman, and whenever he was off the ship he had maturely and purposefully drunk himself into stupor. Nowadays he balanced equally between the two worlds, keeping the mall ship-shape and returning home at night to his wife and drinking two double scotches, straight. On Wednesdays he had his book club, and on Fridays he took his wife out to the movies, except in the winter when he and his wife joined a curling league.

Nordquist's wife was always skip. She had been playing since she was a teenager and understood the game as well as she understood her husband – neither one held many depths she hadn't plumbed. Nordquist was always vice-skip. This was as close an approximation as they could get to their off-the-ice relationship. Nordquist's wife would often point out exactly where the problems were in his life, and it was up to Nordquist to decide how hard to throw the rock to finesse the problem away from the button.

But his real joy, besides a cleanly mopped floor, was his book club. He had started it several years ago and the roster had rotated continuously through whatever current employees happened to be book-minded. Due to the high turnover rate at the mall there had already been over twenty members of the book club. They met every Wednesday night in the small meeting room in the office section on the second floor of the mall. So far this hadn't been a problem because Mo had been a member of the book club since it started, and she had keys to every room in the mall except for Ipswitch's office, which was where the dreaded Wheel of Fun was kept.

Ipswitch himself had no knowledge of the book club, and since he would have shut it down forthwith if he knew, no one told him.

The current members collectively decided what books to read and how much to read each week, according to their schedule. There were weeks where Nordquist could easily have read more than the quota, but with his signature stalwart dignity he would refuse to read even one word over the democratically determined amount.

Seated around the long table, books cradled lovingly or tossed carelessly, as the case may be, they discussed. The current members were Nordquist, Mo, Kel Urquhart, Tamara, Dusty, Easter, and, every full moon or so, Chester. Nordquist didn't mind Chester, but sometimes became enraged by his inability to stick with the group, and often had to disentangle Chester and Kel when they got into an argument.

"Frankly, I think the title is extremely misleading, so far. I don't see why it's heartbreaking, the only staggering thing about it is its size, it's not particularly genius, and it doesn't seem like the author did that much work," said Kel, tossing the heavy hard cover onto the table with a satisfying thump. He crossed his arms.

"Well," said Easter carefully. She said everything

carefully, as if enunciation made her more credible. She was young and very, very smart so she was used to her youth – and her gender, frankly – acting as a barrier to being taken seriously. It was a frustration she had learned to focus in other directions. "I think the connection between the brothers is, or could be, heartbreaking. Here, we have a boy trapped in a man's body taking care of a man trapped in a boy's body."

"Why do you say it could be heartbreaking, Easter?" Nordquist asked. He tended to gently lead the discussion around the room, as if showing off a prize cow. He wasn't ostentatious about it, but the thing he liked about the book club was the ability anyone had to subtly direct the flow of a group's analytical energy.

"Could be, could be," said Kel dismissively.

"I think any strong relationship has the potential for tragedy," Easter answered.

Tamara nodded, "My feeling, you know, is that at this point the author is setting us up. He's just kind of, you know he's kind of cueing the sad music. I have a sort of fear, or anxiety maybe, that something bad is going to happen, which sort of drives me to read more."

"Have you been reading ahead, hon?" Mo asked, smiling, eyes flashing. Usually Mo was the one that read ahead, her curiosity was like a caged animal injected with amphetamines.

"Oh, never!" said Tamara, with mock indignation, because she was the second most likely person to read ahead. Her brittle energy made her restless, and she was the kind of person who succumbed to her indulgences.

"Yes, Dusty?" said Nordquist, because Dusty had raised his hand.

"What about– Has anyone read the chapter heading...things?"

"Things. Exactly," Kel added. "This book is just a jumbled collection of things, there's no through-line, and that descriptive stuff with the chapters is just there to try to give a semblance of order. And what's with that completely spurious foreword?"

"You know, I liked the foreword," said Tamara quietly. They had already had a bit of an argument about the foreword while lying in Kel's bed the previous night.

"Yes, Dusty?" said Nordquist, because Dusty had raised his hand again. It didn't help to tell him that it wasn't necessary, he just always raised his hand.

"Where's Chester?" he asked. Chester tended to encourage Dusty's hesitant analyses of the novel they were reading. Dusty needed that sort of support in the face of Kel's vehement tsks and pffts.

"On a date," replied Easter, smiling enigmatically.

"Oh. With January?" Tamara asked, either impressed or surprised or both.

"With Gina," answered Easter and Mo at the same time. They looked at each other, modestly surprised, and then laughed.

Chester was standing on the cold concrete porch of Gina's house, straightening his shirt collar under his jacket, waiting for someone to answer the door. It was a mild fall night and the wind was electric, blowing russet-coloured leaves about in little whirling circles. Chester looked around the neighbourhood, the tree-lined street, the house next door. He blinked in surprise because he recognized it as Modesta Mae's bungalow, where she held her Oscar party every year. He'd never realized they were neighbours.

He stepped back from the door and looked up and down the street, wondering if he had the right house. He glanced up to the second storey and saw a light turn off. A few moments later the door finally made some noise as someone tried to open it from inside.

There was some mild cursing on the other side of the door. The knob rattled again and locks clicked back and forth. There was some kind of exasperated conversation between a frustrated male voice and Gina's angry female one. Chester rocked on his heels and puffed out his cheeks as he waited. Finally the door clicked and the knob turned and a square of warm yellow light fell on Chester's smiling face. Gina stood on the other side of the door, holding it shyly, looking partly around the edge of it.

"Sorry about that," she said. Her hair was up and she was wearing more make-up than Chester was used to. He was suddenly touched by the effort that she must have put in to what, he believed, was something of a fake date.

"Don't worry about it."

Chester stepped forward but Gina put a hand on his chest. "No, don't come in, I just—" she began, but it was too late, Chester had stepped inside.

"Gina, bring your friend in here so we can meet him," yelled Gina's dad from another room. Gina sighed, put a hand to her face.

"Dad!" she yelled, annoyed.

Chester looked around. From where he stood the house was a study in the shade of green. The carpet was a sort of overcooked pea colour, which ran up the stairs to the second floor and spilled into the adjacent rooms, of which Chester could see few details. Three walls of the foyer were painted with striped bands of deep, dark jungle green and creamy mint. The wall to Chester's right, which continued up the staircase and curved at the top, was wallpapered with a sea-foam green broken up by tiny red and yellow roses.

"We just want to meet him, just for a second," said Gina's mom, yelling from somewhere upstairs.

"No, mom, we've got to go," Gina yelled back. Then softer, slightly desperately, she said to Chester, "I just need to get my coat on and we can go." She opened the closet door, and Chester looked at her, touched by her embarrassment of her family.

"Where are you kids going?" yelled her father.

Chester smiled, and said to Gina, "Have you guys ever thought about getting an intercom system?"

Despite herself Gina smiled, and rolled her eyes. She yelled to her dad, "Out!"

Chester leaned closer, "You look lovely," he said.

"Thanks, let's go," she said, pulling out a long, reddish-brown wool coat. It was luxurious but old, with woolen fuzz sticking out haphazardly.

"No, I mean," he paused, smiling at her, "you really look beautiful."

"Gina!" yelled her dad.

"Oh," she said to Chester, and became abashed. Then, not quite knowing how to respond to Chester, she yelled to her parents, "We're going, I'll see you later!"

She pushed him out of the door as her mom began coming down the stairs. Chester caught a glimpse of a short woman, wearing a skirt and green pantyhose. He didn't see her face, and then the door was closed and Gina was pulling on her coat.

"I don't mind meeting your family," said Chester.

"No, it would just be too much," she said. She pulled her auburn hair out from under the coat. It was curly, and bounced as she moved her exquisitely cute head. Her skin was like new-fallen snow it was so smooth and pale. "So where are we off to?" she asked.

"That bus stop over there," Chester replied, pointing down the street.

"Oh, you don't have a car?"

"What do I look like? A millionaire?"

She stopped him with a hand to his chest. He liked her hand on his chest, and thought that it was probably dangerous that he liked it. It was like falling in love with someone's most angry expression, or enjoying the sound of their voice only when they were yelling. He felt more obliged than usual to stir up trouble. "Wait here," she said.

"For what?" he asked, but she was already moving around the side of the house, sneaking along. He went after her, moving carefully, treading quietly. When she ducked her head down to avoid being seen through a window he did the same, after quickly glancing through it.

That's how Chester saw Gina's dad for the first time. A thick-shouldered, short man with a balding head and a thin, aquiline nose wearing a plaid shirt, watching TV and laughing, that was all he saw. But he liked the look of the man's laugh, teeth like newly-popped popcorn, eyes closed and head back.

Moving like two people who had failed their ninja training course, they arrived at the back door, which Gina eased open. She slipped inside, reappeared only a few seconds later and quietly shut the door. She turned to go down the steps and ran into Chester.

"Ah!" she yelped.

"Shh, shh," said Chester very quietly. "I'm just me."

"Goddammit!" she whispered angrily, swatting him. "You scared me!"

"Sorry."

"I told you to wait there."

"I wanted to see what you were up to," he whispered, smiling. They were slowly and silently making their way back around the house to the driveway. Gina dangled car keys, handed them to Chester.

"Can you drive stick?" she asked.

"What do I look like? A genius?" he replied, handing the keys back.

"Chester..." she said, pouting, her elfin features pulled down, making her look like a child who had found that Christmas morning had been grinched.

"What can I tell you? Now I wish I'd learned."

She sighed, unlocked the doors, got into the driver's seat. She put the key in the ignition, then looked at the dash for some time. "Okay," she said. She steadied her hands on the wheel.

"Do you know how to drive stick?" Chester asked, worried.

"Well," Gina began. She looked at the various parts of the dash, at the gearshift, and adjusted the rearview. She started the car. "Theoretically..." she said.

"Theoretically?"

"It's like an airplane," she gulped. Chester was silent, nervous. She continued, "The hard parts are takeoff and landing."

The car lurched forward out of the driveway and then stalled in the middle of the street. Gina got it started again and turned to Chester. "You okay?'

"Never better," said Chester, his hands gripping the seat and the door handle. He tested his brow to see if there was sweat there. His hand came away dry, for the time being. Gina shifted gears, revved the engine, popped the clutch, and the car rocketed forward and then stalled. She got it started again and brought the engine up to a near-screaming level, then released the clutch and Chester's head bounced off the headrest. The houses became a blur and the engine sounded like it was an angry nest of giant hornets, ready to attack, and then Gina shifted and everything calmed down.

"See?" she said, "Once you've got the takeoff you're fine."

"Good work," Chester said, smiling tightly, refusing to mention anything about landings.

They did arrive safely at the restaurant, not without some knuckle-whitening moments. Chester shakily gave his name to the maitre d' and once they were seated Gina tried to apologize by laying her hand gently on his. He jumped slightly and yanked his hand back.

"I'm just trying to calm you down," she said, miffed.

"I'm okay," he said. "I'm okay." And he tried to remember the one yoga class that he'd gone to. They had been big on relaxation, but he couldn't recall any of the calming exercises, which made him sorely frustrated.

Chester began humming to himself as he looked through the menu. Gina took an opportunity to look over at him, and the corners of her lips curled up as she watched him. He had shaved, and was wearing a mellow hint of something that smelled nice: aftershave or cologne. It was diffuse enough that you could only smell it when you were concentrating. His hair was all a-muss but Gina thought that was cute, and she liked the way his lips changed expression as he contemplated different menu items. Chester was not classically handsome. What Gina found enchanting about him was his vitality, which bordered on agitation, and his lack of self-consciousness. He was like a cute little crackpot, blazing trails he didn't even realize had not been blazed before.

Chester looked up from his menu, caught Gina smiling at him with a kind of immature slyness.

"What?" He looked at his shirt. "What are you looking at?"

Gina shook her head, making her curls swing, "Oh, nothing."

"Do you know what you're getting?"

"Of course."

"You didn't even look at your menu..."

"I've been to East Side Mario's before," she replied.

"Am I losing points?" he asked sarcastically.

"Well, there are better date restaurants," she said matter-of-factly.

"So if I go out with January, I should take her to one of those?"

Gina sighed. He would have to bring up her ruse and ruin the moment she'd been having. "Can you just," she began, "pretend like you want to be on a date with me?"

Chester noticed something sad in her expression. "Oh. Sure." He nodded. "You really do look beautiful," he added. She was wearing a kind of lip gloss that made her lips look extremely shiny, like she'd just licked them with a Vaseline tongue, and a soft-looking fuzzy green turtleneck that matched her large, arrestingly direct green eyes. Her small features – the button nose, the narrow but full mouth – looked even smaller compared to her eyes, which were demurely downcast so he was looking at them through the fringe of her fragile lashes.

"Say that again," she said, looking up at him.

"You really do look beautiful."

She began to blush slightly. She felt the sensation slowly tingle her forehead, and then her ears, and then her cheeks. Gina always felt that she blushed too often, a fact that made her very remotely embarrassed, which caused her to blush.

To combat the sensation she said, "So why did you think we could take the bus?"

"Why didn't we take the bus?"

"Cause it's not very cool, when you're going to go on a date, to take the bus."

"It's cool every other time," Chester retorted.

"It's not cool every other time."

"It's not?"

"No. It's cool to have a car."

"Why is that cool?"

"I don't know, it just is."

"Well that's not a reason," Chester muttered. "Listen, how many dates have you been on?" he asked, putting his elbow on the table and leaning forward.

"Plenty. I've been on hundreds of dates." Gina crossed her arms.

"Oh." He hadn't realized he was talking to an expert. He shrugged, and abandoned his line of argument. "Who did you go out with?" Chester asked, genuinely interested.

"My last boyfriend was Puck, actually." Gina said it like it was a source of pride. She wasn't sure why it would be, exactly, but felt it was a good defensive strategy.

"What happened?"

Gina blushed again. "He said something that I didn't appreciate," she said airily.

Chester didn't catch on. "What did he say?"

"Chester."

"What?"

"I don't really want to talk about it."

"Oh, come on. Here's your chance. You tell me what he said, and I say oh, that's awful, and then you agree and then we smile together and feel a bit closer to each other." He was nodding, sincere. "So, shoot."

Gina thought about it, pursed her lips, looked at Chester's expectant and guileless face. "He told me I was a bad kisser," she said.

"Oh, really?"

"Yeah."

"That's not very cool," Chester said, frowning. "He should have said maybe like, hey, I think we need to work on our kissing technique: let's make out."

"Yeah." Gina chuckled.

"So, okay, who else did you go out with?"

"Um, before Puck I went out with Jasper."

Chester stopped. "Jasper?"

"Yeah." She paused, and then sarcastically added, "He works at the Shopper's Drug Mart. He's got brown hair and brown eyes. Kinda gullible, but sweet."

"I know him."

"I know. You guys order from me, like, every day."

"I'm just a little...surprised, I guess. Jasper? He doesn't seem...experienced. I mean, is he experienced?"

"I don't know. Not really. It was quite a while ago."

"Jasper," Chester muttered to himself. Then he asked, "So what happened there?"

"Oh," Gina winced, looked sheepish.

"What?"

"He...he also told me that I was a bad kisser."

"Jasper did?"

"Yeah." She looked like she was bracing for a pie in the face.

Chester paused. He was still trying to process the information. Jasper and Gina. He shook his head. "Well, what the hell does he know?" he asked. "What is he, teaching a class in professional kissing?"

That made Gina laugh, and Chester smile, and then the waiter finally came to take their drink order.

They talked and Gina felt like she understood where the phrase making conversation came from. It was like they were working together on a detailed mural, adding small bits of colour over broad sweeps of expressive statements. It was easy and peaceful and each tidbit they added to the conversation seemed to lead naturally to the next and the next. There was a sort of shared goal they were both working toward, and without telling each other what it was, they both understood where they were going. She wondered if that was what making love was like.

Gina wanted to reach across the table and interlace her fingers with Chester's, and look at their hands holding each other as she smoothed the surface of his palm with her thumb. She kept imagining it, but kept her hands to herself. Chester was mostly oblivious, wondering why she kept blushing ever so slightly. When he would ask, it would make the blush burn her skin and she would stammer some excuse, and he realized he should probably stop asking.

They avoided talking about work because it made Chester irritable, and then he'd say, "Bah, let's not talk about work." So Gina told him about her years as a figure skater, and Chester told her about his fear of ice, and Gina told him about her fears of loneliness, and Chester told her about the time that he went camping by himself for a week and was sorely lonely.

Gina talked about her parents, who really were nice people, just effusively overbearing. She was an only child. They worried about her too much and protected her too much and she wanted to save up enough money to move to the city. Chester, who had moved from a tiny farming community where he had lived with his parents and two older brothers, thought that they were living in the city. He had moved in with his grandmother, in her apartment, until he could save up enough for his own place. He told her about how he used to dream that he was an only child, and didn't have to suffer the thousand small injustices played upon him by his siblings just because he was the youngest and most naïve. She told him about how she used to dream she had any kind of siblings at all, even evil stepsisters, just so she had a de facto playmate or two.

By the time they left the restaurant it didn't seem all too much for Gina to lace her arm through Chester's and lean her head against his shoulder. They got in Gina's car and she managed to drive to the mall, where she parked in the unlit back corner of the empty parking lot. She felt like she was almost getting the handle of driving stick. They slowed until the car suddenly jerked forward and died, and as Gina turned off the lights and set the parking brake Chester looked at her, confused.

"What's up?" he asked.

Gina looked at him sidelong, her eyes reflecting the haze-shrouded, golden streetlights. "We're parking," she said.

"Are we...going into the mall?"

"No," she said, chuckling.

"Well what are we doing?"

"We're," she began, trying to emphasize the double entendre with vague hand gestures, "parking."

"Well, I can see that," Chester said patronizingly, because he thought she was patronizing him. "But why?"

"Will you just shut up and kiss me," she said exasperatedly.

"Oh." He turned towards her. She raised her hands and put them on his shoulders, and he caressed her smooth jawline with one hand as his other hand settled on her hip. She slipped her arms around him and pulled him closer. Their lips came together gently, sweetly, hesitantly. Gina felt a tingle that seemed like a blush, but had an entirely different character, and it raced down from the edge of her hairline down her cheeks through her neck and she could feel it gather in the top of her chest and slowly diffuse down her breasts to her nipples. Chester felt a different electricity jump from his fingertips down through his arms and into his torso and spread to the inside of his thighs making him acutely aware of the pulse in his loins. They both took in a breath, smelling each other's skin as their lips caressed.

They separated, Chester opened his eyes and saw Gina was biting her lower lip, her eyes closed.

Chester cleared his throat. "I don't know what they were talking about," he said huskily. "You're a good kisser."

Gina smiled, opened her eyes. "Really?" she said.

She turned her face away in embarrassment. “I’ve been practicing.”

“So, does this mean that I can go out with January?”

Gina’s large, moist eyes trembled slightly as she frowned. She looked up at Chester and her eyes gathered moisture from somewhere, became pools of wetness reflecting the orange glow of the parking lot lights. The tingling feeling in her chest felt sour, and she said, “Chester.”

“What’s wrong?” he asked.

Gina blinked, which made a tear roll over her lashes and trickle down her cheek. “You can be a real idiot sometimes, Chester,” she whispered, wiping at her cheeks quickly.

“What are you talking about?” He was confused. “What did I say? What’s wrong?”

“Nothing.” It was hard to not be mad at him, but she realized that she’d done it to herself. She shook her head. She started the car, let the clutch out and it lurched, stopped, lurched again, and stopped. “Fuck!” she yelled.

“The parking brake is—” began Chester helpfully.

“I know what the fucking parking brake is doing, okay!” Gina shouted at him. Chester flinched back, looked at her like he just wanted to jump from the car and run for it. Tears burned her eyes and rolled down her cheeks. She took the parking brake off and the car roared out of the parking lot.

When they got to Gina’s house, though, it was she who jumped out of the car and ran into the house, on the brink of sobbing. Chester got out of the car, one hand on the open car door as he watched her retreat and wondered what the hell had just happened.

“I’m sorry!” he called to her. Then, “I had a lovely time, really. I didn't mean to screw things up. I...I shouldn't have mentioned her, I know. It's just— Was this about January or was this—?”

Gina stopped just as she was about to open the door to her house. She turned around, eyes red and quivering, her body straight as a ramrod, her jaw clenched. “Don’t you worry about January, Chester, I’m sure the two of you will have a wonderful fucking time and a beautiful fucking life together.”

She wrenched the door open, ran inside, and slammed it hard enough to make Chester wince.

“Well,” he said to himself, “I guess that's that.” He sighed, confused, and he closed the car door, turned to the bus stop, and began walking. His shoulders slumped under the peculiar weight of self-loathing, and he muttered to himself bitterly, “The ol’ Chester magic strikes again.”

Chapter 11 - Guy Tuffray

Guy Tuffray was all about recognition. And synergy. And teamwork. He was all about catchphrases, too. And mottos, and slogans, and high-energy motivational speaking. He was the kind of person who clapped his hands together and said, “All right, people, let’s gather around.” And the desultory employees of the Mega-Mart would either take a few steps toward him and cross their arms, or simply cast a witheringly disrespectful glance and keep talking to their friend about the party last night, or, in the case of Chester, simply leave and go see whether Polito had that camera angled so he could see into change room 17 yet.

Tuffray was not a commanding figure. His head was shaped like a potato, and on top was an uncombed collection of meagre orange-red hair. He had very pale lips to which he regularly applied Chapstick, and in the no-man’s-land between his upper lip and his thin, wheezy nose there was an unkempt bristle of mustache that looked like it had been grown by a 13-year-old girl on testosterone therapy. He also fidgeted, and this attribute, in part, accounted for his lack of ability to command respect.

Ipswitch, by contrast, was as steady as a laser-guided level. He was unswerving and direct, firing a long, terrible stare at whomever he was talking to. Tuffray was like a nervous animal. He would look side to side, stare at the ground, tilt his head this way or that, talk into his hand just before coughing. He gave the impression that you were something he was thinking about last-minute. It seemed he gave no real thought to what he said or how he said it, but was instead parroting some obscure book-on-tape about management that he'd heard in the early '80s.

Tuffray took a marker and wrote the word "symbiosis" on the whiteboard that was tacked to the wall next to the employee bathroom in the Mega-Mart stockroom. It was a bare moment after he had written it that he realized it was a permanent marker, not a whiteboard marker, and he cursed into his mustache.

He turned around, clapped his hands together, and said "Okay, team, let's gather around." No one paid any attention.

"Gather up," he tried. Then, after a pause where a few employees shuffled their feet without moving, he added, "Gather in? Let's gather together, people. Come on, gather closer."

He picked up his clipboard, glanced at it, flipped the pages back and forth, then said, "Watson."

"What?" Watson asked, as if he clearly had better things to do with his time.

"We need to re-organize the linens aisle. I want you to actualize that. Take some time and creatively re-focus your energies. Think like a customer. Be the product. You know? Just take some breaths and really understand how the customer is going to approach the product. Okay? You follow?"

Watson stared at him and blinked. He opened his mouth. He had no clue what Tuffray had just asked him to do, and at the same time it wasn't important to him to make sure he understood. So he shrugged and said, "Yeah, sure."

"Easter," said Tuffray, looking back down at his clipboard, then scanning the group. "Easter," he repeated.

Easter stood in front of everyone, but she was short and often overlooked. It took Tuffray a few moments to find her, calling her name in the same over-enunciated manner.

"Oh, there you are," he said as she sighed and crossed her arms, standing hipshot. "Can you—"

"I'm going to be helping Watson, so...no, I can't," she said.

"Easter, I need you to work with the team here, honey." Tuffray sometimes referred to female employees by the slightly offensive "honey" and referred to the male employees by the slightly offensive "pal".

"Oh well," said Easter sarcastically, like she was mock-apologetic that she couldn't follow his orders.

Tuffray shot glances into all the corners of the room and went back to his clipboard. "Um, Shorsky," he said, looking up and quickly spotting the tired, wrinkled face of Shorsky with the goiter just under her right jaw. "Excellent work yesterday with the customer-oriented approach to achieving your personal goal set."

"What?" said Shorsky.

"I said good work with your customer-oriented service. It really helped us re-focus our, um, strategies and build up our relations manifest, so..." Tuffray nodded. "Kudos to you."

"What?" said Shorsky. She still had no idea what he was saying.

"Team," said Tuffray, raising his voice as a few people at the back began filing slowly and stealthily out of the stockroom, "that's the kind of attitude we should all have. A complete customer-focused orientation, okay? We've got a lot of synergy that we're building between the client faction and us. We need to keep building on that, turning over our resources, and taking client-side issues and making them our own. You know? Gain ownership, take ownership," he paused dramatically, "and actualize that problem to a gainful solution for, you know, all sides."

The remaining employees stood and stared blankly at him.

"What's today's motivation word?" he said, trying to

psyche everyone up.

No one said anything.

"That's right, it's symbiosis," he said, pumping a fist in the air and turning to the whiteboard. "Symbiosis," he repeated, "is how we interact with the customer. They want service, they want a product. They get those things from us and we..." at this point Tuffray raised his finger and was nodding, smiling like he was about to reveal the great secret of existence. "We provide it. That's symbiosis."

"That's not symbiosis," said Easter.

Tuffray ignored her. The employees, with some hidden signal or herd mind survival instinct, began shuffling as a group toward the door. Tuffray tried one last, valiant effort to be managerial, calling out, "All right, let's get out there people and...well, let's just get out there. I like that enthusiasm. Symbiosis!"

The employees left, gladly, and took nothing of Tuffray's speech to heart. In fact, they served every customer with an undercurrent of scorn and an air of defeatism.

Easter turned to Watson as they shuffled out. "That's not symbiosis," she said.

Watson put a finger to his lips, cocked a warning eyebrow at her, and said "Shh."

Easter made a face, stuck her tongue out at him, and blew a raspberry. Watson chuckled, shaking his head in a forbearing way, and proceeded to have one of the worst days of his life. In the course of it he got his tooth knocked out and couldn't make it to work the next day, which was ultimately lucky for him. That was the day Chester ended up borrowing Watson's uniform and proceeded to have one of the worst days of his life, which wound up being lucky in its way as well. Perhaps the uniform was cursed, or blessed.

Chester was sitting in Polito's back room, on the chair in the corner, legs stretched out, trying to get some sleep before lunch. Polito's daughter was on the floor colouring, crayons strewn about her, trying to stay rigidly inside the lines. She was breathing loudly through her mouth because she had a cold, and would sniffle as she dropped the emerald green to pick up sienna. She was four years old. Her name was Samaria.

"Hey, you know I saw Tamara come in today," said Polito.

"Hm," said Chester. He wasn't in the mood to talk. His heart was still smarting from the bruising it had received earlier in the week from January.

Polito looked over his shoulder at Chester. "She was with someone."

"Okay."

"Hey, what's up, man? You don't seem yourself."

"Aw, fuck it," Chester sighed. He kept his eyes closed.

"Hey, don't say fuck in front of my daughter," Polito said.

Samaria looked up at the two adults.

"Oh, fuck. Sorry." Chester sat up, he looked down at Samaria, whose mouth was slightly open as she breathed loudly. "Sorry, Samaria. Don't say fuck okay?"

"Okay," she said. She went back to colouring.

"Why is your daughter here?"

"It's Take Your Daughter To Work Day."

"What?"

"It's Take Your Daughter To Work Day," Polito said louder, turning back to the monitors. "All around the country fathers are taking their daughters to work with them so they can see what daddy does all day. Right, sweetie?"

Samaria kept colouring.

"The moms don't take them?"

Polito swiveled in his chair, stared hard at Chester. "I'm not letting Eden take her to the goddamn strip joint."

"I thought it was a gentleman's club."

"Shut up," said Polito.

Chester leaned back, closed his eyes. "So you're showing Samaria here the ropes?"

"Yeah," said Polito, intent on the screens.

"It looks like she's colouring."

"Well what the hell do you want her to do, she's four years old."

"She's four? You're four already?" Chester asked, sitting up.

"Yeah," said Samaria. "Look at my picture."

"Oh, that's nice. The frog has purple legs."

"Yeah, he's a jumping frog," said Samaria.

"Cool."

"He goes jump jump jump!" Samaria sang out. She proceeded to make her crayons jump around.

"So what did you want to tell me about Tamara?" Chester asked, settling back.

"She came in with someone this morning," said Polito, doing a Groucho Marx with his eyebrows.

"Stop trying to build suspense and just tell me."

"It was Kel."

Chester's eyes opened slowly. "What?" His tone was sepulchral.

"Kel Urquhart."

"I know his last name. What are you trying to say?"

Polito shrugged. "I don't know, man. All I know is they came in together and he went to give her a kiss when he left."

"What did she do?"

"She leaned away. But then she looked around and made sure no one was looking and gave him a peck."

"Where did you see this?"

"On the monitors."

"Son of a bitch," Chester said slowly. He looked into the distance. "Can you show me?"

Polito pressed some buttons on his console, one of the monitors began rewinding, the time code in the upper left corner jumped and flickered as it ticked backward. After a few moments Polito hit a few more buttons and the monitor showed Tamara and Kel walking in the doors of the mall, too close for Chester's comfort. They weren't touching, but they were obviously coming in together.

Samaria watched with Chester and Polito. They watched Kel lean in and Tamara put a hand on his chest to stop him. She looked perturbed, looked around quickly, then gave him a quick peck on the lips and a stern look. She was saying something. The cameras didn't pick up sound, but she waved a finger at him and he looked suitably dressed down and apologetic. Then he left and she went in to the Mega-Mart.

"Jesus Christ, that son of a bitch is dating my aunt," Chester said. Polito pressed a few more buttons and the monitor went back to recording.

"Told you," said Polito.

"That son of a bitch." Chester ran a hand through his unkempt hair. His heart was hammering at the door of his chest like an ill-tempered bill collector, vigorously and jittery.

"Son of bitch," Samaria echoed.

"Honey, don't call people sons of bitches," Polito said, putting a fatherly hand on her shoulder. Chester was still in shock. Polito picked Samaria up and put her on his knee. "Now, do you want to help daddy try to see into change room 17?"

"Okay," she said, looking intently at the monitors.

"I've gotta go," said Chester. He stood up, dumbfounded, and pushed his way out the door of the small room. He felt untethered, and he wandered through the Mega-Mart out into the mall with no clear direction or purpose. At least, none that he could discern through the fog of his thoughts.

Polito looked over his shoulder, and frowned after him in concern.

"Daddy?" said Samaria.

"Yes, sweetie?"

"Your friend smells bad."

Polito kept his eyes on the door, realizing that he could smell something now as well. Just a faint taste. Chester was drunk.

"Daddy?" said Samaria again.

"Yes, sweetie?" He turned back to see her pointing at the monitor showing change room 17.

"Why don't you just raise the mirror?" she said.

Tuffray opened the door. "Where's Chester?" he

asked. Polito shrugged. Tuffray was often oblivious to what happened in the Mega-Mart in general and the back room in particular. He wasn't aware of how the majority of the staff saw him, which was as a blundering imbecile on a power trip. He didn't know about the tapes Polito had made of him picking his nose, adjusting his underwear, or any of the thousand moderately embarrassing things that he did on a daily basis. Those tapes were compiled around Christmas time and edited, culled for the best material. They were Polito's gift to the employees.

He had one tape, though, that Tuffray had actually confiscated. Tuffray's conversation with the Texan. Directly after he had talked to the Texan, Tuffray marched straight back into the backroom, his face red, his shirt decorated with sticky chocolate sauce, his hair dusted with confectioner's sugar, to see Polito clutching his sides laughing.

"Give me that tape," Tuffray had wheezed angrily.

"What tape?"

"Give it to me!"

"You can't confiscate the—"

"I can do whatever I bloody well want! Now give me the tape or you're fired!"

Polito shrugged, gave Tuffray the tape, and Tuffray promptly smashed it on the ground. He stomped on it, obliterating the episode from the face of the earth.

"Don't you tell anyone," Tuffray whispered menacingly to Polito. And then he'd left to go to the bathroom and clean himself up, taking the remains of the tape with him.

Polito had watched the whole thing with incredulity and amusement. The Texan had wandered in on a slow Wednesday afternoon, as he usually did, and began lazily cruising the aisles. He was almost the only customer in the whole store and, due to his reputation, he was left completely alone. If he entered an aisle where an employee was working, stocking shelves, pricing, what-have-you, they would instantly find a reason to leave. Everyone except Tuffray. He elbowed Hoginberry, who had since quit to move to the city and go to college, and said, "Go get team-motivated and actualize that customer's priorities."

"What?" said Hoginberry.

"Go ask that guy what he wants," Tuffray hissed, annoyed.

"You do it."

"Don't be impertinent."

"Listen, old man, I'm not talking to that guy," said Hoginberry, holding his hands up. Tuffray sighed, exaggeratedly. He walked over to the Texan, who was standing in the baking supplies aisle, looking at muffin mixes. He sidled up beside him, looking at the muffin mixes as well. He allowed a quiet moment to pass.

"Can I help you find anything, sir?"

The Texan turned his head slowly to look at him, squinting. "I think I'm fine, son," he said carefully. There was an edge in his voice.

"Are you sure there's nothing I can help you find? Perhaps you're looking for cake mixes? They're just down here—" Tuffray put a hand on the Texan's shoulder to direct him down the aisle to the cake mixes.

"I don't need your help, and I'd appreciate it if you wouldn't touch me," the Texan replied coldly.

"But sir, any questions you have I could answer. I'm the manager here at the Mega-Mart," Tuffray said proudly.

"That's great. Leave me alone." The Texan was now standing square to Tuffray, looking directly into his eyes, trying to burn a hole into them.

"It's just that I've seen you come in here before, sir, and I was just hoping that perhaps this time I could help you find—"

"Listen, son, I'm telling you one last time. Turn around. Walk away."

"If you just let me know what you're looking for, I can certainly direct you—" Tuffray began, and the Texan slapped him. "Sir," said Tuffray, his face blossoming red in embarrassment.

The Texan slapped him with the other hand.

"But I—"

The Texan reached out, grabbed a squeeze bottle of chocolate sauce and unscrewed the cap, dropping it with disdain.

"Excuse me, sir, but I'm afraid—" Tuffray began, but he didn't have time to finish. The Texan used his thumbnail to split the foil safety guard covering the opening of the chocolate sauce. He squirted the thick, dark, sticky liquid onto Tuffray's shirt as Tuffray backed up quickly. The Texan waved the bottle, getting the chocolate sauce on the floor as much as on Tuffray.

"Sir, excuse me—" Tuffray said, and then slipped as he was backing up, the chocolate sauce getting under his heel. He crashed to the floor with a girlish yell and the Texan grabbed a bag of icing sugar from the shelf and tore it open over Tuffray's head. The white powder dusted down on Tuffray like a miniature, sweet avalanche. Tuffray sputtered, kicked his feet trying to get back up.

The Texan leaned in and slapped him again. "If I ever see you in here when I'm in here, there'll be plenty more where that came from. Now don't bother me ever again." There was a hard glint in the Texan's eye, and Tuffray quailed, mouth agape, face and hair dusted in fine white sugar, his shirt and hands sticky with chocolate sauce.

Tuffray flipped over, crawled away quickly as the Texan pursued him. He got to his feet, trying to escape, and the Texan shoved him with a well-placed boot on his rounded flabby butt. Tuffray collapsed on the tile floor, and picked himself up quickly. When he turned to look over his shoulder the Texan had gone back to looking at the spice selection. Tuffray hurried away quickly and went straight to the back room.

Chester only heard the vaguest details third-hand from Kipling, and had no idea what exactly had happened between the Texan and Tuffray. Still, he was impressed.

"See, I think I've got to be more like that," said Chester.

"Mean? Ornery?" Kipling asked, slowly re-wrapping his chicken soft taco.

"No, no, no. No. I've just got to be...more confident."

"Mm," Kipling nodded.

"You know what I'm going to do?" Chester asked, nodding, winking.

"Ask January out?"

"I'm going to— Hey, how did you know?"

Kipling shrugged. "I thought things went badly with Gina?"

"Yeah, they did. I still don't completely understand what happened, and Gina won't talk to me."

Kipling blinked and ate and said nothing. Gina talked to him. He knew exactly what had happened, but for Gina's sake he stayed quiet. In his opinion Chester was a bit thick for not seeing the possibility, but that was Chester's nature: he did not dissemble. He was blunt. He didn't really understand that people might have motives behind their actions other than the ones they clearly stated. He never saw the point in that kind of behaviour.

Chester jogged his knee. He was suddenly nervous. "Should I do it today? I don't know. I've had too much coffee today. I need to balance out. What's the opposite of coffee?"

Kipling thought for half a second. "Tea?"

"What are you kidding me?"

"Um. Something sugary? Apple juice?"

"No, they're both stimulants."

"Whiskey?"

They both considered it. Chester looked at his watch. Five minutes to noon.

"No," they both said together.

Jasper walked smoothly across the crowded food court and set a tray down on the table beside Kipling as

Kipling took a large bite of his chicken soft taco.

"What's the opposite of coffee?" Chester asked.

"Warm milk," Jasper said without hesitation. He sat down beside Kipling and glanced at Kipling's tray. There was one wrapped soft taco left. "Down to two now, huh?"

Chester looked back and forth between the two of them, completely confused, and then said, "Warm milk, you say?"

So Chester warmed a litre carton of milk from the Mega-Mart by putting it on the heater in the staff room. He left it there thirty minutes. When he came back he took a gulp and said, "Ugh!" and poured the rest of the litre in the sink. Feeling slightly nauseous he went to see January.

She was by herself at Candida's Fashion, leaning out on the cashier counter with her hand on her chin. She was close to falling asleep, and was bored out of her mind, wishing that anyone would come along to make her feel less lonely. Besides which, it was hot in Candida's. Sitting down in that store in the afternoon was like two sleeping pills with a hot toddy chaser.

The night before she had spent in her room re-organizing her clothes in different ways. First by colour, alphabetically, so black came before brown and so forth, then by season, and finally by how often she wore them. She had an aching chasm of time to fill, and she didn't have anyone to call to chat with or go to coffee with or anything.

So when Chester walked up to the counter and saw January with her eyes half-closed almost dozing and said, "Hey," she had woken up with a start and then smiled widely at him.

"Hi, Chester," she said warmly.

"Listen, January," he began, "I know you may have heard some bad things from Gina. I know my date with her didn't go well, but I don't have any idea what happened, you gotta believe me. She just kinda went... kablooie...I don't know. I'm not a particularly good date, I guess." He shook his head. January's brow was furrowed. She had no idea what he was talking about. He continued, "And I...I just hope that there still might be a chance that we could maybe go out sometime. Nothing crazy, just, y'know, hanging out, chatting, maybe just get to know each other a little better and see what happens." He looked her in the eyes, nervous, concerned. "What do you think?"

January was silent, processing for some time. Chester began to nervously chew his lower lip.

"Is it hot in here?" he asked, to break the silence.

"Are you asking me out?" January said, frowning. She wasn't sure what was happening, but in her confusion Chester only heard imminent rejection.

"You know what, it's okay," Chester said, raising his hands, putting a small buffer between them. "I'm sorry." He turned to leave.

"No, wait," said January. "Um. We can go out." She smiled encouragingly.

"Oh," Chester said, walking back quickly. "You don't care what happened between me and Gina?"

January shook her head, her lips trying to form the proper response to that question. "I don't know why—I mean, I guess not. What happened between you and Gina?"

"Nothing," said Chester, smiling, "nothing at all. It's..." he sighed with some relief, "nothing."

"Oh, hey, I have an idea. Do you wanna go to the casino?" January had overheard Puck once telling his friend that the casino was the best place for a first date. According to Puck you either celebrated together or commiserated together, plus with the lights and the sounds and all the red, it was a pretty exciting spot.

"Uh, sure. Whatever you'd like. When do you want to—"

"How about tonight?" she interrupted.

Chester nodded, "Okay, okay, that's good." They were smiling at each other. Chester began backing away. Instinct told him now was a good time to leave, before he put his foot in his mouth. "So I'll see you tonight, then," he said.

"Okay, come by my place at eight." She gave him a wave, holding up her hand and just bending the fingers, like she was illustrating the art of one-handed clapping.

Chester felt exultant, roaringly powerful, hugely and careeningly successful. He beamed his smile to everyone he passed. He was still grinning ear to ear when he got off the bus near January's house, and walked up the street. He had a fairly pathetic bouquet in his hand that he thought was quite something. He walked up her driveway, her charming Tudor-style home looking like a small mansion compared to his grandmother's house. He used the doorknocker just to be insouciant and waited with his hands folded in front of him, holding the flowers sideways.

The door opened.

"Yes?" said January's father.

Chester's jaw hung open.

It was the Texan.

Chapter 12 - Dove Anquanita

Chester found Kel at the front desk of the Barnes & Noble, where he was serving a customer, an older woman with a tired stoop to her shoulders and a hat with a stuffed bird on it.

"Hey," Chester barked. Kel looked up, the old woman slowly turned her head. "Keep your hands off my aunt."

"I'm with a customer, Chester!" Kel retorted angrily. The old woman was slowly counting out change.

"Oh my god, you're two-timing on my aunt? You son of a bitch." Chester was shoulder to shoulder with the old lady, and she was getting nervous, trying to count faster.

"Chester, please, can't this conversation wait? Have a little professionalism, man!" Kel was trying to reach over the counter and hold Chester back from shoving the old lady over. She held up her hand defensively. Chester saw that he was upsetting her and calmed down. He put a gentle hand on her shoulder and tried to smile at her. It came across as a wolfish grimace; she counted faster. Chester jabbed his finger at Kel.

"You should talk. Professionalism. You've got your horny little hands all over an older woman."

The old lady looked at Kel.

"Chester, why would I touch your aunt? I don't even know who she is."

"I saw you. I saw you with your grubby little mitts all over her."

The old lady listened, now that she wasn't being shoved around.

Kel tsked and said, "I've never touched your aunt." He shook his head and his baby cheeks made small jowly sounds.

"I've got video proof, Kel!" Chester said.

Kel closed his eyes, held up a finger for Chester to wait a second. "Who...who the hell is your aunt, anyway?"

"Tamara, you idiot."

"Oh. I didn't know she was your aunt!"

"How do you think I got the job at the mall, stupid?"

"Geez, I don't know," Kel said sarcastically, "maybe you actually applied for it, the old fashioned way."

"Old fashioned way? Is that some euphemism for you dropping your sad little boner in my goddamn mother's sister?!?"

"Will you calm down?" Kel indicated the old lady, who was losing her patience and holding a great handful of change. "Customer!"

The old lady had been watching the back and forth, but she swatted Chester's arm with her gloved hand and said, "Out of the way, out of the way!"

"Hey watch it, lady."

"Just cool it for a second, Chester."

She dumped a clinking waterfall of change into Kel's hand and took her purchase, season one of *Sex and the City* on DVD, and harrumphed her way out of the store.

As soon as she was out of the way Chester launched forward, the counter the only thing keeping him from throttling Kel. "Yeah, I saw the two of you," he said, breathing hard through clenched teeth. "So keep your filthy paws off her."

"But, wait, she doesn't even have the same last name—"

"She was married, you giant bowl of ass water," Chester said, pounding a fist on the counter.

Kel looked slightly sheepish. Then he cleared the air by waving his hand between him and Chester and said, "Listen, she's a grown woman, she can make her own decisions."

"Yeah? And if I see you with her I'll beat the living hell from you. So, you know, make a decision you fat-necked freakbag. Fuck my aunt or live a long healthy life."

"Chester, will you keep it down? This is a family store, for crying out loud."

"Don't think you can assistant manager your way out of this, you nincompoop. You're my goddamned nemesis, for Christ's sake!"

"I'm your nemesis?" Kel was surprised.

"One of them, yeah, of course you are! Don't play dumb with me, Kel."

Kel frowned, his brow furrowing the baby-soft smoothness of his forehead. "I thought," he said slowly, "that I was Kipling's nemesis."

Chester was equally taken aback. "Why would you think you were Kipling's nemesis?"

"Well," Kel explained, "he's my nemesis, so I kind of assumed. I mean, I thought it was like a reciprocal—"

"Wait a second," Chester said, putting a hand in Kel's face. He pursed his lips. "Kipling is your nemesis?"

"Yeah."

"Not me?"

"Why would you be my nemesis?"

"Because you're my— Listen, this is getting confusing." Chester put both hands flat on the counter. He tried to get a grip on the situation. "I hate you," he said. "Don't touch my aunt."

"Chester, she's a grown—"

"Uhtutut," he said quickly, stopping Kel from saying another word. "Don't touch my aunt."

"But—"

"Uhpupup." He waved a finger in Kel's face. "Don't touch my aunt."

Kel shook his head and sighed exasperatedly.

"And," added Chester, "whatever we were before, we are now officially nemesisses."

"Nemeses," said Kel.

"I will hit you in the mouth right now, so help me!"

"I'm just—"

"I know what you were just." Chester shot him a warning look and left the Barnes & Noble with a purposeful stride. He went to go have a talk with his aunt.

Dove watched him, swinging his arms manfully as he swept past the HMV. She was standing in her signature pose, looking uncaring and cool, her knee twisted in awkwardly, her hand on her waist just as it curved out to her sensual hip. She wore trendy jeans, rolled up, and a long tight-fitting black shirt with a diaphanous pink scarf tied around her waist. Her body was well-proportioned and her clothes were always form-fitting, revealing as much as they covered, because Dove thought being modestly immodest was the sexiest paradox of all.

She was tall, but not as tall as January, and everyone thought her straight dark black hair was beautiful, but not as beautiful as Areola's curly coif, and people complimented her on her style, but not as often as they complimented Mya. Dove felt that she was in a constant competition over every aspect of her personality, and she kept coming in second place.

Mostly she hated Areola, who was sunny and sweet where Dove was dark and bitter, and was ostensibly Dove's best friend. Dove subscribed to the Machiavellian notion that you keep your friends close and your enemies closer. The day she had met Areola she knew they would be close.

It was when Dove was dating Puck, and Areola had just started working at VictorStyle, the salon in the mall owned by Victor, the flamboyantly depressed gay salon owner cliché, who named everything he owned after himself. His toy poodle, for example, was named

Victor Jr.

Areola had worked at VictorStyle for about a week and had only really met Polito out of all the employees of the mall. Polito was interested in Areola, but was nervous about dating someone. He hadn't dated anyone since his daughter had been born and his now ex-girlfriend Eden had decided to become a stripper.

Polito asked Puck if the four of them could go on a double date, just to ease the nervousness he felt. Puck agreed without consulting Dove first, which made her temper flare up like a rattlesnake on a dance floor.

"Like, why can't he just go out with her himself?" she asked, disgusted. "He's totally not even, like, a man anymore."

"I'm just trying to help out a friend of mine," Puck explained.

"You should have asked me if it was okay. Why do I want to go on a date with another couple? It's, like, totally lame."

"Maybe it'll be good for us," said Puck, who was already formulating his exit strategy. He had a fairly good idea of how and when he was going to dump Dove. He wanted to date Gina next.

"This isn't good for us. This is, like, a step backward for us. We've gotten to the point where we can totally just hang out by ourselves and be comfortable. God, you, like, don't understand anything."

"Well can you please do it, for me? I would really appreciate it, sweetie." Puck gave her his smile, the one that made babies gurgle.

"Oh, fine," she said, feeling charitable in her way, which meant knowing she would extract some unsavoury task from Puck in the near future.

When they arrived at the restaurant, which Dove insisted on choosing, she saw Areola for the first time. She was smiling brightly, she was so cute, she had reddish-gold curls of gorgeous hair, she wore a funky sleeveless top with a teardrop shape cut out to show her cleavage. She was amazing, she had a laugh that filled the room, and Dove smiled and decided to hate her forever.

That's when she started hanging out in VictorStyle and chatting and gossiping with Areola and using their computer that showed you how you would look with different hairstyles. Areola was happy to have a friend, especially one who knew so much about everyone. Dove kept her ear to the ground, and knew, for example, that Dusty had a crush on Gina almost before Dusty did.

When she heard, she had a powwow with Areola.

"Finally I can get that little bitch back," she said. She blamed Gina for Puck dumping her, and felt a need to prove that she was more desirable than Gina.

"How does that get Gina back? Dusty has a crush on her, she doesn't have a crush on him," Areola said.

Dove gave her a withering look. "When she finds out that I stole him from her, even though he had a crush on her, then she'll know that I am totally way hotter than she is. Duh."

"Oh," said Areola. She didn't really understand Dove's thought process, which centred on her insecurity over her large, hooked nose. Dove wore sexy, revealing, clinging clothes so that when people did a double-take at her she could believe it was because she looked amazing.

The most embarrassing was when she was making out with someone and her nose got in the way, smudging their glasses or bumping against their cheek or being prominently noticeable when she wished it would just disappear. She couldn't pass a mirror without looking to see if maybe, hopefully, a miracle had happened and her nose looked normal. She had visited many plastic surgeons, and the best price she could find for a rhinoplasty for her indelicate shnozz was over ten thousand dollars. There was no way she could afford a ten-thousand-dollar nose job. But ten times a day, or more, she would imagine that she had won the lottery and could fix all of her problems.

Until then, she wore a sexy, slinky, black sparkly dress to the employee Christmas party and watched as

Dusty took a glass of eggnog over to Gina and offered it to her. She imagined that their conversation was filled with double entendres and witty bon mots, and when Dusty went to the drink table for refills she struck her signature pose and whispered, "Dusty."

He turned and saw her and walked over, slightly confused.

"Did you call me?" he asked.

"I ordered something hot and spicy," she said, coyly.

"Um," he replied, completely unsure of himself in this erotic new territory. "Do you want some eggnog?"

"No," she said, "I want to talk to you."

"Oh," he said. "Really?"

"Yeah, we've never, like, really talked before."

"Well, uh, I always kind of thought you didn't want to talk to me."

"Dusty!" she said, feigning being hurt. "Why wouldn't I want to talk to you?"

"Well, I don't know..." Dusty was not the most voluble and eloquent at the best of times, and now words escaped him. He was looking slightly toward the floor and so all he could see were Dove's hands framing her hips and her long, smoothly muscled legs.

"Gina seemed to totally want to talk to you," she alluded.

"Um, well," he looked over at Gina, who was looking at the sprig of mistletoe in the middle of the ceiling and edging away from it. "Not really," he said.

"Well, then we can talk." She smiled. "I want you to tell me something about yourself. Something, like, no one else knows."

Dusty was at a loss. Anything he could think of that no one else knew about him was something that he didn't want anyone else to know. Nobody knew, for example, that he liked to look up Gina's phone number, spreading the thick phone book across his bedspread and just looking at her number for a long time. He did that sort of thing with every girl that he developed a crush on. Nothing overtly menacing – he was a wistful stalker. And Dove's sudden, jarring burst of attention was making him develop a swift attachment to her.

He found out about a five-part documentary on cosmetic surgery and taped the episode that dealt with nose jobs, intending to give it to her because he knew how she felt about her nose. He didn't understand it. He thought her nose was perfect. But he could never find the right time or the right words to say to give it to her, so he kept it in his backpack and every month or so he would watch it over again.

He also bought her a small charm bracelet and a couple of charms. Dove was interested in religious iconography without being involved in any organized service except for Christmas Mass with her family. Dusty bought three charms for the bracelet: an ankh, a cross, and a Star of David. And he kept it in his room, on a shelf next to his desk so that whenever he turned his head slightly to the left while he was at his computer, he could see it.

And when he managed to obtain Gina's coat from the Lost and Found, he felt guilty about wearing it. He felt that he wasn't being true to Dove. He explained this kind of thing to Rose, but she was not terribly sympathetic. After Puck had broken up with Rose he had begun dating Dove. Puck had planned on dating Ameesha, but she had started dating the drummer from Hanson, who had turned up at one of Peoria's weekend parties. Peoria, who herself had designs on Puck. For the employees of the mall, nothing occupied more time than untangling the past, present, and sometimes future relationships of the other employees.

Rose, who had a relatively fragile heart, could only forbear Dusty's talks about Dove for so long before she would say, "Enough!"

"Sorry, Rose," Dusty would mumble, glumly. He was glum most of the time, and had an arched neck from looking down at the tops of his shoes so much.

"Can we talk about something else?"

"I just can't stop thinking about her."

"And last year you couldn't stop thinking about Gina. And the year before that it was Piper. And so on and so on. We all get crushes, Dusty."

"Yeah, but mine are meaningful."

"Dusty," she said tenderly, and put a hand on his shoulder. "You've got a very strong heart, Dusty. You know? You're lucky, that you feel so much. Some people walk through life like zombies and don't care who they hurt and are so goddamned insensitive."

Dusty thought about it. "I don't feel lucky," he said. "It sucks being so...lonely and desperate all the time."

"I know," Rose said, and sighed from the bottom of her lungs, bringing up all the old stale air from way down there and trying to get rid of it.

"I just wish someone would like me, even once. I don't care if they're not pretty or not cool or whatever, it would just be nice to have someone want to be with me for a change."

Rose's heart went out to him. She knew exactly how he felt, but she also knew that it wasn't commiseration that he needed. At that moment Guy Tuffray breezed into the Grand & Toy and bee-lined for the counter, startling Dusty's reverie and making Rose jump into customer service mode.

"Do you have staples?" he asked, brusquely.

"Yes, indeed, Guy, aisle three just halfway down on the left," said Rose sweetly, giving a smile.

Tuffray did a double take. "What did you call me?" he asked. No one had called him by his first name before. And she had even pronounced it correctly.

"Guy..." she said hesitantly, but saying it the correct way made it look like she was smiling. A shy little smile, making her cheeks lift and her slight freckles redden just a little.

"Oh," he said. "Thanks."

He walked away, watching her for a moment. His left shoe wheezed every time he put his weight on it. It had been doing that since his conversation with the Texan, many moons ago. It had developed a small tear in the sole.

Dusty noticed none of the slight sparkle of sexual chemistry between the two, but realized that when

Rose had a customer he should shove off. He mumbled a goodbye and Rose gave him a supportive wave.

Tuffray watched her as he stood in the aisle in front of the staples, trying to make a show of not watching her. She noticed, and fixed the hair at the nape of her neck.

He found the staples and walked slowly back to the counter. He tossed them onto the counter, devil-may-care, but they hit the front of the counter and landed on the ground. The box sprang open, and staples spilled everywhere. Tuffray cursed and dropped to his knees, his face getting as red as his frivolous mustache. He tried to pick up the staples, but it was difficult to do with his thick clumsy fingers.

Rose came around the counter to help him, getting down on the floor with him and using her delicate fingernails to gather up the loose staples.

"Goddamn it," said Tuffray. "Sorry about that."

"No, no, no problem," said Rose. They were on their knees facing each other, peering intently at the ground.

"Christ, they're so small. Slippery little devils," said Tuffray.

"Yeah, but at least they're better than paperclips," Rose replied. "The little rows sometimes manage to stay intact. I dropped a thing of paperclips and I had to go get a magnet to pick them up."

"Aw, that sucks," said Tuffray, smiling with the camaraderie of the accident-prone. He looked up at her.

"It was all right, with the magnet," she said, looking up at him.

Their faces were only inches apart, their eyes locked. They wordlessly gazed at each other for a few moments, small piles of staples in their hands.

Tuffray broke the silence. "Can I just say? You look beautiful."

"Oh," said Rose, her delicate heart touched for the first time since Puck had dumped her. She knew she was rebounding, even after all this time, but she didn't care.

She dropped her staples and he dropped his and she flung her arms around his neck and they kissed each other passionately, on their knees on the floor. Rose didn't even mind his mustache pricking her upper lip.

They broke off, Rose was breathing hard, searching Tuffray's eyes. "That...magnet is in the back room," she said.

"Oh, yeah?"

"Can you...help me find it?" she asked.

They got up quickly and she took his hand and pulled him into the back room where she stopped and turned around, leaning back against stacked boxes of printer paper. She put her arms up around Tuffray's neck again as they embraced and kissed. Rose let her hand slide across his shoulder and grip the back of his arm as he put his hands behind her shoulder blades and pulled her in. He kissed down her body and she ran her fingers through his wiry, carrot-coloured hair. She pushed his head gently downward until he was on his knees.

She leaned even further back against the boxes, and spread her legs slightly. He undid her pants and pulled them down along with her panties, which were a lavender colour with a tiny bow on the front. She gripped both sides of his head and closed her eyes, gasping as he began kissing and licking.

After some minutes of his tender and insistent lapping and fingering she let go of his head with her hands and gripped it instead with her knees. She used one of her free hands to caress her breasts, her eyes closed, her mouth open as she gasped. Her other free hand slapped down on top of a box of printer paper like a referee counting a knockout.

"Yes, oh yes," she said each time she slapped the box of printer paper. Then she gripped it, and tried to dig her nails into the cardboard. She groaned deeply and Tuffray nearly passed out as her knees squeezed his head.

Afterward they came out of the back room, Rose slightly bedraggled, tucking her shirt back into her pants, Tuffray turning his head this way and that trying to fix the ache in his neck. Neither of them noticed the Sumerian watching them with his jaw clenched.

He had seen the whole thing, or at least, he had seen what happened in the store and had heard the muffled sounds of what had happened in the back room. Venomous bile filled his chest where his heart used to be.

Besides Ipswitch and Chester, Rose was the only person that the Sumerian felt remotely comfortable with, and would allow to talk to him. She would always sing-song a chipper hello in the morning when she would unlock the Grand & Toy, and a wistful goodbye at night as she wandered her tired way to the parking lot and her car with the crumpled driver's side door.

The driver's side was dented in the first day after Ipswitch had the parking lot repainted to prove a point, and make Tuffray's life that much worse. Rose's door was so buckled and twisted that she had to get in the passenger side and slide over. Fortunately it had bench seating – it was a Ford Galaxie.

But ever since Rose gave up her dreams in her second year of college, thanks to Puck and Kel Urquhart and an expired student card, and had started working full-time at the mall, the Sumerian had seen her almost every day and had fallen into a kind of hypnotic trance over her. It wasn't exactly love, but when the Sumerian saw her coming out of the back room in a state of post-coital disheveled satisfaction, his heart splintered, fractured, and fell apart inside him.

When Rose locked up and walked past the info booth, smiling wearily at the Sumerian and saying goodnight, he stared mutely at her the way he always did. But inside he was a churning morass of sadness, loss, anger, regret, and hurt. And after that, whenever Tuffray would find some tiny article of clothing or a ticket stub on the floor or a piece of lint, and he would rush to the Grand & Toy to put it in the Lost and Found, the Sumerian would shoot daggers of hatred at him from his eyes. Tuffray never seemed to notice, he would just breathlessly jog up to the counter holding his latest excuse to come to see Rose. She would take it, place it in the box behind the counter that marked the Lost and Found, and then take Tuffray into the back room.

After a few weeks of this, with Tuffray jogging to the Grand & Toy every couple of days, he stopped Rose shortly after she'd pulled him willingly into the back room again.

"Um, listen," he began tentatively. He didn't want to hurt a good thing, but he had noticed some inequities. "I wonder if maybe, um, I don't know. Do you think that you might, maybe, go down on me? After? Or before? Or something?"

Rose sighed heavily. She realized that she sort of had been taking advantage of the situation, but she was hoping that it could go on that way. She looked into Tuffray's pleading, insistent, watery blue eyes and said, "Oh, all right."

"Oh, thanks!" he said enthusiastically.

So he took the position, leaning back against the stacked boxes of printer paper, legs slightly spread, and watched her as she got down on her knees and undid his pants. They slid to the floor, pooled around his ankles, his belt clanking on the concrete. His legs were milky white, with thin little curlicues of reddish hair, and she decided to keep her eyes closed as she pulled his underwear down and took him into her mouth.

She'd been bobbing her head, working her hand, for about a minute when Dusty came into the backroom, saying "Hey, Rose, are you back— Holy sweet mother of god!"

Rose pulled her head back, looked over her shoulder at Dusty, who had a hand covering his mouth as he gaped in surprise at the pair. Tuffray tried to cover up his exposed genitals, but Rose still had her hand wrapped around him, holding him straight out, so he had to make do with putting a hand between Dusty's line of sight and his manhood.

"Dusty," said Rose, breathing a little hard. "Wait!"

But Dusty averted his eyes, held up a hand, and escaped at full speed. Rose made to get up, go after him, but Tuffray cleared his throat.

"Um," he said. "Can we just—" he began, nervously.

Rose turned to look up at him. "He saw us," she said.

"But, well, he can't un-see us, right? I mean..." he floundered for the words to convince her, because he was close to satisfaction. "If we, um, finish up, then, you know, you can talk to him after...? He probably wants to be alone right now, anyway. I think."

Rose sighed, letting her shoulders sag. "Fine, fine," she said. "Is it going to be much longer?"

"Oh, no," he said shaking his head vigorously.

She went back to giving him head.

The Sumerian saw Dusty leaving at a dead run, and his eyes narrowed, and he clenched his jaw, and a miniature explosion decimated the remains of his heart, and steam whistled out of his ears. His vision clouded for a moment, then cleared. He knew what he would have to do.

Chapter 13 - Polito & Modesta Mae

"That's Shorsky there, behind the cash register," said Chester.

"Which one?" Jasper asked. He had a small notebook in his hands, open, with a pen poised. So far he had taken no notes.

"The one with the big lump there, on her jaw," Chester pointed. He was showing Jasper around, having decided to allow Jasper to become his intern. "Now stop asking so many questions."

"Sorry."

"The key to being a good intern is watching," Chester said, pausing for emphasis, "and remembering." He tapped his temple. Jasper was nodding. "Write that down," Chester said, indicating the notebook. Jasper scribbled.

They were walking slowly through the aisles of the Mega-Mart and Chester was educating Jasper in equal parts on his personal philosophy and the employees of the mall. They passed Watson Huffernanny, pricing bottles of baby food.

"That's Watson Huffernanny," Chester said as they sidled past him. Watson lifted the pricing gun to his brow, gave a little salute.

"Huffernanny," Jasper echoed quietly.

"He's a good guy. I mean, he's all right. Actually, he's kind of a jerk."

"What? Why?"

Chester shook his head vigorously as he pushed ahead, walking faster. "No, no," he said, "this isn't a time for you to be asking questions. Remember the key to being a good intern is..."

"Watching and remembering," Jasper replied, reading it from his notes.

"Is it?" said Chester, mildly surprised. "Let me see that." He took the notes, flipped the page over and then back and saw that there was only one note. "Well, I'll be damned," he said. "That's a pretty good rule, I think."

They stopped in the toy section, Chester looking at all the board games, scanning the names carefully. Jasper stood behind him, arms folded over his notebook as he watched.

"Ah, here we go," said Chester finally. He pulled out a slightly battered box of the Game of Life. He set it on the ground and sat down cross-legged. "Have a seat," he said to Jasper.

"What's this?" asked Jasper.

"This is the Game of Life, a very fun board game that I like to while away the hours playing." He opened the box, began setting up the board, and explained the rules to Jasper. They'd been playing for fifteen minutes when Tuffray wandered by, did a double-take, and came back to stand with his hands on his hips over them. Jasper looked up at him, but Chester kept playing.

"What are you doing, Chester? This is not a Mega-Mart team activity," said Tuffray angrily.

"Jasper, this is Guy Tuffray. He's an idiot, but you don't have to write that down, it's self-evident."

Jasper nodded.

"Chester, I asked you a question. What are you doing?" Tuffray barked, trying to sound intimidating.

"Playing the Game of Life, Tuffray," Chester replied, unperturbed.

"I can see that," Tuffray blustered. "You have action items that require implementing. Why aren't you working?"

"I'll work when you inspire me to work," Chester said, flicking the spinner.

"How's about this to inspire you: you're fired!" yelled Tuffray.

"You can't fire me, Tuffray."

"Fine, then you're fired." Tuffray leveled a finger at Jasper, scowling.

"I...I work for the Shopper's Drug Mart," said Jasper, quailing slightly before Tuffray's wrath.

"He's my intern, Guy."

"Well, the two of you can't just sit in the middle of the aisle playing a board game! This is beyond insolent, even for you, Chester! I swear I will bring Ipswitch down here personally. Do you want that?"

Chester sighed. "Hey, I'm on the fast track to success here," he said, indicating the board. "Can you just—" He waved Tuffray away with his hand.

Tuffray, stymied, let out a frustrated growl and began muttering under his breath. He went to see Ipswitch, yet again, and again he was told to wait in the outer office by Ipswitch's sour-faced secretary, Consuela. This time he legitimately had to wait, because Ipswitch was having a meeting with Polito and Modesta Mae. He was telling them that they would be replacing their firearms with taser wands.

"With what?" Polito asked.

"Taser wands," Ipswitch repeated. "These little babies." He held up a short stick that had two small metal leads sticking out of the end and a rudimentary handle. He pressed a button and a short bolt of electric blue snapped between the two leads. "They are effective, and safe, and most of all, cheap. One of these babies can bring down a rampaging bull."

"That's great, just in case we have a stampede run through," said Polito. "No one respects a goddamn taser wand. How are we supposed to be taken seriously?"

"I have to agree with Polito," said Modesta Mae formally. "Our job and the security of this mall are based on respect. We don't got respect, then this mall don't got respect and everything goes right into the Almighty's rear end, pardon my French. It makes it very hard to do our job."

"What is all this negativity?" Ipswitch said. He tried to laugh lightheartedly but it came out like the sound of a cement mixer that has just eaten a shovel-load of hot gravel.

"You're taking away our primary tool of law enforcement," said Polito hotly. He was angry about two things: having his gun taken away and being pulled from the monitors for this ridiculous meeting when he was very close to being able to see into change room 17.

"Listen, numbskull, the primary tool of law enforcement is up here," he said, tapping the side of his pumpkin-sized skull.

"No," said Mo, "the primary tool of law enforcement is in here." She pointed to a spot just above her left breast.

"In your boob?" Polito whispered to her.

"In your heart, Polito, damn," Mo whispered back.

"Irregardless, the decision stands, so get used to it. You will be issued your taser wands by the end of the week. I will need you to hand over your firearms now, however."

"I've got half a mind to just right up and quit!" Polito said, standing up and unclipping his holster and gun from his belt and slamming them down on the desk.

"Polito," said Mo, putting a hand on his shoulder.

"Don't think I can't replace you like that," said Ipswitch, snapping his fingers. His eyes flashed as Polito's nostrils flared.

"Your daughter," said Mo quietly. Polito put his hands up, turned away, cursed roundly. Mo surrendered her gun and holster and took a long, disparaging look at the taser wand that Ipswitch still held.

"This is a mistake," said Mo squaring her shoulders. "I'm telling you that now so when the shit hits the fan you know exactly where the blame rests."

Ipswitch was unimpressed. "You can go," he said disdainfully. Polito wrenched the door open and hit the wall with the heel of his hand as he left. Mo slammed the door behind her. And then Ipswitch tortured Tuffray as long as he could.

Ipswitch's campaign of cost reduction made the mall almost impossible to work or shop in. He ran the air conditioner at the lowest possible setting during the summer, until everyone's uniforms clung to their skin like heated Saran Wrap. He ran the heater at the lowest possible setting in the winter until everyone had goosebumps and suffered a permanent loss of one degree of body heat from their core temperature. And, most infamously, he repainted the parking lot so that the parking slots were angled and slightly closer together, to increase the amount of available parking.

Part of the reason for the parking restructure was so Ipswitch could move Tuffray's official parking space out of the manager's section around behind the mall and put it at the furthest corner from the mall entrance. Tuffray, of course, had no idea why this had happened.

"There was no room in the manager's section, Tuffray, now suck it up like a man," Ipswitch barked at him when he asked.

"But sir, there are several vacant spots—"

"Those are not vacant, they are being held for future residents. Understand? Now stand there and think about how your negative attitude is affecting this entire company," Ipswitch said, fists on his desk, leaning across and glaring hard into Tuffray's puffy face.

Tuffray's bladder shivered, and the muscles in the lower part of his abdomen started going into spasms. Despite his every effort to maintain control he could feel that he was on the edge of explosion. With a high-pitched little yelp he turned and ran from the office, heading for the bathroom.

Ipswitch chuckled. He had proved a point, but his decision to repaint the parking lot was disastrous. All it really did was make the parking lot into a constellation of surefire accident hotspots, and it became something of a miracle to escape the parking lot without a ding, dent, scrape, scratch, or gouge on your vehicle. The paramedics at the nearby hospital learned to swing past every fifteen minutes or so in case any pedestrians found themselves staring down the business end of a bumper. Fender benders were so common in the labyrinthine confines of the angled parking that people started parking on the street outside the mall parking lot. The spots were so close together that even when you were directly in the middle of your spot, and the two cars on either side were directly in the middle of their spot, you could barely squeeze out of your door without tapping the side panel of the car next to you. And the sightlines were horrendous.

Rose had backed out of a space right next to a corner space and was rammed directly in the driver's side by a minivan trying to turn the corner. She got jounced around the inside of her car and suffered a sprained wrist, bruising all up and down her left side, and a minor concussion. Dusty had taken her to the emergency room in her car, which was still drivable, albeit difficult to get in and out of.

Whenever Ipswitch heard of yet another accident in the parking lot he would say, "Bah, they oughta watch where they're going." He had no patience for the problems of others. Even when Modesta Mae almost got into an accident – she nearly hit a young child running in between the cars – Ipswitch had no remorse or condolences or apologies to make. And Modesta Mae gritted her teeth because she was the most conscientious driver in the mall, and had never been involved in any kind of traffic accident. She drove meticulously, often infuriating her son and two daughters, who would say, "Drive faster, mom!"

It was almost a miracle that Ipswitch himself didn't get into any accidents, considering how accident-prone he was. The day before the staff Christmas party he and Polito and another security guard named Desmondo Pontchartrain were moving supplies up to the meeting room where the party would be held. They were using the security doors to shuttle between the van, loaded with the same decorations as last year, and the meeting room.

Desmondo gathered a giant Gordian knot of Christmas lights that would undoubtedly take a legion of maze designers to untangle and hurried back to the security door before it closed. Ipswitch was supervising and thought that Desmondo could carry more than just one giant strand of lights, so he strode briskly after him. Desmondo didn't notice Ipswitch behind him and reached back to pull the security door closed as he walked into the corridor.

"Wait!" Ipswitch barked. But Desmondo didn't hear him. Ipswitch put his hand into the tiny gap that was left, intending to fling the door wide open and sear Desmondo with a scathing indictment of his ability to transport Christmas decorations. But Desmondo was leaning forward, hand on the door handle, pulling the door closed. Ipswitch's finger was in the way, and his index knuckle made a sound like a cockroach being crushed. Ipswitch bellowed so loud that it felt like the building shook. A car alarm went off.

Desmondo opened the door with his foot and looked around, puzzled, the string of Christmas lights still in his lanky hands. Ipswitch went down on his knees in the parking lot, clutching his wrist because he dare not touch his finger, which was throbbing and already turning a mutant purple.

"What happened?" Desmondo asked. Polito was just coming up behind him, back from a trip to the meeting room. He had no idea what was going on.

"You filthy sonnuvabitch! My finger, oh god I think it's broken!" Ipswitch's face turned colour from a rampaging, angry, burning red to a nauseous pale, pasty green.

"Oh my god, are you all right?"

Ipswitch let loose a furious yell of indignation. "Of course I'm not all right!" he yelled. He pointed at Desmondo with his good index finger and said, "You're fired!"

"Hey, Ipswitch, it was an accident," said Polito, coming forward and trying to calm the wounded man.

Ipswitch levelled his one good pointing finger at Polito. "And you: you're suspended, one week, no pay," he added indignantly.

"What the fuck..?" said Polito.

"I'm fired?" said Desmondo.

"Ah, goddamn it!" Ipswitch sucked in a breath as he tried to flex his finger. Bright throbbing pain replaced all the other feelings he had in his hand. He threw up onto Desmondo's shoe. His face was pale, and cold sweat trickled down his back.

"Which one of you idiots is gonna take me to the ER?" he asked in a whisper that was frightening for its lack of vitality. Polito ended up taking him. Desmondo cleared his belongings out of his locker in the back room and left the mall, despondently hanging his head. He'd thought that he was finally good at something.

Ipswitch received prompt service at the emergency room because they all knew him quite well there. They set his finger with clinical detachment while he spewed a roll call of expletives, and asked Polito quiet questions, and nodded and smiled at him gently. The hospital staff were always curious to know about the person that brought Ipswitch to the emergency room because it was a different person every time.

When Ipswitch had to come in to get his neck brace, it was Candida who brought him in. The staff at the hospital had stopped asking her polite questions almost as soon as she had arrived, with Ipswitch barely cogent and nearly unable to stand on his feet.

"What is this? Why are you asking these questions?" she spat in her slight east European accent. "This man is hurt, you stupid cow! You with your questions. You must fix this man."

The nurse had tried to calm her down by putting a

hand on her shoulder and leading her to a seat while they took Ipswitch in to be x-rayed. Candida would have none of it, threw the nurse's hand off with a sharp shrug of her shoulder, and paced back and forth nervously. Three times she tried to smoke a cigarette and had to be scolded each time.

"Why is this? This country, where you cannot even smoke in a hospital."

Ipswitch had visited Candida's Fashions ostensibly to gossip about the problems the Bulk Barn was having with raccoons. In reality he was trying to flirt with Candida, who had a trim and hard figure, bright brassy blond hair, and a scathing candidness to which Ipswitch was drawn. It was another part of his campaign to exact revenge on his wife's imagined affair with Guy Tuffray. They stood among the piles of turtlenecks and bouclé cardigans and the racks of well-pressed button-up blouses in bold colours, talking like giddy teenagers. Candida had her arms wrapped around her and was turning her torso and swaying back and forth at the same time. She had a powerful internal battery that gave her excess energy she had to frisson off in frivolous movement. Ipswitch folded one arm across his body and rested the elbow of his other arm on it so he could stroke the chin of his massive head and look down at Candida and smile and wink with his deep-set green eyes.

January was behind the cashier's counter, watching with a kind of morbid disgust.

Ipswitch, perspiring gently, said, "It's pretty warm in here, isn't it?"

"Maybe only for you because you are so hot on the inside," Candida said, cocking her eyebrow seductively.

Ipswitch chuckled in his deep bass roll. "Maybe it feels hot because I'm standing next to you," he said. January, mercifully, could only hear a bit of what was being said, but she rolled her eyes when she heard Ipswitch's lame come-on.

Candida laughed, though, and her laughter was like a breaking plate – a sharp smash of mirth followed by a few tiny chuckles as the pieces skittered across the floor.

"Seriously, though," said Ipswitch, pulling on his collar. "It is warm in here." He was beginning to suffer from the localized atmosphere of Candida's, which was humid, oppressive, stifling, and perfumed to the point of near-strangulation.

Candida was used to it. "Oh, don't you be such a big baby," she said, swatting him playfully on the arm.

"You're having quite the effect on me, Candida," he said, trying to be boyish, smiling. "I feel like I...can't really...breathe." He coughed. He felt light-headed. Darkness rolled over the top of his head, drifted down into his eyes, then lifted again as he swayed.

"What is wrong? You are drunk?" said Candida, putting her hands on her sharp hips.

Ipswitch swayed like a tree being axed and his eyes fluttered. He drifted sideways in slow motion, his feet staying still, and crashed into a rack of blouses, hitting his neck on the steel bar. The rack of blouses pushed him sideways and he smashed the back of his head on the edge of a bin of fuzzy sweaters and twisted and landed cheek-first on the tile floor. Candida made a strange yipping noise and put her hand to her mouth.

"January, call the 911!" she yelled. She knelt over Ipswitch, lightly slapping his face, saying, "Wake up, now you wake up now."

The paramedics had arrived forthwith – they hadn't been far away thanks to the parking lot's reputation – and Jasper watched them put Ipswitch on a stretcher and wheel him out with Candida traipsing along in their wake on her absurdly high heels yelling at them to be careful with Ipswitch. It was only after a battery of tests at the hospital that they found out Ipswitch had suffered a mild stroke.

January watched them leave and then twisted her hair around her finger and went back to the counter and leaned on it, bored.

Jasper stopped a young boy that was passing by, on his way to the arcade.

"Hey, kid," he said. "Can you do me a favour? Can you go to the Mega-Mart and tell the cashier there to page Dr. Pendleton?"

"What's in it for me?" said the boy warily.

"She'll give you whatever candy bar you want, okay?"

"And what else?"

"What do you mean what else? You get a candy bar. That's it. You're not delivering a priceless artifact to the British Museum, kid."

"Eh, not interested," said the youth, dismissing Jasper with a wave of his hand.

"Hey, wait," said Jasper desperately. "Okay, what do you want?"

The kid swivelled around and said, "Quarters," and his eyes lit up.

"Okay, fine, she'll give you a dollar's worth of quarters, okay?"

"I want two."

"Two? You little—" Jasper shook his head, stymied. "Jesus, you kids." He quickly wrote a note and gave it to the boy, and said, "Who are you going to get her to page?"

"Dr. Pendleton. I'm not a moron, thanks."

Jasper straightened up as the kid walked away shaking his head. Jasper blew a lock of hair out of his face and shrugged. He felt sure he hadn't been that insolent when he was that age. In fact, the only time that he didn't honour someone's friendly request was the day he said his goodbye to Chester.

Polito heard the page for Dr. Pendleton and paused the camera aimed at change room 17. He turned around in his chair to lightly hit Chester's knee with the back of his hand. Chester came slowly out of his slumber.

"Hm? What?" he asked.

"They just paged Dr. Pendleton," said Polito.

"Oh, so what," said Chester, frowning sleepily and shifting into a more comfortable position to resume his nap.

"Listen, you can't just keep avoiding it, you've got to talk to her. You've got to tell her how you feel."

"What do you know?"

"I've got an ex-girlfriend who is now a stripper, Chester. Learn from my mistakes, okay?"

Chester opened one eye.

"Get it off your chest, man. You've got to. Christ, you're back here all the time and it's getting sad, man," Polito stared him in the eye. "You're taking it out on yourself, doing god knows what kind of damage to your liver, you look like hell, and I don't know if you've been showering or not, but it smells like not. And," he added, "she's probably got things she needs to get off her chest, too. So do it. Go talk to her. Don't even do it for yourself, do it for me. I'm sick and tired of you."

For a moment Chester didn't move.

"Don't make me use my taser wand," Polito said with a smirk.

Chester made vague annoyed grumbling sounds, but he got to his feet and opened the door to the back room to leave. He turned around and looked, bleary-eyed, at Polito. "Thanks," he said.

"No problem," said Polito, spinning back around and hitting play on the monitor showing change room 17.

Chester strode, half scared and half angry, to Candida's Fashion and saw January behind the counter by herself. She was staring off into space, so she was startled when he came up to her and said, "We should talk."

"About what?" she said defensively, straightening up, folding her arms.

When the door to January's house opened and Chester saw the Texan, back-lit by the hall light, his jaw had dropped. The Texan, too, had the welcoming smile wiped right off his face.

"This better be a joke," he said. Chester gulped.

January came bouncing to the door, excited and

nervous out of her mind for what she saw as her first real date, and immediately sensed the electric tension between Chester and her father. "Daddy?" she said. "Chester?"

Her father turned to her. "Is this the boy who's taking you out tonight?"

"Yes, dad, this is Chester."

The Texan shook his head, hands gripping his hips, and said, "No. No way, no how. No daughter of mine is going to go out with this lazy, slack-about goof-off."

"Dad!" said January, upset, her eyes already brimming with tears that threatened her immaculate and understated make-up. She hadn't foreseen this possibility, and she immediately felt betrayed by her father. He had never been particularly over-protective, that had been her mother's chosen position, and even now her mother had mellowed significantly in the face of her daughter's somewhat desperate social situation.

"No, no, don't dad me," he said, pointing firmly at his daughter. "Every time I come to pick you up I go through the Mega-Mart there, and I see this boy," here he tossed a thumb over his shoulder to indicate Chester, "playing board games in the middle of the aisle or asleep in a chair in the furniture department. He's got no respect for his job, and no respect for himself, and I'll be damned if I'm going to allow him to date my daughter, whom I'm sure he has no respect for either!"

"But that's not fair!" said January, stamping her foot. Her relationship with her father had not changed much since she was four – a fact she now found infuriating rather than endearing. "We agreed to go on a date tonight and I'm a grown woman, I can make my own decisions."

"You are not a grown woman, I don't care how old you are. Grown women do not live with their parents, January. And while you live under my—"

"...roof you'll live by my rules. I've heard that before, oh my god, I'm so sick and tired of it!"

"Don't you start disrespecting your father, young

lady!" roared the Texan.

Chester cleared his throat. "Excuse me," he said.

They both turned to him and, if nothing else, Chester felt vindicated in turning their anger away from each other, even if it was now directed at him.

"I just, uh, wanted to say...to January." Chester swallowed. He was having a hard time thinking of what to say with the intense scrutiny of her father beating at him like a steel bat. "Um, that you look really lovely, this evening," he finished.

She gave him a reassuring smile, and said, "Thank you, Chester."

The tension somewhat mollified for the time being, the Texan sighed through his nose like he was making a tough decision. He looked at his daughter, who was wishing with all her heart that she could spend a night out with someone and not have to sit up in her room just to escape the pitying looks of her parents. The Texan, after such a long time of hoping that his daughter would make some friends and get out of the house more often, was now confronted with the irony of wanting her to stay home in order to avoid the certain erosion of her character that Chester would cause.

Eventually he said, "Well, you've made a commitment. And your mother and I always raised you to be—to live up to your responsibilities." He sighed, rubbing the back of his neck as he looked at Chester. "So I guess that – this one time – you can go out together. But I'm afraid that is the end of it as far as I'm concerned. And if I see you anywhere near my daughter after tonight," he said, turning to level the full force of his menace at Chester, "I will end your life in the most painful and humiliating way you can imagine."

Chester paled slightly, but clenched his jaw and stood as firm as he could. "I understand, sir," he said, partially adopting the Texan's menacing quiet manner of speech, "but I respect your daughter's wishes above your own."

January, sensing danger, pre-empted any further exchange by jumping down from the door onto the porch and pushing Chester with her hand as she swung her purse over her shoulder. Chester turned and they left, January tripping lightly down the stairs of the porch and calling out, "Thank you, daddy!" She waved over her shoulder as he stood in the doorway for a moment before pushing it closed with a quiet click.

"Oh, god, I'm sorry about that," said January. She wondered if Chester would want to call everything off, so she tried to distract him. "Where did you park?" she asked.

"Um," Chester looked sheepish. He winced. "I don't have a car," he said, wondering if January would want to call everything off

"Oh, okay, don't worry, I've got the keys to my parents' car." She whisked them out of her purse and jingled them, smiling. She crossed to the garage and pressed a button by the door. In Chester's experience the garage door opener was always the most spastic machine in any household, prone to fits and starts. Garage doors tended to open groaning and jerking like a geriatric getting out of a recliner. January's garage door might as well have been over the entrance to the Batcave, it opened so smoothly and cleanly. January pressed the button that made the car chirp, and unlocked the doors. And Chester got to sit in the dark green Volkswagen he had seen the Texan get into and out of in the parking lot of the Mega-Mart.

"Will they be mad you took the car?" asked Chester.

"Oh, god, I think they're just glad to finally have me out of the house," January laughed. Then she froze as she pushed her seatbelt buckle in and it clicked.

"Are you home a lot?"

"Oh," she said, feeling her cheeks redden and glad for the darkness of the car. "No, it's just I was home a lot this week, but normally, you know, I'm out all the time, so...you know." She started the car, backed it out quickly, switched gears, and jammed the gas pedal to the floor, accelerating away from her all-too-familiar home.

"Yeah, I guess you probably have something happening pretty much every night, hey?" said Chester. He watched her drive, resting an arm on the windowsill and steepling a finger against his temple. She drove with furtive glances at her mirrors, like she was afraid she was being followed. She chewed her lip slightly and kept her hands firmly at 2 and 10. Finally she noticed Chester watching her and glanced at him out of the corner of her eye and smiled.

"What?" she said.

"Huh?"

"What are you looking at?"

"Oh, I'm just—" Chester looked around, searching for an excuse, "I was just, uh. Well, just looking at you, actually."

She smiled. "I know," she said. "Look at my legs, I have really good calf muscles. Look." She leaned over and watched herself flex her calf muscles. Chester watched with a sort of detachment. It was like he was only partly there, like she was almost talking to herself.

"They're...nice," he said. "Very nice."

"Yeah, guys tell me they like my legs all the time."

Chester smiled sadly, "Yeah, I guess you're pretty popular."

"Oh, yeah. Of course," said January. For some reason there was a tear forming in her left eye. She could feel the water brimming against the edge of her eyelashes. There was a blurry smear in her vision.

"So what do you say to them?"

"Hm?" She forced herself to take long deep breaths, which seemed to help her body absorb the tear without shedding it.

"What do you say to those guys, who say they like your legs?"

"Oh, nothing," she said breezily and laughed lightly to show that it just amused her. She tucked her long silky brown hair behind her ear. "So do you have a girlfriend?"

Chapter 14 - Watson Huffernanny

“I heard you went on a date with Gina,” January continued. “Are you two...?”

“Listen, that date with Gina. I don’t know exactly what she told you about that but I – honestly – I don’t know what happened. One second everything was fine and then I said something about you and she just flipped out.”

“You...what? You told her you had asked me out?”

“No, I was, like, asking her advice. I said something like oh, is this how I should ask January out? Or something.”

“Why would you ask her?”

Chester looked at January, looked at the road through the windshield, looked back at January, opened his mouth, closed his mouth. “I’m confused,” he said. “Did Gina tell you anything about our date?”

“Our date? This date?”

“No, my and Gina’s date.”

“Oh, no, I mean you said something when you...when you asked me out, and so I went and asked Dove about it. She told me that Easter told her that you guys went on a date, so, that's how I heard about it.”

“Why didn’t Gina tell you? Are you guys having a fight?”

“I don’t...” said January, not sure how to answer that question. “I don’t even really know Gina that well.”

"What? She told me, I mean, she told Jasper that if I wanted to ask you out I had to...to ask her out."

January scoffed. "That doesn't make any sense, why would you do that?"

"She said it was, like, your screening process. Because you get asked out a lot and—"

"What? She said that?"

"Yeah."

"My screening process?"

"Yeah," Chester said, nodding his head.

"I don't have a screening process," said January, frowning.

Chester was trying to connect the dots, moving his hands in the air like he was working at joining tenuous strings together. "Then why would she say that?" He was mystified.

"Well," January began slowly, "I think she wanted you to ask her out."

"What? No." Chester made a kind of a sour face as he shook his head. "That's impossible."

"Why is that impossible?"

"Why would she do that? I don't understand."

January smiled at him, poked him in the side, and said, "Because she likes you."

"Gina? She doesn't like people," Chester replied. Then he realized what he'd just said and laughed at himself. "I mean, she doesn't like me. Not like that."

"Well, then why did she trick you into asking her out?"

Chester thought about it. "It seems really weird, doesn't it? Why didn't she just ask me out herself?"

"I don't know," said January, shrugging, "I can understand why she might do it. It takes the pressure off. Especially if you have a crush on someone."

January knew about the pressure of a crush because for a short while she had had a crush on Jasper. She saw him sometimes, across from Candida's in the Shopper's Drug Mart, making notes studiously in a ringed notebook. She had wanted to ask him what he was writing that was so important, and she thought it was cute the way he stuck his tongue out a little when he was trying to write quickly. She could never find the courage, though, to just walk right up to him and ask. He might have said anything, and she imagined some terrible things that he could have said. For no reason at all she thought everyone knew deep down that she was terribly lonely and sad. In reality no one knew, because they were all too worried that everyone else knew, deep down, exactly what their darkest secret was.

That was how Watson Huffernanny felt, and it was exacerbated by Easter's candid and unrepentant nature. When Tuffray, at the morning staff meeting before the worst day of Watson's life, asked her a question and she responded with, "I'm going to be helping Watson," he had to bite his tongue to stop himself from shushing her. Did she want the whole world to know?

Shushing wouldn't have worked anyway. Every time he shushed her she would stick out her tongue at him and blow a raspberry and make it even more obvious that they were stealing into the change rooms and having sex at every possible opportunity. She was sixteen, he was twenty-one. There was not much of a gap in maturity, but there was certainly a gap in the legality of their union. And even though the sex was dynamite, he couldn't stop feeling guilty about that.

Easter seemed to take it in stride, partially because she couldn't care less for the rules of society, and partially because she felt that she was in love with the tall, stick-limbed, and hyperactively cynical Watson. What had, for her, started as a kind of experiment in seduction had evolved into an experiment in pleasure, and was now an experiment in the depth of tender feelings, as well. Watson knew none of this, but then Watson wasn't too bright, and Easter had the IQ of a genius.

Watson's worst day ever started with the morning staff meeting, which set a bitter tone to the day. Easter walked beside him as he left to re-organize the linens aisle, her short frame bouncing along as she hurried to keep up with his lanky stride.

"That's not symbiosis," said Easter as they pushed through the swinging door and onto the main floor of the Mega-Mart.

Watson put a finger to his lips, cocked a warning eyebrow, which he was especially good at, and said, "Shh."

Easter stuck out her tongue at him and blew a raspberry. Watson always thought that her face looked adorable when she stuck her tongue out at him. She squinched up her eyes and tilted her head way over to one side. It always made him chuckle. But he was still, at the core, a solitary individual. A loner.

So he said, "Listen, you can't help me today."

"Why not?" asked Easter.

Watson saw her, in a way, as a puppy that had attached itself to him and wanted to go wherever he went. According to Watson there was a time to be together and a time to be separate, for the purposes of individual growth. The time to be together was any time that there was physical intimacy being explored. The time to be separate was any other time. He was not up for late-night bonding sessions, walking the desolate streets of the downtown area where the wind was always blowing some kind of garbage around. Watson was a pragmatist, and the long philosophical discussions – which were more lectures by Easter than discussions, truth be told – were best left for people who cared to discuss the nature of reality and thought and abstract truth and a fair way for humans to live on the planet. Watson had weed to purchase, and roll, and smoke, and complex role-playing video games to master, and his mother's cooking to avoid. He had parties in abandoned train yards to occupy his time. He had the Internet, and its glowing bastion of humour-related websites, file-sharing websites, and instant punditry websites. There he could troll anonymously, without having to defend his ideas the way he did with

Easter.

Easter, on the other hand, thought that the de facto standard was for partners to spend time together. After all, each had strengths and weaknesses, and it made a natural kind of sense that two unique individuals should balance each other out to create a sort of super-normal pair. There is yin in the yang, and yang in the yin, she thought. She sometimes thought it during sex, and would silently snicker to herself. But because of Watson's outlook it was generally up to Easter to foster and maintain the pair-bond they had established, as well as fill the air with intelligent rhetoric. The only time she felt no need to say a word was directly after sex with Watson, but that was partly because after sex with Watson he often leapt into an angst-riddled speech about something or other, pacing around, his eyebrows leaping and cavorting like dolphins in the sea of his forehead.

She loved that part about him – when he was ranting about the socio-economic effects of not increasing minimum wage once in eight years, or about video game developers who created new worlds for their RPGs when there were already abundantly rich RPG worlds that could be mined, or about the loss of coherent character development in Spielberg movies. When he was passionate, animated, and seemed to be taking charge and taking responsibility. Sex made him a new man, it seemed.

She had, in fact, tried several measures of positive reinforcement when he leapt into one of his tirades. First she tried giving him oral sex right when he was becoming most fervent, but that just seemed to really throw him for a loop. He found it hard to handle two sets of passions blooming in his body at one time. Then she tried exhorting him to action with impassioned zeal of her own, but that also confused him. He did not understand collusion as well as he understood confrontation. And so finally she became devil's advocate, which seemed to really incense him and sometimes even provoke forward action from him.

He had actually written a letter to a senator about minimum wage. And it was a well-written and thoughtful missive. It was a shame that the senator he had sent it to replied with a form letter about economic issues, but still, Watson had been goaded to action. There was hope.

So when Watson said things like, "Listen, you can't help me today," Easter would demand reasons. Unfortunately Watson could always play the jailbait card, leaving Easter to storm off, angry at her inability to refute that argument. Unfortunately, on this particular day she did not want to give up so easily, and kept pursuing it until they had a muted shouting match in the linens aisle.

"Listen, I do enjoy hanging out with you," Watson said through gritted teeth, "I just don't understand why it has to be right now, when our every movement is being captured on closed-circuit camera!" He pointed to the ceiling, dotted periodically with black domes under which Polito's cameras buzzed, whirred, and collected evidence.

"Oh come on, Polito is the only one who sees those monitors," Easter whispered hoarsely.

"Still, still," said Watson, emphasizing his point by driving a finger into the palm of his hand, "you're not the one who would get tossed in the hoosegow for cavorting with a minor!" Watson's eyebrows climbed over each other at the end of his emphatic whisper.

"Do you think I'm not risking anything for this relationship?" Easter demanded.

"Oh, oh yeah, I forgot. Your precious reputation," said Watson, making quotations in the air.

Easter slapped him. It was a touchy subject with her. Most of the girls her age were making the culturally appropriate choice to experiment with sex with boys their own age. The fact that she had decided to approach an older man, albeit an inexperienced and downright mean one sometimes, had labelled her a slut. Things might have been different if Watson Huffernanny was cool. Perhaps she would have been called a slut out of jealousy. Still, the situation galled her, and made her lose her poise.

Watson's face turned a bright pink where her hand had slapped him. He looked down on her from his exaggerated height, but she didn't back down at all.

"Get away from me," he whispered darkly.

She spun on her heel and walked away, still angry at Watson.

Halfway into the afternoon she came back to the linens aisle to find Watson surrounded by different piles of assorted linens. Tuffray had just come by to see how he was progressing and told him that he was doing everything all wrong and he would have to start again from scratch, but still managed to provide no direction at all. And so Watson was still at a loss as to what to do with queen-sized fitted separates versus shammies and dust covers, not to mention dining accessories and the tyranny of thread counts.

"What do you want?" Watson asked huffily as she approached him silently. She simply grabbed his hand and pulled him back to the change rooms, where they secreted themselves in their favourite change room and proceeded to disrobe each other with lightning speed. Their hands were fumbling over each other's bodies, touching, rubbing, exciting tingles along nerve endings.

At one point, impassioned, Easter pushed Watson away in order to pounce on him. Watson, unfortunately, still had his pants down around his ankles and so he fell backwards in slow motion. His back hit the mirror and he began sliding down the smooth surface. He reached up to grab the top lip of the mirror – a move that normally would have saved him – but he missed it because someone had recently moved the mirror up six inches. His hands scrabbled at something, anything to find purchase. He found nothing and half-turned as he slid and mashed his face off the small bench in the corner of the change room. His tooth snapped and he felt his mouth fill with blood as he yelped. The tooth clattered on the floor.

"My tooth!" he said.

Easter found the bloody, small, white chunk of tooth and they hurried to the back staff room to find a glass and some milk to transport the tooth to Dr. Pointree. They burst into the staff room and were getting the glass and milk when Polito came in, his face flushed with embarrassment.

When he saw the two, he immediately stammered, “I—I didn’t see nothing!”

They both knew immediately what it was he had not seen.

Easter, caught in the middle of pouring the milk over the tooth, looked from Watson to Polito and back. “You won’t say anything, will you, Polito?” she entreated.

Polito shook his head. “You guys,” he said, shaking his head. “You know Tuffray sometimes reviews the tapes.” His words hung in the air.

“You won’ leh him, will you?” Watson asked, trying not to move his aching jaw too much.

“There’s not much I can do,” said Polito. “I mean, chances are he won’t see it, but he might and then you two are pretty screwed.”

Easter put the milk away. She took Watson by the arm and said, “Can you erase it? Or lose it, or something?”

Polito shook his head. “No, then it’s obvious, if Tuffray watches the tapes, that I tampered with them. That’s way worse.”

“What about taping over it?” she asked. “You find a spot where there’s no one in the frame and then start taping and just let it tape right over.”

Polito thought about it. Watson’s head was throbbing, he moaned slightly as he put a careful hand to his jaw. Easter patted his arm comfortingly, looking at him, brow furrowed in concern.

“Oh, baby, I’m sorry,” she said.

“What happened to him?” asked Polito.

“Didn’t you see us...?” said Easter

Watson closed his eyes as he cradled his aching jaw.

“I saw the first bit but then I turned away. I was...

kinda shocked. How old are you?"

Easter pulled Watson forward until she could pluck at Polito's lapel. "Please, Polito, we need your help." She gave him her best puppy-dog eyes, but Polito had a 4-year old daughter and had built up something of an immunity. "If we get caught," she added hesitantly, looking to Watson for support, "we won't just be fired. We're kind of, it's kind of—"

"She's sissteen," said Watson, looking pale. His jaw was already starting to swell.

Polito gave Easter an appraising look, and thought about his own daughter, and hoped that she wouldn't ever find herself in any situation that was remotely similar to this one. "I'll see what I can do," he said eventually, "but I'm not going to put my job on the line. I've got a daughter to think about." He looked pointedly at Easter, who normally would have given a severe tongue-lashing to anyone who questioned her personal choices, but held herself in check for Watson's sake.

Instead she said, "Thank you," and kissed her fingertips and pressed them to Polito's cheek. Then she turned to Watson and whispered, "C'mon let's go, sweetie."

Polito watched them shuffle out the door, Watson moving tenderly as Easter pulled him along and carried the glass of bloody milk with the tooth clinking around in the bottom. He pursed his lips and couldn't wait to be finished work so he could go home and spend time with Samaria.

Watson sat down in Dr. Pointree's office as Easter went to the front desk. The waiting room was disconcertingly quiet, with a few young children desultorily playing with blocks or reading books or pushing trains around half-heartedly. Their mothers or fathers sat reading magazines. No one seemed all too overjoyed to be visiting the dentist, including the receptionist, a heavyset young woman with short blond hair that she had styled so it flipped out at the sides, making her look a bit like a blond version of Jane

Jetson.

"What do you want?" she asked.

"My friend over there just hit his jaw and lost his tooth," Easter explained. "I've got it here in this milk." She held up the glass, with the reddish swirls of blood drifting lazily through the milk. The receptionist made a face.

"You'll have to wait," she said.

"But this is an emergency!"

"Yes, and this is a waiting room," the receptionist snapped.

"Can you at least tell Dr. Pointree that there's an emergency in here?"

"I could," said the receptionist, "but I won't."

"What is your problem?" said Easter, raising her voice. "This man over here just lost a tooth, all right? He fell and banged his jaw and his tooth popped out. Okay? That requires serious attention, and I mean right now. And if you don't go tell Dr. Pointree that we are here and we need help, then I'm going to do everything in my power to make sure that this dentist office gets shut down and she loses her licence and never touches a fucking tooth again! Now get off your ass, please!"

The receptionist narrowed her eyes and gave Easter the most smouldering look an overweight, high-and-mighty, but essentially powerless peon could give. Then she stood up and went to get Dr. Pointree.

Easter went to sit next to Watson and comfort him, but as soon as she sat down Dr. Pointree came hurriedly out of the back and said, "What happened? Come with me, quickly, quickly."

Watson and Easter followed her as she whipped down the hallway, her coat flowing out like a superhero's cape, past rooms both lavish and sterile, always with the great chair in the middle surrounded by lights and instruments. They looked like extremely well-appointed torture chambers. Finally Dr. Pointree whisked them into a room and told Watson to lie down on the chair as she set out instruments and readied herself. A dental hygienist slipped into the room and began setting out gauze and needles and equipment.

Finally Dr. Pointree whirled on Watson, with Easter by his side holding his hand. She gave them an extremely serious and mesmerizing look, her doe-like brown eyes, which were almost hypnotically large, seemed to make time stand still.

The hygienist took the glass of milk from Easter's numb fingers and set it aside.

"So," said Dr. Pointree. There was a significant pause. "Do you know Chester?"

"Um, yeah," said Easter, confused.

"Are you friends with him?"

Easter looked at Watson. "Not really, no."

"Yes or no!" yelled Dr. Pointree.

"No, I guess," said Easter, taken aback. She was beginning to wonder if maybe Dr. Pointree hadn't snapped.

"Good then," she said, and smiled. When she smiled the features of her face seemed to arrange themselves in subtly beautiful and warm ways. "Now let's fix that tooth."

Not twenty feet down the hallway, Gina was on the tail end of a good flossing. Debbie, a young and pleasantly puritanical dental hygienist, was smiling down at her, and rubbing her gums with the thin mint-flavoured string. All Gina could taste was the latex of the gloves Debbie was wearing.

"There," said Debbie, taking her hands out of Gina's mouth and unwinding the floss, "all done."

Gina ran her tongue over her teeth. After the bit of a fiasco with Chester she had been more self-conscious than at any other time in her life. She wondered if she was pretty, if she would ever find happiness, if she should just stay inside for the rest of her days. She questioned her ability to inspire love in others. But she didn't seclude herself, she kept coming to work, and began hanging out with Kipling more and more often.

He was willing to listen to her talk about all her worries and concerns, and would walk around the mall with her before her shift or afterward. She would come by the Amphibian Emporium and begin talking to him about nothing and he would say, “Do you want to go for a stroll?”

“Um, sure,” she said, and watched as he walked out from behind the counter and out into the mall.

“Are you coming?” he asked.

“Don’t you need to...lock up? Or something?”

Kipling blinked at her. “Why?”

She walked out to join him, worrying at her fingernails with her teeth. “Aren’t you afraid someone will steal something?”

“Oh, no. I mean what would they steal?” he said, strolling in a random direction.

Gina followed, and said, “I don’t know, money?” as if it were obvious.

“Oh. Yeah I guess they might,” replied Kipling. He shrugged.

Gina chuckled to herself. “You can be a weird one, Kipling.”

“Yeah,” said Kipling.

They walked past the news stand and smoke shop, and Gina scanned the covers of the magazines. So many beautiful people, she thought to herself. Kipling stopped as she browsed, and did some calculations on his calculator watch. He said, “Hmm,” to himself.

“Oh, what’s wrong with my body now?” said Gina, reading a headline that said “How to make yourself look good: the 20 things that are wrong with your body”.

Kipling looked up. “What?”

“I don’t know, I’m just feeling very unattractive, you know?”

“Hm,” said Kipling.

“I mean, we’ve talked about it, but look at me and then look at these women on these magazines. I mean what the f, right?” Gina had toned down her f-bombs to just the letter f since her date with Chester. She didn't want to be the kind of person who only expressed themselves in a pure stream of expletives.

"You think those women are prettier than you?"

"Well duh."

"Why?"

"Well because of what happened with Chester. I don't know. It hurts being rejected like that."

"When did he reject you?"

"On our date! I told you that already." She sighed and looked sad. "Do you even listen to me? Or am I just talking to myself?"

"Hm. You told me that he kissed you, and then asked if that meant he got to date January."

"Exactly."

"That doesn't sound like rejection, that sounds like confusion." He took her by the arm and they kept walking. "You didn't give him a chance to know how you felt. He was reacting to the situation as he understood it."

"But he didn't even care about kissing me!"

"From what I understand it was not that he didn't care about kissing you, but rather that he didn't know that kissing you meant anything about his relationship to you, only his relationship to January."

"But he was kissing me," she said, slightly petulant.

"But he thought," said Kipling gently, "that you were only doing it for January."

"It's still getting rejected," said Gina dismally.

Kipling nodded. "You could choose to see it that way. Or maybe you rejected him."

"What?"

"Well, when he said what he said about January you had a choice. You could have told him the truth and seen what happened, but instead you cut the date short. I think you rejected him."

"I don't know, Kipling." Gina folded her arms and watched the ground as she kicked at invisible spots on the floor.

"It's just a theory," said Kipling. They were just starting down the hallway where Candida's was located. Kipling searched ahead and spotted Chester standing at the counter in front of January, talking to her. It didn't look like a romantic conversation, but still he quickly grabbed Gina's arm and steered her in a different direction. "Hey, let's go down here," he said. "There's something I'd like to tell you."

Inside Candida's the atmosphere was loaded with a fog of disappointment.

"I'm sorry, Chester," January said. "It's not that I didn't have a good time, but I just...my family is very important to me. I can't let my father down. I can't disobey him."

Chester tapped his fingers on the countertop. He was trying to invent any argument he could that might convince her. He couldn't think of anything.

"But you did have a good time?" he asked quietly.

January sighed sadly. "I really did," she said.

"Doesn't that mean something?"

January looked at him for a moment, then said, "Couldn't you try harder? I mean...my father, my dad, his problem is that you have no motivation. No ambition. And, you know, from what I see he is kind of right."

"What are you trying to tell me?"

"I think, I mean, I feel like, if you feel strongly about someone, that you would at least try."

"Okay, then," he said and smiled briefly as he glanced up at her. He immediately looked down again and his smile dropped off the face of the earth. "I guess I'll..." He turned slowly and walked away, leaving his sentence unfinished.

Jasper had watched the exchange, and his heart went out to his friend. He stopped a middle-aged man in mid-sentence, and said "I'm sorry sir, but I have to go right now," and followed Chester as he hurried away. Jasper caught up with him just by the food court. He was moving quickly towards the Mega-Mart, fists in his pockets, unaware of his surroundings.

"Chester!" he said.

Chester ignored him.

"Hey, wait up a sec," said Jasper as he came up beside Chester. They walked in stride for a short while, Jasper scrutinizing his friend's darkly tense face. "Are you okay?"

"No, not really." Chester came to a stop. They were just outside the Mega-Mart, looking in on the bright, fluorescent crowds of shoppers. It was less than a month till Christmas and the mall was bedecked in bunting and holly and tackiness. Saccharine versions of Christmas favourites were being piped gently and continuously through the public address system. The mall had become a pornographic version of itself. It always happened around the holidays.

"What happened?" Jasper asked gently.

Instead of answering him, Chester said, "Tuffray," and indicated the jouncing, pear-shaped body of Tuffray as he greeted customers entering the store. Tuffray's tie was fastidiously knotted, and had reindeer cavorting all over it. "Remember how I was going to tell you why Tuffray is such a jerk?"

"Um, yeah," said Jasper. "But, you know, that was a couple of months ago. I'm pretty familiar with his jerkiness now."

"Last year about this time, there was a cashier named Appolonia," Chester began, almost in a trance. Jasper felt like Chester hadn't even heard him. "She was a nice lady," Chester continued, "and a good worker and all that, you know. She didn't sell cigarettes to minors or anything. You see what I'm saying – just really conscientious. Anyway, she gives Tuffray a month's notice that she needs a day off. It's her son's birthday party, blah blah blah, she's got to be there, etc. etc., and there's gonna be clowns and food and party games and all that."

Jasper nodded slowly.

"So Tuffray says okay, you can have the afternoon off, but I need you here up to 11am. Which is all fine, Appolonia's got the party starting at 2pm so she's got time in between for everything. So everything is hunky-dory, and time passes and we get to the day of the birthday party.

"Appolonia comes in in the morning and gets to work and, I shit you not, it comes up to 10:50 and Tuffray comes around to her and he's like, oh I'm sorry but I can't let you go early. You're going to have to work until 3pm. Obviously she gets upset, she's like, hey, it's my kid's birthday, you said everything was okay, yadda yadda yadda. And Tuffray, with his stupid fucking little clipboard, says, oh well you didn't file a 940 request for leave form, so there's nothing I can do for you. Then she's like well what if I just leave right now? And Tuffray says you leave right now you won't come back. And remember, you got that little boy to take care of."

"Jesus," said Jasper.

"Yeah, exactly. Super prick, right? But it gets even worse. Because she has to work until 3 she's calling all around trying to find someone who can go to her place and make sure everything goes off all right. She's still working, too. So she's, like, scanning items and making phone calls and scanning and calling and on and on. She can't find anyone to help her look after the birthday party.

"Finally she gets hold of one of the parents that's coming and convinces them to go a little early because she's stuck at work. The parent is like, okay okay, I'll go at 1pm or so and help set things up and stuff. So everything seems better, a little, you know, she's got it under control. But then she gets the call at just after 1pm, and it's the other parent and she's saying oh my god your house is on fire!"

"Holy..."

"Yeah. Her house is on fire. Apparently her son found the birthday cake and he put some candles in it and lit them and dropped one and the kitchen started to just go up like the devil's own underpants. So she panics, obviously, and she runs to Tuffray and she's like my house is on fire! And Tuffray says, yeah right Appolonia, now go back to your station and finish your shift."

"Damn."

"So she just hauls off and smacks him one," Chester laughed. "Oh, lord, that was sweet to see. She gives him such a hard smack that he goes down on one knee and then she's like forget you I've got to go save my son. And she tears out of there and gets home just as the fire department is getting the last of the fire. There wasn't all too much damage, but, I mean, it's a goddamned fire. You know? The house is smoky and burnt and water-damaged, and basically she can't live there for a couple of months while it's getting fixed."

"Hm, yeah," said Jasper. "Tuffray really is a jerk."

"Well, yeah," Chester nodded. "I mean he fired her after that, too. I think she's a cashier at the Discount Dollar now."

"Hm," said Jasper. He felt reluctant to bring up January again, watching Chester staring at Tuffray, lost in some kind of reverie. Neither of them saw Dr. Pointree come striding up to Chester, her heels clicking loudly on the tiled floor of the mall.

She tapped Chester on the shoulder. He turned to her, surprised to see her.

"Dr. Pointree?" he said.

"You are the worst human being I've ever had the misfortune to meet," she said angrily, shaking her finger at him, making the shiny bracelets on her wrist jangle.

Chester opened his mouth but found that no words were coming out. Dr. Pointree gave him a long evil eye, her beautiful face twisted in scorn. Then she hauled her hand back and slapped him hard.

Chester stumbled, clutching his jaw. Dr. Pointree nodded satisfactorily, and whipped around and strode off, her coat flowing out behind her.

"Ow, fuck!" said Chester.

"What was that about?" Jasper asked, dumbfounded, trying to help Chester stand up straight.

"Ahhh," Chester winced, his jaw was stinging. He flexed his jaw, opened his mouth, closed it. He sighed heavily and said, "Probably just another healthy dose of that ol' Chester magic."

Chapter 15 - The Sumerian

The day that Jasper said his final goodbyes to Chester and Kipling dawned beautifully, with the sunrise touching the new-fallen snow, tinging it a delicate pink and orange and blood red. Watson Huffernanny lay asleep, his jaw swollen and tender and his bloodstream still coursing with painkillers that would leave him groggy when he woke up. Chester was just limping his way home to get changed and go to the Mega-Mart for the start of his shift. He'd spent his nights in the same place for the past month since January refused to date him on strict orders from her father. He was drunk and would nurse a terrific hangover until the afternoon, when he would get a sudden burst of adrenaline about twenty minutes before Jasper had to say goodbye.

Most everyone else was asleep; quietly, peacefully, each alone. Kipling, Gina, Rose McDougall, Jasper himself. Puck, Dove Anquanita, Consuela, January, Shorsky, Easter, Peoria, Modesta Mae; Polito was nestled next to Areola, and his daughter was comfortably drooling on her pillow in the next room. Tuffray, Zari, Singer, Piper; Ipswitch and his wife; Stanswick, and the other Stanswick. Homelina was currently asleep, but would wake periodically with cramps from the cervical cancer that was just beginning to ravage her body. Horne Outhwaite was on his computer, playing online chess and chatting with a 22-year-old woman who was pretending to be a 38-year-old man. Kel Urquhart was on the couch at Tamara's house, and she was upstairs in the bed. They'd had another fight about the book club's current novel, but they would both be apologetic in the morning and they would seriously discuss plans for Kel to move in. Mya was awake, but drifting on the edge of sleep, dreaming about Lucy Liu. Dusty was also half awake, looking at the swirls of stucco on his ceiling, thinking about Dove and Gina intermittently. The Sumerian was wide awake, looking at his hands, sitting on the edge of his bed in his cramped, dirty, confused apartment. He was dressed in the same uniform he wore every day. He was ready to go to work.

No one knew much of anything about the Sumerian. Rose probably knew him best, but even she had never heard him talk. Ipswitch had hired him for his taciturnity. He had been remarkably impressed, in the interview, that the Sumerian had answered none of his questions and had, in fact, sat there impassively while Ipswitch demanded he talk. After thirty minutes Ipswitch threw his list of questions on the ground, stood up, walked around his desk and held out his hand.

"Congratulations, you've got the job, you son of a bitch," said Ipswitch begrudgingly. Only Ipswitch, with his penchant for random and unnecessary cruelty, would hire a mute to work at the information booth at the mall.

The Sumerian looked at his outstretched hand and stood up and clasped it once, briefly, and then turned and went directly to the information booth. Later that week Ipswitch had Chester deliver his uniform.

"I'll tell you, friend, don't get caught working here for long," said Chester. "Management is ridiculous. Look at that doofus over there," Chester pointed to Guy Tuffray, "I'd like to blow his brains out sometimes. Christ."

The Sumerian said nothing.

"Anyway, spiffy uniform. Take care of it. I see you put your full name on the name tag. Sam E. Ryan. What's the E stand for?"

When the Sumerian didn't respond, Chester waved and wandered away to go talk to Kipling. The Sumerian watched him go, slowly took his name tag off and dumped it in the garbage, and then when he turned back around he saw Rose McDougall for the first time.

She was unpacking pens, hanging them carefully in rows upon rows, bending so that her pants were pulled down slightly. The Sumerian could just glimpse her underwear, which was a pink thong. His face remained immobile, a weathered topography of fissures, valleys, folds, and wrinkles, but his eyes softened slightly and his heart was filled with the desire to protect this beautiful young woman that no one else thought was beautiful.

He watched her day by day, taking care not to watch her too overtly. He just enjoyed being able to be near her, and to experience life through her eyes. When she was bored he was bored, and when she was smiling and helping a customer he was happy for her. The day when she noticed that he was looking at her as she left, and she waved and said, "Have a good evening," he thought he might finally be able to talk to someone. Since then he'd been quietly building his courage up.

Now the Sumerian sat on the edge of his bed and believed that maybe today, maybe today he would be able to talk to her.

Kipling woke up and immediately turned onto his side and stared vacantly at his packed bags. He knew that the morning would come where he would do this and feel that today was the day. He had managed to save enough money, but something held him back, some small fear in the deepest region of his brain. He just needed the impetus, the last step, the little push. Reaching over his head he fumbled by his clock and got his calculator watch and strapped it on. Idly, sleepily, he punched a few buttons, made a few calculations. Yep, he could leave any time he wanted. He had always thought that as soon as he could leave he would. He had every reason to leave, and only a sparse few reasons to stay. The only person who knew why he was leaving was Gina.

When he had pulled Gina away from Candida's, and said, “There's something I'd like to tell you,” she had perked up slightly. Kipling didn't speak about himself often, he was generally the sounding board for other people. He had decided, though, that he could confide in Gina. Part of his decision came from a deep crush that he had developed on her ever since her date with Chester had gone south.

They found an empty bench down the unpopular branch of the mall's four corridors. It was a slow afternoon anyway, and so they had their privacy. Kipling sat first, Gina next to him, and she waited patiently. She watched him playing with his fingers nervously, running his hand through his unruly dark hair. He sat with his shoulders slumped forward, looking at the ground.

“I'm going to leave,” he said quietly, almost as if Gina wasn't there. But when he looked up at her with his very direct stare she knew that he had spent some time rehearsing these words.

“What? Leave?”

“I've got to go. I've already made the decision.”

“Where?”

“Fiji.”

“Fiji?” she said, incredulous.

Kipling nodded. He looked back down at his hands. He was very nervous, she could see, because he was fidgeting. Kipling was not one to fidget.

“Why are you going to Fiji?” she asked, quieter.

“I've been thinking, planning this for a long time. I haven't told anyone, not Chester, not Jasper. Not my family. Especially not my family.” He paused. “I need to escape. I need freedom, Gina. I can't live anywhere near here anymore. I just can't do it.”

“Why are you telling me? I'm—I mean we're friends, but you have closer—”

"I want you to come, as well. Not right away, but," he looked at her, "eventually."

"Geez, Kipling, I...I'm not sure. I don't really know what to say."

"You don't have to say anything. I'll be in touch, and you can make your decision when it feels right for you." He looked up at her again, and there was that direct stare that made her feel like he knew everything she was thinking. "There will be a time," he said, "when you don't want to be around here anymore. You and I, we're alike in that way. We don't live here, we're passing through."

Gina was silent for some time, thoughts piling over each other until her brain felt like a clumsy, cluttered mess. "When are you leaving?"

"I'm not sure. Soon."

"What about your family?"

Kipling looked away. His knee started to bounce, a nervous tic. "My family," he said, in a far away voice. "My mom and dad, they're— Well, I'm not even sure they will notice. They've got issues."

Gina nodded. She had heard about it from other people, and she didn't want to pry. His mother's depression, his brother's lack of ambition, and his father's listlessness were all fodder for the town gossip mill.

"My brother," Kipling began, and then stopped. He flexed his hands and made fists and then opened them again. He was staring very intently at the ground now. "My brother," he said again, deliberately, "is not someone I care to have in my life."

Gina could sense that Kipling was struggling with what to say, how to say it. She watched him with her lips slightly parted, frowning a little, concerned.

"He used to come into my room," Kipling said slowly. "When I was young. He's twelve years older than me, so I thought," Kipling paused. "I thought he knew. You know, I thought he was wiser. That he...that whatever he— I looked up to him, at one point, in my life. I did. He's my older brother.

"It was a, kind of a, game. I was 'special' to him, and he wanted me to do things and I, we would—

"It was always at night. Always in my room. He would come in and he would wake me up and he would be, you know, happy about it. He really, I mean he made it out to be a special thing. It was secret, obviously. I wasn't supposed to tell anyone...ever. But I didn't really understand that it was wrong." Kipling was looking blankly at the floor.

"It," he began, and faltered. "It hurt. I didn't like it, and so, so many times I asked him to stop, and he always—" Kipling stopped, his voice trembling, and he waited until he had mastered himself.

"Well," he said. "He always...got his way. And he kept coming into my room, not every night, but... A lot of nights. Most nights. I thought, you know, for a while I just thought: this is normal. This is what brothers do. To each other. I didn't— How could I—? He was my brother.

"You know the first thing I ever bought for myself? I was fourteen years old. I had an allowance for the first time. I had my own money. I bought a deadbolt for my bedroom door. I put it on myself. I used it." Kipling took a breath, and his shoulders relaxed slightly. "It was the first time I had, for myself, any freedom. Any nights that weren't just absolutely rigid with terror, because if he came it was bad but if he didn't..." Kipling shook his head slowly, still unable to look at Gina.

"I would just lie there. Listening for the door to open. I just— It was... That lock was everything to me. He was mad, of course, but I could deal with him during the day. I could avoid him, or I had places to be and I had my own, you know, responsibilities."

"God. I'm so sorry, Kipling," Gina began. He glanced at her with a sad smile.

"I want to tell you all of it." He took a deep breath, and said, "When I was twelve, I, I got my first— I mean I was old enough and my body was, well, maturing. I had my...first erection. And I was just— I felt terrible. I was scared. I was scared that I, that I was going to have to, or that I would succumb to my own...

"I didn't want to hurt anyone like that. I didn't really know anything different. I just thought, if you had one, that you, that you would have to do that. It was the only thing I knew about them, about erections. They could only be used to, just to hurt, and hurt and I — Oh, god, I didn't want to hurt anyone.

"So, I went downstairs. I went to the basement. And I tried, I mean, I found my dad's tools and in there I found his—I found his drywall knife." Kipling's hands were shaking. He had tears streaming down his cheeks. "I found his drywall knife," he said again, "and I, I just, I couldn't stand myself. I cut it. I didn't know what I was doing, but I..." Kipling could barely speak. "I, I cut at myself until I—" He stopped. His shoulders were shaking as he wept in silence.

"Kipling," Gina put her hand gently on his shoulder. They sat like that for minutes, until he could finally speak again.

"My dad found me. I was— They took me to the hospital. I have, I have scars, but there was no permanent damage. Not there, at least. But I'm, I am not right, Gina." He looked up at her. "I've never had a real relationship, and I honestly don't know if I can. My life— I'm messed up. You know? I'm just really...I'm really messed up."

"I know," she said. She still had her hand gently on his shoulder. "It's okay to be messed up, you know? I... I'm so sorry to hear it, but I'm glad you told me. Now you have someone you can talk to."

Kipling looked at her, and covered her hand with his own.

And on the morning of the day Jasper said goodbye, Kipling threw the covers off and got up to feed the salamanders, toads, and frogs in the large glass case on top of his dresser. Then he unlocked the deadbolt on his bedroom door and went to have a shower.

At the same time, Chester was dragging himself

sleepily out of the shower, which had not rejuvenated him at all. His eyes were sunk and dark, rimmed in red, and his head felt encased in a block of concrete. It was too heavy for him to hold it up straight, so he looked at himself in the mirror with his head crooked over. He couldn't remember much of last night, which was how things went when he got drunk.

Looking at himself in the mirror he felt ashamed. He rubbed his face blearily. His conversation with January two weeks ago had resolved nothing, and so he resolved to kick Polito directly in the balls the first chance he got.

January woke up when her father stuck his head in her room and said, "Time to get up, sweetie."

She sat up, hair delicately tousled, and yawned. "Daddy," she said, stopping him from closing the door.

"Yes?" he asked wearily.

She asked the same question she had asked every morning for a month. "Why not?"

"You know why not."

She pouted at him. Her eyes were dry, and felt thick, and had collected a thin salt film from the tears that had pooled there as she drifted off the night before.

Her father stepped into the room again. "You know how your mother and I feel about that boy. You can do so much better, pumpkin. You deserve better."

"Yes, daddy," she mumbled. She wondered if she could do better. She wondered if Chester was really all that bad.

He stayed in the doorway for a second. "Get ready for breakfast and come downstairs."

January got up and got ready to have a shower, taking off her pyjamas. Meanwhile, still in her own pyjamas, Gina was watching cartoons as she ate a bowl of Choco-Disaster Puffs. It was an episode of the *Care Bears*, the one where Tenderheart Bear has to overcome his fear of heights in order to save a little girl locked in a tower by No Heart. Gina wished that someone would be brave enough to save her. But when she thought about it, she felt that she was too ugly, too dumpy, too clingy, too emotional to deserve saving.

Depressed, she turned off the television, tossed the bowl into the sink with a loud clatter that elicited a “Hey!” from her mother at the kitchen table, and went upstairs to shower.

Polito, Mo, Gina, and Areola all arrived at the mall at the same time. This was less coincidence and more car-pooling. Polito and Mo unlocked the mall doors, let in Mr. deHavilland, and went in to turn off the alarm system.

The employees of the mall began arriving like tumbleweeds, rolling along with early morning weariness to their appointed stores. It was to be an auspicious day at the mall – the newly finished Starbucks was opening its doors for the first time. For those few who didn't know what the Starbucks was all about, they were told it was a coffee place that charged three dollars for a medium coffee, except they didn't call it a medium coffee. It was all pretty exciting.

Chester and Kipling arrived at almost the same time, and Kipling held the door while Chester slumped through it.

“You look like hell,” said Kipling.

“Thanks,” said Chester, his voice rough and hoarse.

“What’s up? Where’s your uniform?”

Chester looked down at his body, closed his eyes and dropped his shoulders in exasperation. “Aw, Christ,” he said. Under his winter coat he was wearing the same clothes he'd had on the previous night, a soiled t-shirt and jeans.

“What did you do last night?” Kipling asked, concerned.

“Oh, I don’t even know. I went out. I had a drink or two. Maybe two and a half.”

They crossed to the Mega-Mart entrance and stopped there.

“Be careful,” said Kipling.

“Listen I don’t need your help, okay?”

“I’m not trying to help you, I’m trying to make sure you don’t destroy yourself.”

"Well, I don't need you to stop me from destroying myself." Chester levelled a weary look at Kipling.

"Are you sure?"

Chester sighed. He let that one pass.

"Don't you think you've punished yourself enough?"

Chester's eyes flashed darkly as he looked suddenly into Kipling's calm gaze. "No," he said thickly.

"Do you love her?"

"I... How could I know?"

"Do you know what love is, even?"

"Do I know what love is?" Chester was suddenly angry. His head still pounded and the morning sun felt like it was stabbing through his eyes as he turned on Kipling. "Of course I know what love is. Love is aching and longing and hurting and a big fucking empty space sitting on your heart. Love is looking at yourself in the mirror and hating what you see because you know, you goddamned well *know* that you aren't ever going to be good enough. And you make yourself sick, and you can't stand the feeling of being alone because you are absolutely aware, so goddamned aware, of exactly how much you would let her down. Every day you would be just, just that fucking shy of being someone she could respect." He shook his head. "Do I know what love is," he muttered.

Kipling put a hand gently on Chester's shoulder. "You're fucked up, Chester."

Chester nodded. Then he said, "Do you ever wonder why we get crapped on so much?"

"No," said Kipling.

"You mean you know?"

"No," said Kipling, shaking his head slowly. There was a long pause.

"What am I supposed to do?" he asked, clenching his fists. He would have banged a countertop if one had been nearby.

Kipling shrugged. "Go to work, sleep through the day, piss off Tuffray."

Chester chuckled. "Do you want to meet for lunch?"

Kipling blew out a breath, puffing his cheeks. "It

might be hard for me to get away."

Chester punched his shoulder and said, "Oh, Christ. We'll get some lunch, we'll play some video games."

"That sounds like you," said Kipling, turning and wandering toward the Amphibian Emporium. Chester shook his head, felt a little bit better, and went into the Mega-Mart, where Tuffray immediately attempted to call down the thunder.

"Why aren't you properly attired in regulation uniform, Chester?" he barked.

"Oh, will you please shut your face, Tuffray," Chester said as he walked past the pudgy manager, whose face was almost as red as his hair.

"You cannot be on the floor here if you don't have a proper uniform, Chester. I won't allow it," said Tuffray, trailing after Chester as he walked to the back room.

"Fine, send me home."

"You are scheduled to work today and you will work your full shift, Chester! And in uniform!"

Chester shrugged. "Well, it's at home, Tuffray. And my shift starts in ten minutes. What do you want me to do?" He pushed open the door to the back room and tossed his coat on the back of a chair. He turned to face Tuffray, who had his hands on his hips.

"Well let's actualize and expedite this problem, Chester. What can we do?"

"Oh, god." Chester collapsed back into the chair he'd just tossed his coat on. He closed his eyes.

Tuffray looked around. He spotted Watson's shirt and smock hanging over a chair, which Watson had left with Easter yesterday when his parents came to drive him home. "Here," he said, taking Watson's uniform down and handing it to Chester, "wear this."

Chester opened his eyes. "What? Isn't that Watson's uniform?"

"Well it will have to do for today, Chester, so make do!"

Chester grabbed the uniform from Tuffray's sweaty, ham-like hand. "Fine." He pulled the button-down shirt on over his t-shirt and shrugged into the smock, did it up, and put his hands in the front pockets, feeling something odd.

"Good," said Tuffray, and turned around and whisked out of the back room.

Chester pulled his hand out of the pocket and came out with package after package of empty condom wrappers. "Jesus," he said. He looked around, making sure no one had seen. He stuffed the empty condom wrappers back in the pockets. "Maybe this is a lucky uniform," Chester said to himself. He went to join Polito, sit on the chair in the corner, and get some sleep.

By the time Jasper arrived it was past mid-morning, but he had a surprise for Kipling in two mid-sized boxes wrapped in string that he carried into the mall. He went past the new Starbucks, where a long line had formed, and headed straight to the Amphibian Emporium. He spotted Kipling, who was peering intently into one of the glass cases filled with hopping, croaking frogs and feeding insects into the case one by one. Kipling was murmuring something to the frogs, who festooned every surface in the glass case, from wide mossy rocks to angular lengths of tree branch to the surface of the case itself. They hopped over each other to shoot their tongues out and nab the insects. Jasper set the boxes on the counter and came over beside Kipling.

"See that one?" Kipling said quietly. Jasper followed his finger and saw a tiny frog with olive-green skin and mottled black patches. The frog made a high-pitched peeping sound. "The ornate chorus frog," said Kipling. "Somewhat related to the barking treefrog. The only difference is the size of the diaphragm, which makes the ornate chorus frog peep and the barking treefrog bark."

"Cool," said Jasper. "Hey, I got a surprise for you."

"Hm?" Kipling looked up at him.

Jasper jogged back to the counter, proudly

displayed the boxes, and said, "Ta-da!"

"What's that?" asked Kipling, joining him.

"One thousand postcards," said Jasper, beaming.

"Seriously?"

Jasper untied the string and lifted the top off of one of the boxes. Inside were ten bundled packs of postcards, glossy in the muted overhead light of the Amphibian Emporium. "Each one has fifty postcards in it," Jasper said, indicating the bundles.

Kipling, quietly overawed, reached in and pulled out a bundle of postcards. "These are perfect," he said. "Where did you get them?"

"I got Rose to order them in special at the Grand & Toy," Jasper explained, enjoying his friend's reaction.

"Just let me know how much I owe you, man," said Kipling carefully replacing the bundle. "Thanks so much."

"Actually," said Jasper, "they didn't cost anything."

"What?"

"Rose told me. Apparently they're all discontinued and the company just had overstock, so the only cost was shipping. And since they were already sending her an order they just put it in with that, so..." Jasper shrugged.

Kipling looked into Jasper's eyes for a moment. It was moderately disconcerting for Jasper because Kipling had very intense blue eyes. Suddenly Kipling hugged Jasper hard, and squeezed the breath out of him.

"Okay," wheezed Jasper, trying to clutch at Kipling, his arms pinned to his sides.

"It's the best gift anyone ever gave me," said Kipling, letting Jasper go. "I'd given up on getting them."

"What do you need them for, anyway?"

"A little thing I like to call 'you'll see'," said Kipling, making his fingers into a gun and pointing at Jasper. His thumb went down and he made a clicking sound with his tongue on the roof of his mouth.

Jasper laughed, and said, "All right, keep your

secrets then."

"I will."

"Have you seen Gina yet?"

Kipling was thumbing through the postcards, whistling under his breath. "No, but she's supposed to come here before she has to open up for lunch."

"Okay, well...tell her I said hi," said Jasper cagily. Kipling, looking at the pictures of wide expanses of sky or evocative sunsets or windswept mountains, noticed that Jasper was being deliberately nonchalant.

"Sure," he said. For Kipling nonchalance came as easily as a nice slow, laconic blink. There was no effort. The eyelid did all the work.

Gina found herself behind schedule, though, and because of her fear of being on the receiving end of one of Clyde Saphoria's brutal haranguings she didn't get a chance to visit Kipling or receive Jasper's hi. She did, however, see Ameesha as she was arriving, looking tired and formless with the Canton Kitchen uniform draped over her usually curvaceous body.

"Hey, Ameesha," she said brightly from behind the Taco Bell counter.

Ameesha winced. "Yeah, good morning. Oh, Christ, I hate starting early."

"Long night?"

"A bit." Ameesha was about to stumble on her way, eyes half-closed in tiredness when she turned back to Gina. "Hey, by the way, what's up with your boyfriend?"

"My...what?" Gina stopped stirring the preprocessed ground beef for a second.

"You know. Chester. What the hell is his problem?"

"Oh," Gina sighed. "He's not my boyfriend, actually."

"I thought you guys were dating?"

"Well, we only went on one date and that was kind of a disaster, so...I haven't even talked to him in more than a month." She shrugged, playing with her fingernails and not meeting Ameesha's eye.

"Well, okay, I'm glad that you're not dating him

because he's kind of a huge jerk."

"Yeah, I know."

"No, seriously," said Ameesha, warming up to her subject now and becoming more animated. "He comes into the Paradise Club, like, every night and just hoots and yells and calls all the girls names and stuff. He's so rude." Her lip was curled in distaste.

"That doesn't sound like Chester," said Gina, frowning, slightly concerned.

"Oh, it's him all right," said Ameesha, nodding. "He's worn his stupid uniform there before. His name tag and everything. Actually, I think he left it there last night."

"Oh." Gina felt equal measures of pity and sadness. Chester, sitting in an exotic dance bar night after night, getting drunk and yelling at the girls while his heart refused to mend. She felt a certain kinship to him, because her heart was refusing to mend, too. But, then again, he was the complete horse's ass who had hurt her feelings in the first place. It was confusing sometimes. The only thing that made her feel better was spending time with Kipling.

"Yeah. Anyway, if you see him, tell him that if he comes in again he's gonna be thrown out and banned for life, okay?"

Gina nodded and Ameesha scuffed her shoes across the tiles as she walked, to indicate how she felt about having to work so early. It was 10:30.

Ameesha was the reason that Dr. Augusta Pointree hated Chester. Ameesha's tendency to over-exaggerate didn't help matters either. She had been in the dental care aisle of the Mega-Mart, searching for a new toothbrush, using the knowledge she had gleaned after being taken under Dr. Pointree's wing. Chester, who was mopping the aisle, stopped briefly and watched her as she compared different brands and styles.

"Aren't they pretty much all the same?" Chester asked.

She turned to him and said abruptly, "Of course not."

"Oh, and how would you know?" he challenged.

"Because I'm going to study to be a dentist, duh," said Ameesha sharply.

"I thought you wanted to be an exotic dancer?" Chester asked innocently. He didn't mean anything by it, that was just what he had heard from Puck.

"Oh, so you think I can't be a dentist?"

"Well, no, I didn't—" Chester began, but got cut off before he could finish the sentence with "mean that."

"Do you think I'm stupid?" she asked.

"Of course I—" he started, but got cut off again before he could add "don't."

"Well fuck you too, Chester!" said Ameesha, and threw the toothbrushes on the ground and stormed off to cry on Dr. Pointree's shoulder.

As she walked away Chester said, "What just happened?" to no one in particular. And then an hour later Dr. Pointree walked up to him and gave him a piece of her mind.

"You are a terrible human being," she said matter-of-factly, and turned around and walked away with such dignity that Chester was completely at a loss as to how to respond. She had never talked to him before.

Ameesha also explained to Dr. Pointree what Chester had done and said at the Paradise Club. And, even though he was under the influence and couldn't remember a thing about those long, terrible evenings, the terrific slap he received from Dr. Pointree was indelibly imprinted in his mind. From now on, said Chester to himself, I'm going to live my life to avoid that woman.

"God, I'm a wreck," said Chester. He was sitting next to Jasper and across from Kipling at the food court. His head was still pounding, even after wolfing down a full complement of chicken soft tacos.

Everyone was sitting in front of a localized pile of taco wrappers. Kipling was still slowly eating his only one, re-wrapping it and chewing thoughtfully. Jasper had taken the opportunity to talk quickly with Gina while he was ordering.

"I'll have three chicken soft tacos and I'm sorry," said Jasper.

Gina looked up at him. "Huh?"

"Three chicken soft tacos, please?"

"And what else?"

Jasper shifted his feet. "And...I'm sorry."

"Where is this coming from?" asked Gina, tilting her head. Behind Jasper the line groaned, seeing a long potential wait ahead. Gina held up her finger to the line, trying to get them to behave. Stomachs growled.

"Well, Chester, he...a while ago...I mean," Jasper sighed. He straightened his shoulders and tried to sort his thoughts out. "Chester told me that he kissed you, and he also told me that you felt like you weren't a very good kisser. And I think partly I am to blame for that. And so, I just wanted to say I'm sorry. I wasn't very mature when I said that to you."

Gina smiled at him. "Thanks, Jasper. I mean, it wasn't that big a deal, you know? But...but thanks."

Jasper smiled back, took his order and skedaddled to the delight of the line behind him. Now, sitting across from Kipling, who was punching numbers into his calculator watch with a slight line of concentration across his forehead, Jasper felt at ease. He felt like he had done something right.

Chester, his elbows on the table and his hands pressed over his eyes, groaned like the opening of a crypt.

"Do you want to go play video games?" Jasper asked.

Kipling looked up at the two of them. "I'm in," he said.

"You're always in," muttered Chester.

"Not always, but, as it turns out, I'm still twenty four dollars and seventeen cents over budget, so I'm in."

"Over budget?" Chester asked.

"Yeah."

Jasper and Chester waited. Kipling waited too. Jasper and Chester leaned forward, expecting Kipling to talk. Kipling looked back and forth between them.

"So...video games?" said Kipling.

Chester banged his fist on the table, then immediately regretted it and held his forehead in the cool of his palm. "Oh, I'm just going to go back to the Mega-Mart. Sorry, guys."

"No problem," said Jasper, "we'll go with you."

They walked with Kipling and Jasper on either side of Chester, making sure he didn't collapse onto the ground.

"What are you doing to yourself?" asked Jasper.

"Don't ask," said Kipling quietly.

They got to the Mega-Mart and had walked Chester halfway to the back room when there was some kind of explosion near the cash registers and a huge, bellowing voice yelled, "Nobody move! You. The security button. Now."

And then there was a clanging bell and Chester grabbed his head and fell to his knees as the security gates came crashing down over the doors to the Mega-Mart. Kipling and Jasper whipped around, trying to help Chester up and looking to see what was going on.

Everything was in panic. Shoppers were dropping to the ground covering their heads or running pell-mell not knowing where to turn or what to do. The loud bells of the security system were still banging away, making it nearly impossible to think. Steel grates lowered over the doors to the Mega-Mart, locking people in.

There was another explosion from the cash registers and Kipling, Chester, and Jasper moved to the broad main aisle where they could see what was happening. The bells kept ringing, and they saw people everywhere lying on the floor with their hands over their heads.

At the cash registers they saw the Sumerian, brandishing a shotgun in one heavy hand and an assault rifle in the other, his legs wide in a broad stance as he looked around at the scurrying shoppers. His eyes were wide and tense, his face red with rage, his whole body shaking. He had two pistols jammed into the front of his pants. He yelled, “What part of 'don’t move' do you people not understand!” and fired the assault rifle a third time into the ceiling.

Everyone froze.

Chapter 16 - Jasper the Friendly

Jasper had never seen a gun, except in movies, and had never known the gut-wrenching feeling of being near one when they went off. It was like his stomach leaped up and grabbed onto his heart and clung there for a minute, swaying, not ready to let go. And then there was the sick, prickling feeling of fear crawling along his spine. Real fear, not the mild nervousness of heights, or the vague trepidation of asking a girl to dance, but the kind of fear that tenses every follicle in your body and makes your heart palpitate like a galloping horse with a lame leg.

The feeling only intensified when the Sumerian swung his attention to them, the only people in the main aisle who hadn't collapsed to the ground with their hands over their heads, huddling, weeping, terrified. The Sumerian levelled the assault rifle at Jasper, who suddenly felt his limbs turn numb.

"You," said the Sumerian, in his surprisingly loud voice. "Go get Polito." Then he turned his attention to Kipling. "And you," he said, and his eyes clouded over and he developed a startlingly nasty sneer, "find Tuffray."

Neither Jasper nor Kipling moved.

"Now!" yelled the Sumerian, and the assault rifle fired a fourth time, putting a sizable hole in the ceiling tiles of the Mega-Mart.

Jasper still couldn't feel his limbs, but he managed to step lively toward the back room with Kipling. They ran into Polito coming stealthily down the toiletries aisle, his back against the glycerin soaps and the taser wand in his hand like a pistol. Both Jasper and Kipling had grey faces and eyes as wide and scared as frightened animals. Polito looked rather sickly himself.

"What's it look like up there?" he said, just loud enough that it was on the brink of audibility over the klaxon haranguing.

"It's not worth it," said Kipling, edging past, looking for Tuffray.

Polito shot a questioning look at Jasper, who shook his head. "He's got a couple of really big guns," said Jasper. "He means business, and I think it's probably wise to just come quietly with me. I don't think he wants to hurt anyone."

"Then why the fuck does he have the guns?" said Polito.

Jasper had no answer for that, but gave Polito a helpless look. "Think about your daughter," said Jasper. Polito put the taser wand back in its holster and followed Jasper over to the front cash registers.

Kipling, meanwhile, had edged open the doors to the back room area and said gingerly into the vacant space: "Tuffray?" It was impossible to hear any sound except the deafening clanging of the alarm bell, which was located in the back room somewhere, so Kipling said it louder: "Tuffray!"

He stepped further into the back, looking around the flats of Mega-Mart merchandise, stepping carefully and leaning around to look between boxes, over boxes, under boxes. Anywhere he thought a Tuffray-sized object could find a place to wedge itself.

Suddenly the alarm stopped, although Kipling could hear it echo around inside his head for another couple of minutes. He sighed in relief from the auditory onslaught and pushed open the door to the employee men's room. The only stall was occupied, and there was a desperately muffled whimpering coming from behind the door.

"Tuffray?" said Kipling.

The muffled whimpering stopped.

"It's me, Kipling."

"Go away," said Tuffray quietly. "Pretend there's no one in here."

"I can't. He's looking for you, specifically."

"Tell him I left."

"How? The alarm went off, the doors are all sealed."

"Tell him I went out the window."

"Are there any windows?"

"No."

Kipling sighed. "Wouldn't he know that?"

"Who is it?"

"It's the Sumerian, geez, don't you even know who you're hiding from?"

"I just thought it was some nutcase."

"Well, it's not just some nutcase, it's a very specific nutcase, and he very specifically wants to see you, for some very specific reason, so come on."

"No no no," said Tuffray. "No no, he wants to hurt me."

Kipling paused. He let his fingers touch the door to the stall, comfortingly. "You don't know that for sure. Maybe he just wants to make sure everyone is accounted for. He asked for Polito, too."

"He did?"

"Yeah."

"But Polito is the security guard, right? He's the only one who's armed."

"Well...okay, yeah," Kipling conceded. "But only with a taser wand."

"Still."

"Listen, if I don't bring you out he's going to be upset, I think, and maybe hurt someone."

"But you don't know, for sure."

"Well, no, but I don't really have much choice here, Tuffray. Neither do you, really. He'll get you out of here at some point, if he has to come in here himself." Kipling stopped for a second. He felt like he was being carried on the crest of a gigantic wave, about to be plunged under by it and held down and sucked out to sea by the riptide. He didn't feel very good. "Listen, let's go out there together. We'll face whatever is coming together, okay? Otherwise I think he might go ape and hurt a lot of people."

"Better them than me," said Tuffray. He was sitting on the toilet, feet tucked up, hugging his knees. He was sweating.

"Tuffray."

"What? It's true."

"Stop being selfish."

"You stop being selfish!"

"Listen, this argument is not going to happen right here, okay? You're coming out, now."

"No!"

"Come out, now!"

"No!"

Kipling squared his shoulders. With a sharp little intake of breath he lifted his leg and kicked the stall door, which popped open and barely missed taking a chunk out of Tuffray's knees. Tuffray gasped and squeezed himself into an even tighter ball.

"Hey, that was locked!" he said.

"Shut up," said Kipling. He stepped in and grabbed Tuffray by the shirt and hauled him out.

"No no, don't make me go!" said Tuffray, but he couldn't keep his feet and fell as Kipling dragged him by the shirt out of the bathroom.

"Get up!" he said as he let go of Tuffray's shirt and panted slightly from dragging the heavy, weeping, blubbering mass of selfish micro-manager. Tuffray hesitantly got to his feet, his shoulders sagging, his head tucked into his chest. "Now, let's go," said Kipling, shoving Tuffray's shoulder, pushing him ahead.

They came out of the back room. The store was quiet and customers were still on the floor with hands over their heads, not daring to move. Some had crawled into one aisle or another and had found a place to hole up, waiting on their knees until they could think of how to escape. Tuffray looked at them as they walked past, his face wet with tears. Kipling tried to murmur comfort to them.

At the front of the store Jasper, Chester, Tamara, Gina, Shorsky, Easter, and Polito were all on their knees with their hands clasped behind their head in a semi-circle about fifteen feet from the Sumerian, who was watching them carefully and shooting glances to the back where he had sent Kipling. When he spotted Kipling and Tuffray approaching he aimed the rifle at them and yelled, "Double time, come on!"

Kipling hurried to join the group, getting down beside Polito and putting his hands behind his head. Tuffray hesitated, holding his pudgy hands nervously in front of himself.

"Move!" yelled the Sumerian, and then Tuffray jumped and got down on his knees next to Kipling, lacing his fingers behind his tufted strawberry hair. His mustache twitched nervously, it was prickly with sweat.

"What are you doing here?" Kipling whispered to Gina as quietly as he could.

"I was looking for Chester," she said helplessly.

"Shut up! No talking, from now on," said the Sumerian. "It's my turn to talk and I've got some things to say." His voice was surprisingly strong, clear, and controlled. Everyone clammed up.

"Now," said the Sumerian. Then there was a long pause. The Sumerian shifted his guns, pointing them at different people as he searched their faces. "I've got something to say..." he said, less confidently. "Fuck! I've forgotten what I wanted to say. Anyway, fuck it. Tuffray dies." He pointed the assault rifle deliberately at Tuffray, whose eyes widened.

"Wait!" yelled Tuffray, "No! Please!" He held his hands out, pleadingly. "Oh, god, why? Why do you want to kill me?" He said it like it was inconceivable to want to kill someone of so little importance.

"Why?" roared the Sumerian. "Why?! You broke Rose's heart, you little piece of– I knew I should've killed you as soon as you two started having sex in the back room! But no, I didn't, I waited, like an idiot, and now you've gone and broken her heart, you complete horse's ass! That means you have to pay." The Sumerian aimed the rifle again, straight and true.

"What?!?" said Tuffray. "I didn't break her heart, she broke mine!" The Sumerian lowered the rifle slightly.

"What?" he said.

"Yeah, she broke up with me. She told me that we could never see each other again. She told me that I make her sick!" He laughed a sickly, high-pitched, nervous laugh. "I—I make her sick!" he repeated.

The Sumerian narrowed his eyes. "Then why was she crying?"

"I don't know! Oh, please, I swear to god I don't know. Maybe she felt bad about the whole thing, or...I don't know!" Tuffray began weeping, he covered his face with his hands.

Everyone else was stunned, looking from Tuffray to the Sumerian and back.

"Did you know Tuffray was seeing Rose?" Gina whispered to Chester.

"No, I had no idea."

"Did you?" she whispered to Jasper, on the other side of Chester.

"No, no clue."

"Tamara?"

"I'm...flabbergasted," said Tamara.

They turned back to watch the Sumerian, who had just levelled his gun at Tuffray again.

"It doesn't matter. You're going to die anyway! I should have killed you when I found out you were sleeping with her." The Sumerian's face was red and tense, he pointed the rifle at Tuffray and his jaw flexed as his eyes narrowed.

Everyone was frozen. Tuffray had shuffled forward on his knees and so was separate from the rest of the semi-circle, his hands clasped in prayer before his face, his head lowered as he begged for his life. Kipling's mouth was agape and dry and his body wouldn't respond to the screaming directions coming from his brain. Polito was wincing, pulling away, eyes closed. Shorsky was bent double, hiding her face against her knees. Tamara had unclasped her hands to hug Gina, who was hugging her back. They both had their faces against each other's shoulders, crying helplessly. Chester was unable to look away as the Sumerian began to pull the trigger, his lip curling as his body shook. The rifle only wavered slightly, still drawing a bead on Tuffray's lumpy, potato-shaped head.

Suddenly Jasper was between Chester and the Sumerian, and he could no longer see exactly what was happening. Jasper roared as he leapt from his knees and pitched himself headlong between Tuffray and the Sumerian. The Sumerian saw him at the last second and in his surprise he didn't pull the trigger right away. Jasper managed to hit the rifle at the same moment as the Sumerian tried to step back and pulled the trigger. The rifle exploded, the sound deafening, and Chester and Kipling were both up and moving after their friend. The Sumerian pulled back further, jogging back until he bumped into the cash register and stopped, staring, the rifle in his hand smoking guiltily. Tuffray raised his head and opened his eyes.

Jasper lay on the ground, blood pooling around him. Kipling and Chester reached him at the same time, one on each side of him, both cradling his head.

"Oh my god, Jasper. Oh Jesus. Oh Christ," said Chester, his eyes burning with tears as he looked at the raw gaping hole in Jasper's stomach. It didn't look like a big hole, and for a second Chester thought it might not be too bad.

"Shh, it's okay, hold on, buddy," said Kipling, rocking slightly. With one hand he was pulling off his shirt to press it against the bloody wound. Jasper was white, and could barely blink. His whole body was trembling very slightly, the way the edge of a piece of paper trembles when the rest of it is burning, and he couldn't swallow. "Tuffray," he whispered, making a small bubble on his lips burst soundlessly.

“Oh god, hang on, hang on, it’s okay,” said Chester with tears streaming down his face, dripping from his nose. He pulled Jasper’s head close to him, cradling it.

“He’s all right, he’s alive, Jasper,” said Kipling, trying to be gentle as he pressed his shirt against the wound. The blood was spreading around them. Kipling and Chester were both kneeling in the thick, sticky, red pool as it oozed wider and wider. Kipling couldn’t figure out why there was so much blood. His shirt was only slowly soaking through. He pressed it to Jasper's wound a little more, trying to staunch the flow, except there didn't seem to be much flow.

“I’m okay, guys,” said Jasper, and he tried a smile that barely twitched his lips. He could feel his grip on his body slipping, and could no longer make the muscles move much at all. “Hey,” he managed to say, “I’m okay. I’m okay.”

Chester caressed his face uselessly, trying to smooth his hair back, make him more comfortable. He could barely see, his eyes were filled with tears. He swiped at them quickly and went back to holding and caressing Jasper’s white cheeks and forehead. Kipling said, “Don’t move, buddy. You’ll be okay.”

“I think, I should... Goodbye,” said Jasper, his words only barely audible. He closed his eyes and his body shook more violently. “I’m sorry...goodbye. I’m sorry.” Jasper stopped shaking.

Chester collapsed over him, sobbing as he held him. Kipling slumped to the ground, watching as Chester rocked back and forth with Jasper’s head on his lap. He looked over at the Sumerian, who was breathing hard and still pointing the rifle in their general direction.

“Why? Why did he do that?” the Sumerian said.

“You killed him,” said Kipling, and he felt like his voice was coming to him from far away.

“It was an accident,” said the Sumerian weakly.

“An accident?!” said Chester, looking up at him with eyes still weeping tears and his eyebrows knit together angrily. “You stupid son of a— What the fuck did you think was going to happen?” Chester stood up, carefully letting Jasper's head down. He strode directly at the Sumerian, who lifted his rifle until it pressed against Chester's chest. It was the only thing between them, the only thing stopping Chester.

"Don't make me—" the Sumerian began.

"What did you think was going to happen when you brought a fucking assault rifle in here? You knew you were going to kill someone!"

"It was an accident, now calm down—"

"You killed a man!"

"I don't want to shoot you, Chester, but I will," said the Sumerian, but he sounded unsure of himself.

"Shoot me, then," said Chester, a new batch of tears springing into his eyes. He held his hands out. "Shoot me, you goddamned bastard. Shoot me! Pull the trigger! Come on!"

The Sumerian locked eyes with Chester and couldn't say anything. He saw the raw hurt in his eyes and recognized it, because it was the way he felt when he had seen Rose crying. He turned his head away slightly. Chester took a half-step back and grabbed the rifle, pulling it out of the Sumerian's hands and tossing it to the ground.

Then the front window of the Mega-Mart shattered and a grenade clattered across the ground, drawing everyone's attention. The grenade burst, gas spurting from it as another grenade smashed through a different window and burst, and another and another. Everyone dropped to the ground, coughing, choking, eyes streaming painfully. They tried to cover their mouths, noses, eyes, but the gas seeped through, making every part of the face itch and burn and feel like there was raw smoke just under the skin. When the SWAT team finally came in through the windows there was no resistance. And when everyone was outside, being treated for the effects of tear gas, there were only a few who could not stop crying.

The week after Jasper's funeral Chester went to

Kipling's house and rang the bell, but there was no answer. He stood outside for the better part of an hour, but eventually went home and crawled into bed still fully dressed. He dozed off and was awakened by his phone.

"Hello?" he said thickly.

"Can I come up?" It was a woman's voice, calling from his apartment's lobby.

"January?" he said.

"Yes."

He buzzed her up and straightened his clothes as he got out of bed. He felt old, tired, uncomfortable. He shook his head, splashed some water on his face, and went to open the door for January.

She stood in the hallway outside his apartment, holding her purse in front of her with both hands, protectively, and searching his eyes with sad, brown-eyed glances. Chester stood in the doorway and put his hands in his pockets. There was melancholy in the air between them. Finally Chester spoke.

"Won't your dad be upset? That you're here?"

"Chester," January began, her eyes shimmering from the flickering fluorescent light caught in the tears she was forming. She looked at her boots for a second, and then squared herself and looked at him clearly. "I'm so sorry about Jasper."

Chester blinked slowly and leaned against the doorway. Something in him wasn't in the mood to entertain the niceties surrounding mortality. "Oh," he said. "Yeah, thanks. I'm sure you know what it's like to lose someone like that. See you." He stepped back and began to swing the door closed, but January stepped forward and put her hand out to stop the door.

"Wait. Don't be mad, please. I'm sorry."

Chester was still halfway into the apartment, turned away from January. But he wasn't closing the door anymore. He hung his head, sighed, slowly turned to face her, his hand resting on the door. He didn't know if he should open it or close it.

"No one should make a girl choose between her

family and love," said January quietly.

"Love?" Chester watched her smooth cheeks, her down-turned eyes, her long lashes.

She looked up at him. "Maybe."

"Look, if you're just here to give your condolences, well, thanks, but...please go now. I can't really take feeling this thing and feeling for you, I'm just not equipped to handle it."

"Chester, I'm here to say I'm sorry. I'm here to see... if you still...have feelings. For me." She stopped and her hands gripped her purse quite firmly. "This is really hard," she admitted. "I...don't really talk to people, much. I'm not–I'm not good at it." She looked at him. "Do you...still have feelings for me?"

"Would it matter if I did?"

She nodded. "It would."

Chester closed his eyes, sighed again, feeling the dull throb of need radiating out from his chest, centred on his heart. He had lost Jasper, and he hadn't seen Kipling in a week. He felt absolutely lost and so alone. He had moved out of his grandmother's place, finally, because he couldn't stand feeling like a burden on her any more. And the way she looked at him, every night, with pity and sadness, was too much.

"I still do, yes." He opened his eyes. He recognized the feeling that was pulsing in him the way a deep, fresh wound pulses, following the rhythm of his heart. It was the need to be known. The need to be blindly and unabashedly accepted. And when he opened his eyes he saw the same need in January's pleading, lingering look.

They both stepped forward and Chester turned his head slightly and lifted his chin up and January turned her head slightly and lowered her lips down to meet his and they kissed and all they could hear were the quiet sounds that they made together. The small gasps. The little moans. The wordless expressions of being known.

When they separated, still holding each other tightly and gazing into each other's eyes, looking from eye to eye, January said, "I heard what you did."

"What did I do?"

"The way you disarmed him. Stood up to him."

"Oh," Chester said and looked away for a second, shyly. He didn't want to remember.

"My dad was there."

"He was?"

"Yeah. He saw you," she said, biting her lip. "He said you were so brave."

"I..."

"He said he was wrong about you."

"He said he was wrong?"

January laughed. "I know," she said, "I thought they must be setting up ski lifts in hell."

Chester laughed with her. "Yeah, they might be," he said.

The day after January moved into his apartment was Chester's first day back at the Mega-Mart. It was a hard day for Chester, although he kept it to himself. Things had changed. For one thing, Polito's back room had been expanded, and now held a complement of three security guards, none of them Polito. They didn't take kindly to the notion that Chester should have a quiet space to rest his eyes, and wordlessly pointed to the door as he stood there trying to argue.

"Come on, guys, give me a break! Just a little shut-eye."

They pointed at the door.

"You can't give me five minutes? Just five minutes!"

They remained mute, and pointed at the door.

"You know guys, I know people, okay. I'm not going to say who, I'm not going to name drop, because I'm not a name dropper, but I'm going to tell you: if you want Ipswitch to fire you, then feel free to kick me out of here."

They stood, pointing. Finally one of them said, "Sir, we've been instructed not to talk with you."

"Why not?" Chester was moderately offended.

"Mr. Ipswitch, sir, says that talking to you is an exercise in futility. That you don't listen and that you make things up to get your way."

“Well Jesus,” said Chester, scratching the back of his head. He hadn’t expected Ipswitch to have him so accurately pegged. “Look, don’t say no right now, just think about it,” he said to the three security guards. “We’ll talk later. Yeah.”

As he left he bumped into Polito, who was wearing a new, spiffier looking uniform with a sidearm in a shiny new leather holster.

“I like the cut of your jib,” said Chester. “Why the new threads? And what’s up with the automatons in the booth here?” He indicated the back room he’d just left by jerking his thumb over his shoulder.

“Oh, those guys,” Polito chuckled. “Yeah, they’re just following orders. Don’t give them a hard time, okay?”

“Why would I give them a hard time?”

“Just...please. Find someplace else to nap, okay?”

Chester held up his hands and Polito turned and started to leave. “Hey, wait, you didn’t tell me about the uniform.”

“Oh,” said Polito, walking backwards as he looked down at the new clothes. “It’s a bit of a step up. I’m the new co-supervisor of security. Ipswitch promoted me and Mo. How do you like that?” He smiled and opened the door to the surveillance room.

“Hmph.”

“And I heard that Ipswitch wants to talk to you,” he called over his shoulder as he pulled the door closed.

“Oh, hey have you seen Kipling?” Chester called, but Polito was already gone. “Oh.” He turned around a couple of times, thinking of a good place to have a nap. Then he remembered the last thing Polito had said. “Why would Ipswitch want to see me?” he said out loud.

“Because I want to offer you a promotion, Chester,” said Ipswitch, sitting on the edge of his desk, chomping on his cigar. Chester was in Ipswitch’s office, thinking that the plush chair he was sitting in would be perfect for napping.

“A what?”

"Promotion, my boy. You're the hero of the hour! The man of the year! We need you to head up the team at Mega-Mart. You have to know that with Guy Tuffray gone there is a position available. With someone like you at the helm, well, we can expect everyone to feel a little safer, more secure. What do you say? There'll be an increase in your pay scale, of course, and more vacation time, benefits, sundry and so on." Ipswitch was leaning forward, grinning wolfishly, a bluish cloud of cigar smoke around his oversized head. "Well come on, son, what do you say?"

"Um, no thanks."

"What?" The cigar fell right out of Ipswitch's mouth and bumped across the carpet. He hopped after it, picking it up before it could scorch the knap.

"I'd rather not. Take the promotion. Thanks anyway," Chester explained slowly.

"Listen, boy, you take that promotion or you can say goodbye to your days here at the mall!"

"Okay, fire away. I'm not much of a fan of this job anyway. With Tuffray gone it doesn't seem as much fun as it once was."

"No, no, wait. Now, hold on. I don't think you understood me," said Ipswitch, placatingly. "Cigar?" He offered his own half-smoked and wet-nibbed stogie.

Chester shook his head.

"How's about this? You keep your same job as you have now. Sound good?"

"I don't know," said Chester. "I mean, it seems kind of dangerous these days."

Ipswich smiled and ground his teeth together. "All right, then how about a little pay raise? Ten percent?"

"Twenty-five."

"What? Twelve is more than generous."

"Twenty."

"I can't possibly afford to give you any more than fifteen."

"I think I said twenty."

Ipswitch looked at him, startled, and said, "That's not negotiation, son."

"Well, maybe you can send me on a course or something."

"Fifteen."

"Twenty."

Ipswitch glared at him, his deep-set eyes glowing like kryptonite. But his hard stare left Chester completely unfazed. Ipswitch tossed the cigar down on the carpet. "Fine! Twenty. But don't you breathe a word of this to anyone."

"Done," said Chester, shaking Ipswitch's hand and promptly leaving his office as the big man jumped after his smouldering cigar and cursed the burn mark that he'd just put in his own carpet.

After Chester left, Ipswitch called Easter in and offered her the promotion, which she wisely accepted. And Watson Huffernanny found out that he enjoyed sneaking around with the boss even more than he enjoyed sneaking around behind the boss's back. He didn't mind that Easter seemed to show less mercy on him than anyone else when he was working. It made the stolen moments that much more passionate.

Surprisingly, the merciful one seemed to be Ipswitch, who, after a relatively short time, began visiting the Sumerian in jail. The two became great friends, fueled by their mutual hatred of Guy Tuffray. It was largely due to Ipswitch's influence that the Sumerian managed to get paroled and back at the info desk in the mall in only eight years. The two large-headed, crinkle-faced, cigar-smoking miscreants were fairly inseparable until the day Ipswitch's wife left him for the Sumerian. The two left town in the early morning just before Christmas and were never seen again.

Shortly after Chester turned down Ipswitch's promotion and left his office he went to the food court to talk to Gina. He found her mixing up the ground beef filling that was used for the tacos, staring at the iridescent orange colour of it.

"Hey," he said, conversationally, "you haven't heard from Kipling have you?"

"Oh," said Gina, slightly startled. "No, um, no, no I sure haven't."

"Hm," said Chester. "Well. If you do, you know, let me know. I'm a little worried. I haven't seen him for, like, a month. It's like he dropped off the face of the earth. I was by his house, his parents don't know where he is either. No one's seen him."

"Yeah, well, you know I bet he's totally fine," said Gina, nodding. "He's pretty self-sufficient, you know."

"Yeah," said Chester, but it wasn't a whole-hearted agreement. He felt like Kipling wasn't quite as self-sufficient as Gina thought. Even Kipling needed friends. Someone to spend time with. Chester shrugged and wandered away, engrossed in his own thoughts.

Gina watched him leave, and then thought to herself for a second and began doing some calculations on her brand new calculator watch. She nodded and smiled to herself. She'd gotten the watch in the mail, along with the very first of Kipling's postcards. He had reminded her not to tell anyone about it, that he would explain to them in due time. He told her the exact amount she would need to save if she wanted to join him. "Fiji," he'd said, "is beautiful. I'm not waiting on you, but I think we both need someone to talk to. Any day."

She had put on the calculator watch, and then begun saving up. When anyone asked her about the watch she said, "Oh, it's a gift from my boyfriend." That's what she told Dusty when he asked her, and because she was smiling to herself she didn't notice that he was suddenly deflated, and unhappy. He started spending more time hanging out with Rose at the Grand & Toy, and so was the first person to notice the Lost and Found.

With Rose's help Dusty worked up the courage to ask Dove Anquanita out on a date. He did it at the end of the day, when she was the only person behind the counter at the HMV. He went up to the counter with a Bjork CD in his sweaty hands. He set the CD down and saw Dove's eyebrow arch over his uncharacteristic selection.

"Will that be all, Dusty?" she said, not even making eye contact.

"Um, no, um, I..." He coughed, wiped his hands on his pants. His lungs felt constricted, filled with fluid, perhaps. He had no difficulty blinking, but couldn't seem to stop himself. He concentrated. He'd rehearsed this with Rose.

Dove looked at him.

"Um, I'd like to...I mean, we don't know each other very well. I, uh, I think...um...you know, I like you, and it's possible, I mean would it be possible to, uh, for us to maybe go somewhere, sometime?"

Dove looked at him like she'd just seen a cockroach run across her kitchen floor. "Ew, no way," she said. She handed him the CD. "That'll be 24 dollars and 74 cents."

A month later Rose managed to work up enough courage in Dusty for him to ask again. They rehearsed again. Things seemed to be smoother. Dusty walked up to the counter of the HMV with a Slipknot CD. Dove rolled her eyes.

"So, okay, I was just, I guess, wondering. Um." Dusty swallowed deeply. "Is there anything that would, uh, I mean, change your mind? About going out with me sometime? Or something? Uh, because—"

"I don't know, Dusty. I'm sure you're a sweet guy, you're just not my taste. Okay?"

"Well, okay, um, will you think about it?"

"Yeah, sure, I'll totally think about it," she said dismissively. "That's 27.89, please."

After that Rose couldn't re-build Dusty's shattered ego enough to convince him to try a third time. He moped around and his depression thoroughly grated on Rose's nerves. He noticed, and began to wander out into the mall instead of heading over to the Grand & Toy. That was how he noticed Mya hurrying furtively into the elevators that led up to the second-floor office spaces. He stopped and waited and watched.

Mya stepped into Ipswitch's outer office and Consuela gave her a slow, sly smile and indicated that the door to the inner office was open with a flourish of her hand. Mya heaved a sigh. This was part of being a manager, she said to herself, and steeled her resolve. She stepped through the door.

"Mya!" said Ipswitch happily. "Just in time."

"Let's get it over with. Who is it this week?"

Ipswitch chuckled languorously and leaned well back in his chair and put his hands behind his head. "Are you trying to tell me you don't like my assignment?"

"Putting me in charge of the Wheel of Fun? No, I fucking hate it. But it's part of the job, so let's get it over with."

"Well, I'll tell you, Mya. With that attitude you only make the Wheel of Fun that much more fun for me."

"Who is it?"

Ipswitch stood up and crossed the room to the closet door. "It's Dove's birthday this week, Mya. I think you know her. She works at the HMV?" He pulled a key ring from his pocket, it was a grandiose ring with dozens of keys. He unlocked the closet and pulled out a rickety wooden structure set on a base with wheels. The dreaded Wheel of Fun. It looked like the Wheel of Fortune from the TV game show, except oriented vertically instead of horizontally. Ipswitch had built it himself, had come up with the entire concept. On an employee's birthday they were made to spin the Wheel of Fun, ostensibly to receive one of the prizes marked on the wheel. What no one had been told but, from experience, now understood was that the wheel was weighted to always land on the marker that read: "Pie to the Face".

Mya dragged the Wheel of Fun to the elevator, down to the mall level, and through the throngs of shoppers toward the HMV. She felt bad, but as one of the few managers Ipswitch had hand-selected to administer the Wheel of Fun, she had immunity from the terrible contraption. The people, noticing something was going on, started to follow her, and by the time she got to the HMV there was a good throng in her wake.

Dove saw the crowd, and then saw Mya at the front with the Wheel. She breathed deeply. She had hoped Ipswitch would forget it was her birthday.

As she got close, Mya said, "I'm sorry, but you know how it is."

"Fuck you, Mya."

In a loud voice Mya said, "Dove Anquanita! It's your birthday! As a special surprise from the mall staff, we are offering you the chance to win a special prize from...The Wheel of Fun!" The crowd applauded sporadically. "Spin the wheel to win your prize, Dove!"

Dove stepped forward. She barely spun the wheel, with a look of such hatred on her face that several audience members discreetly left the proceedings.

"You've won...a pie to the face! How about that everyone," said Mya to the gathered host. "Well, Dove. Come here and get your prize!"

"Wait!" said a voice from the back of the crowd. It was Dusty.

"Dusty?" said Dove.

"Dusty!?" said Mya.

"Let me take it. Give me the pie. I'll do it."

Mya looked at Dove, then at Dusty. She lifted the coconut cream pie – a full pie, made by Ipswitch himself – and hesitated.

"Give him the pie! Give him the pie!" chanted the crowd. She shrugged. Dusty got the pie. The crowd applauded, laughed, and then quickly began to disperse. The show was over. Dusty stood and tried to wipe the pie from his face, but it clung to his features in yellow-white chunks. Dove stepped toward him.

Dusty opened his mouth to begin saying something, but Dove cut him off.

"Fine. Okay? Let's go out," said Dove.

And they went out to a nice restaurant, and Dove talked the whole time and Dusty listened the whole time and at the end of the night Dove invited him up to her place where she talked until dawn and Dusty was content to lie next to her and listen to everything she had to say. No one had ever listened to her in that way before, just letting her tell them every secret thought without judgment.

And when the sun came up, and the sky was rosy pink and beautiful Dove turned to Dusty and kissed him the way that he had always imagined she would. And when they pulled away from each other she said, shocking Dusty more than she shocked herself, “I think I’m falling for you.”

And as soon as she said it she knew she already had fallen, desperately, deeply in love. It wasn't real love, of course, but infatuation is sometimes an even stronger emotion and eventually it matured into something deeper and more meaningful.

The first person Dusty told was Rose, who was ecstatically happy for him.

“This is amazing, Dusty!” she said. “And, honestly, like, really good timing actually.”

“What do you mean?” he asked.

“I’ve decided to go back to school,” said Rose. “I’ve been saving up the past couple of months and I can afford to go back and finish my degree, with my previous savings and what I’ve got now, so...I’m going to do it.”

“Oh, wow, Rose. That’s so good for you,” said Dusty. But he still felt a pang of loss because his best friend was going away, and possibly never coming back. She was right, it was good timing.

She left for the spring semester, so she could take some low-key make-up courses and work a little more over the summer and ease into full-time school in the fall. Tuffray, who had been stalking her incessantly since the incident at the Mega-Mart, followed her.

Up until that point he had been living off his parent’s largesse, which he had extracted easily because his life had been threatened by a madman. When he moved away he had to get a job, and he managed to secure a position as manager of a Blockbuster. The hours were flexible enough that he could sit in on some of Rose's classes, where she studiously ignored him. It didn't seem to dampen his overactive enthusiasm.

Walking home one afternoon, several weeks after they had both moved, Rose stopped dead in her tracks, turned around, and marched up to Tuffray. He was shaking, nervous, looking for any place to hide. He had stupidly believed that she hadn't seen him.

"What do you want?" she demanded.

"I...well...I, uh, I would like to, um, to...be with you," he stammered.

"You want to...be with me?" she said, bewildered. "What does that mean?"

"I don't know. Maybe, and I'm just spitballing here, but, um, wife, kids, a nice home in the suburbs, picket fences, and..." He trailed off. "Maybe an SUV," he added.

"No, Tuffray. No way. I'm sorry. Not now, not ever."

"Okay, well, maybe you might change your mind, so —"

"No, Tuffray," she said firmly. "I'm serious. Not ever. Okay? Do you understand?"

She stared at him until he nodded.

"Yes," he said, "I understand."

"Good." She turned on her heel and walked quickly away.

"If you change your mind, though," Tuffray began.

Rose whipped around and ran at him and he quickly jumped and gave a girlish, "Ah!" and ran away. After that she didn't see him, so he either became a much better stalker or left her alone.

With Tuffray gone from the mall Chester found himself bored and unchallenged much of the time. Sure, he enjoyed trying to sneak around behind Easter's back, but found her to be surprisingly forceful with punishment and somehow able to keep his recklessness in check. Once, after he had snuck off and slept, lying on a pallet of paper towels in the back, she had scheduled him to work next to Shorsky every day for the next week. The old woman's phlegmatic, hacking cough and interminable questions about what price things were had driven him nearly insane. He never snuck off to catch forty winks again.

He did, however, get a postcard from Kipling that settled his mind, if not his spirit. He missed his old friend.

"What's he going to do without me around?" he asked January as they lay side by side in bed. He was reading a Spider-man comic, she was studying for her GRE, which she was going to take at the end of the spring so she could enroll at the college to get her Masters in English Literature.

The answer came when, at the end of the summer, Gina left without a trace. A month and a half later Chester got a postcard from her and Kipling. It made him smile and shake his head, and tack the postcard on the bulletin board next to the ones he had already got from Kipling.

The only person left upon whom to focus Chester's ire was Kel Urquhart, but that was becoming increasingly difficult because it was blindingly obvious that Kel made his aunt Tamara extremely happy after her miserable and long divorce. That and seeing Kel spin his grandmother around the dance floor at his family's Easter weekend get-together made it more and more difficult to reduce him to a mere nemesis.

They began to hang out at the food court, whenever Kel could get away from the Barnes & Noble. Kel and Chester could talk about almost anything, they discovered. It was good, but it was strange, and for all the time since Jasper's death, the one thing Chester couldn't talk about was the incident at the Mega-Mart. Chester still found himself crying without warning once or twice a day. He didn't talk about it with anyone, in fact, and it was straining the edges of his relationship with January. Which he also didn't talk about.

Chester sat down at Kel's table with a tray of chicken soft tacos, holding the pieces of a fortune cookie in his other hand. He'd managed to filch the fortune cookie from under Ameesha's nose while he'd been apologizing to her for a vast array of slights. She'd forgiven him, and promised to keep Dr. Pointree away from him.

"Look at those kids," said Kel, indicating the clotted groups of teenagers around the fountain.

"Hm? What about them?"

"It's all about the cliques, you know? This one doesn't like that one, and these ones won't talk to those ones. It's sad."

"It's petty, is what it is. And immature, the whole idea of, you know, 'these guys are our enemies' or something."

"Intolerance," said Kel, musingly.

"Man, I can't stand intolerance," said Chester. Then he held up a slip of paper: his fortune. "I don't get this. Do you understand it?" He bit deep into a chicken soft taco.

Kel, slowly re-wrapping his own taco, didn't reply right away. "Hm, what do you mean?"

"This says 'The more things change the more they stay the same.' That doesn't make sense."

"Maybe they mean that only change is constant."

"What? That makes even less sense."

"Yeah," said Kel, thinking about it and nodding.

"It's just frustrating. You try to live your life by these adages and they turn out to be meaningless."

"True."

"I mean where do they come from?"

"What?"

"What have we just been talking about? Adages. Saws. Sayings. Wisdom."

"Oh, people just make them up."

"They just make them up?"

"Yeah."

"Like I could just say, I don't know, never kiss an ugly baby, and that's an adage?"

"I suppose."

"Well, geez, that's stupid. I mean then all this common sense mumbo jumbo is just a hodge-podge of riff-raff." Chester put his head in his hands. "Ah, it's just so frustrating sometimes."

"Are you frustrated?"

"Yes! Christ, Kel, isn't that obvious?"

"Yes."

"Then why did you ask me?"

"To frustrate you."

Chester sighed, shook his head. Eventually he chuckled. "Good one," he admitted.

There was a long silence then, and Chester looked around. Amid the chaos and noise he noticed the large potted tree that was positioned under the skylight near the middle of the food court. It was a waxen-looking thing, with thin, gnarled branches and thick leaves. It was such a permanent fixture that Chester had never given it a second thought. He had always assumed it was fake. Looking at it now, he noticed the unmistakable tinge of brown on the edges of the leaves.

ACKNOWLEDGEMENTS

The short list of acknowledgements should read something like this: everyone I know. And while that is true, it gives short shrift to a few folks who were willing and helpful in the first stages of the writing of this novel. Chief among them was Lisa Johnson, who gave the novel its first full edit, and those few who read and commented on early drafts of the text: Doreen, Steve, Monica, and Laura.

Laura, it must be said, also put up with a lot of the standard haranguing that goes with being the wife of a creative/crazy person, and she deserves a zillion pounds of credit for being both fabulously patient and wonderfully supportive.

I also can't give enough thanks to Reid McCarter, who provided the last full edit of the novel. Any mistakes, errors, or radical adverb usage in the final product are thus my own, undertaken in moments of pure what-the-hellfullness.

The design of the cover and iconography was done by Adam Therrien, over many long hours, for which he was paid a pittance. He deserves better. My apologies. But thank goodness for his talent and skill.

And if it's not too presumptuous, thank you for reading. Not just this book, but any and all books. It means more than you might think.

- gj.